Apparition Lake

Apparition Lake

Daniel D. Lamoreux, Doug Lamoreux

Published 2014 by Creativia
Paperback design by Creativia (www.creativia.org)
ISBN: 978-1500332020
Cover art by http://www.thecovercollection.com/

"This we know... the earth does not belong to man, man belongs to the earth. All things are connected; like blood which connects one family. Whatever befalls the earth befalls the children of the earth. Man did not weave the web of life – but is merely a strand in it. Whatever he does to the web, he does to himself."
Chief Seattle, 1854

CONTENTS

viii

Chapter 1

Above the stark silhouette of jagged mountain peaks, daylight shed its lifeblood in crimson streaks across a deep purple sky. The blue of dusk settled like a blanket over the watchful pines. From within that bed of shadowy forest came the rhythmic echo of booming Shoshone drums; red man's thunder amid a white man's storm.

It was the year eighteen hundred and seventy-eight.

For thirteen years, President Abraham Lincoln lay moldering in his tomb; placed there by a bullet from the gun of John Wilkes Booth. Crazy Horse had ascended to the ranks of his ancestors two years past, having massacred General George Armstrong Custer and two hundred fifty-six of his pony soldiers at the Little Big Horn. The Freemen's Bureau, organized to protect the interests of former slaves, had been in operation for one week. Carl Sandburg was a suckling newborn, Annie Oakley a budding tomboy of eighteen. Judge Roy Bean was four years from becoming "the law west of the Pecos" when he would turn his Vinegaroon, Texas saloon into a part-time courtroom. Geronimo and his warriors would have another eight years to plunder and murder white settlers in Mexico before their surrender. Only twelve years of life remained to a discernible American frontier...

...and there was much pain in the ancient Stinking Country.

The streaks in the sky spread into darker hues of red that spanned the horizon. From within the black void below, another light began to glow. As if fueled by the increasing intensity of the pounding drums, the ceremonial fire climbed toward the heavens fighting back the approaching darkness.

A lone Indian brave, feeding the flame, stood within the fire's flickering circle of light. Silently he stirred the coals and added fuel, mindful of nothing but that one most important task. The drums beat while the flames cracked and popped throwing sparks in ever-rising circles to the sky. Beyond the edge of the fire's light stood the few members of the rogue Shoshone party, the Sheepeaters. Flickering shadows danced across their faces, making their sculpted features grotesque and shapeless. Yet, reflected in each staring eye, the image of the fire burned with perfect clarity. Silence ruled all.

Further back, in the gloom, stood their temporary village. Brain-tanned leather stretched over triangular stacked poles created their lodges. Small fires within two of these rounded pyramids cast distorted images upon their leather walls, creating eerie stages upon which their occupants conducted ageless shadow dances.

In the first, Silverbear's shadow dance was one of solitude. Though the drums continued to beat just outside his lodge, they were beyond his hearing. The holy man sat upon crossed legs before his small fire. His weary, chiseled features, the color and texture of hammered copper, spoke of a long and difficult life. He cradled a buckskin bundle in his hands and lifted it forward and up, offering its contents to the Gods. Chanting softly, he closed his eyes for a moment, and then opened the bundle in his lap. From it he removed his sacred crystals and medicinal powders, and lay them on the cold dirt floor at his side. Then, Silverbear removed his medicine feather; a gift given him by an eagle messenger from the Great Spirit. The holy man held it gently, golden and perfect in the palms of his hands, contemplated it deeply, then lifted it high in thanksgiving. Silverbear placed the feather upon the floor with the other charms and, lifting his aged and weathered face toward the roof of his lodge, began to softly chant his prayer.

Confident the Gods had heard him, the holy man lit his pipe, breathed deeply of its smoke, and relished the smooth taste of the tobacco. It would soon be time.

In the adjoining lodge, Silverbear's assistant prepared the ceremony participants for the ancient Bear Dance. He dipped his fingers into a bowl of powder and patted the faces and chests of the two older braves seated on the ground before the fire. With the skill of an artist, he created intricate white patterns on their skin. The young brave, not yet old enough for his own spiritual journey, understood the honor and responsibility given him in being tasked with participation in this most sacred of ceremonies.

A fourth Indian, Norkuk, the leader of the Shoshone band, stood watching the proceedings. He was pleased. After the inaction of the reservation life, it was good medicine to again be the master of his own destiny and that of his people. In bringing his party to this place he had defied the trust of his chief. But in doing so he had done the more important, he thought, honoring the wishes of the Great Spirit and the trust of those who followed him. It was good to be back on their homeland. It was also good that they were preparing for the Bear Dance. They would no longer be inactive while their land was being defiled. They would no longer sit by while the white men slaughtered the animals the Great Spirit had provided for the Shoshone. They would no longer watch while the poachers desecrated all that was holy and good with Mother Earth.

The ritual preparation complete, the painted braves donned thick bearskins and ornaments for the ceremony. They stepped from the lodge and into the chill night air and moved to their places alongside the fire. They stood side-by-side, facing west across the flames, and waited on the holy man.

Norkuk took his place within the circle of firelight, listening to the intensity of the drums. He looked upon the stoic faces of his people circled around and pride welled inside him. It was good to be Shoshone. His people would once again wield the great power of their ancestors.

The drums stopped as Silverbear approached from the darkness. The holy man stood facing east before the fire and his people. The feathers of the golden eagle, tied with colorful beads on leather thongs, dangled in bunches from his flowing gray hair. The massive curved claws of the grizzly bear adorned the necklace encircling his throat and the hide and head of the bear covered his own flesh and skull. The ceremonial garments, illuminated by the dancing flames, gave Silverbear the appearance of a great bear. He raised his arms to the stars and the drums began beating anew.

The painted braves chanted in unison and began the Dance of the Great Bear.

Silverbear watched the beginnings of the ceremony with steel gray eyes. He was pleased. There would be strong medicine in the movement, and a great healing for their troubled homeland. Removing a handful of sparkling crystals from his medicine bag, Silverbear offered them to the Great Spirit, and then sacrificed them to the fire. He handed a second, larger leather sack to one of the braves. The young man danced in a circle around the flame, sprinkling its contents of sacred sand onto the ground. As he completed the circle, the drums ceased.

Silverbear hesitated, taking in the silence of the mountain. The sun's light was shining its last and that was good; the final rays would carry his words to the Creator. Silverbear raised his hands and, in his native tongue, began his invocation. He offered his prayer in each of the four directions; south to north, then east to west, representing the four aspects of Man's nature – the physical, the mental, the emotional, and the spiritual.

The drummers began again, striking the stretched animal skins with fervor. As one, the group took up a chant, interspersed with high-pitched screams. As they sang to Duma Appah, the Great Spirit, the young brave presented the holy man with the centerpiece of the ceremony, the sacred bear fetish. A small statue, roughly carved from stone in the image of the grizzly bear, the fetish possessed magic powers. Silverbear gripped it tightly, showing only its head above his

4

fingers and, lifting it to the red flare of ebbing sunlight, offered his prayers as the drums increased their tempo.

Three Indian women in brightly colored ceremonial clothing approached the circle. The first carried a ceramic jar. She knelt, bowed her head, and laid the jar on the ground at Silverbear's feet. The others, holding baskets of cornmeal, took their place on either side of the first.

Silverbear held the fetish toward each of the women in their turn and blessed the food they offered to the Spirit Bear. The statue was placed in the jar; the cornmeal poured in over it to feed the Spirit. The jar was sealed and tied atop a piece of lodgepole with a leather strap. Silverbear lifted the holy staff above his head and joined in the drummers' chant. The women returned to the crowd, leaving only the medicine man and the two braves dressed as bears in the circle of firelight.

"Appah created the Earth with the help of the animal nation," Silverbear said. "Man's spirit now kills the animal; destroys the Earth. War, oppression, hatred, greed, jealousy," the holy man called out, naming the vices carried to their land by the white men.

The drummers cried, "He-agh, He-aghhhh," in response to each.

Silverbear moved the sacred staff to the four corners of the Earth, asking the Great Spirit for healing. He laid the staff on the fire. Though the flames enveloped it, the fetish jar did not burn.

The two braves stood facing the band of Indians on the opposite side of the fire, and became little more than silhouettes as the darkness increased. Silverbear stood over the fire, the light dancing red and yellow on his weathered face. His assistant lit the ceremonial pipe and delivered it to the medicine man. Silverbear lifted the pipe skyward, drew deeply from it, lifted it skyward again and exhaled. The young brave carried the sacred pipe to the Bear Dancers, who also smoked of it.

Silverbear laid the bear fetish at the feet of the first brave, who had seen wapiti poached near Blacktail Deer Creek. The elk had been killed only for their coats in a senseless waste of their meat, their life, and their spirits. Silverbear waved his medicine feather violently about and repeatedly laid his hands upon the brave's head. He spit upon his hands, rubbed them together, and again placed them on the brave. Taking up the medicine feather once more he swept the air around the brave, and then shook it at the fetish jar.

The medicine man spoke to the Great Spirit and then held his breath. A moment of utter silence followed. No one moved and not a sound left the plateau, save the harsh crackling of the fire. Silverbear exhaled emphatically, leaned forward, and sniffed the air like an animal. The loud, rhythmic sniffs were interspersed with quick, sharp exhalations. Twice, the sniffing stopped and an eerie howling from the forest broke the silence around the campfire.

Norkuk smiled. The howls came from the coyote, the creator of human life, and he knew that Appah heard their prayers.

Silverbear moved far off, outside the reach of the firelight, where he loudly and violently threw up to dispel the evil spirits. He returned to the firelight, placed the bear fetish at the second brave's feet and began the ceremony anew. The second brave and his party had witnessed the result of a wholesale murder of bison; animals killed with no respect of their value as creatures of the Great Spirit. Their coats were removed and their bodies left to rot in the blistering Wyoming sun. He used his hands and the medicine feather, each time directing the spirits captured in the feather into the sacred ceramic jar.

The crackling of the fire became more prominent as Silverbear spoke to the Great Spirit. His words and manner were calm but powerful. He looked into the fire and then to the sky, admonishing in a loud voice the messengers of fear and evil to loosen their hold upon the land. "We ask Appah that the Bear Spirit be made free," Silverbear called out. "To do the work in this world that is meant for him to do."

The braves stared into the fire with stony faces. No one moved.

The despoiler of the land had escaped the hand of white justice at every turn. Those of the blue coats and yellow legs had proven impotent at stopping him. The Shoshone now called on Spirit Bear to stop him.

"We ask Appah that it be this way." Silverbear lifted his medicine feather and pointed it at the braves. From the darkness behind the bank came the shrill hoots of an owl. It was not a random call but focused and insistent, as if made by a child hidden in the trees. All heard it; none turned to look. Silverbear, at first, seemed not to notice but when the owl's calls persisted, Silverbear gazed in the direction of the sound. "We reject your word," the holy man shouted, his eyes reflecting the firelight.

The hooting stopped. When it was apparent the owl had spoken its last, Silverbear raised his hands to the heavens. "Let this not be your sign."

The drums began to beat. The two fur-clad braves circled the fire, crouching, then erect, reaching to the sky and chanting in unison with the rhythm of the drums. Like two dark, enchanted grizzlies, they bobbed and kicked their legs and waved their arms in the orange flickering firelight.

"He-agh, He-aghhhh!"

Frenzy overcame the dancers as the circle of Sheepeaters joined them.

"He-agh, He-aghhhh!" The tempo increased, shrieks and whoops rang out. The fire blazed and the darkness fell.

"He-agh, He-agh, He-aghhhh!"

Chapter 2

The bison's charge erupted from serenity.

The bull had been minding its own business, nibbling the grass on the lawn of the National Park Service administrative building at Mammoth Hot Springs. Minding its own business, that is, until a tourist carrying a video camera had walked to within six feet of the animal and yelled out, "Hey, dummy, look up!" The bison gave him more than he'd asked for. He charged. The camera was tossed skyward and the tourist became a blur of churning white legs and arms.

Having successfully intimidated the pest, the bull ended its charge as quickly as he'd started it and returned to grazing. The tourist, meanwhile, covered one hundred yards of open ground despite losing his camera and his left shoe. He came to a stop, bent at the waist, panting for breath and staring at the shiniest pair of boots he'd ever seen. Still gasping, he followed the polished footwear up past pressed olive pants, a perfect military gig line, an olive duty jacket over a starched khaki shirt with a glittering gold badge, and a well-shaved square jaw below an icy stare, topped by a trooper's hat. The tourist, had he tried, could not have found a worse way to introduce himself to Yellowstone's Chief Ranger Glenn Merrill.

"Had that bull been anything more than mildly irritated," Glenn told him, "or you a split second slower to react, we would this minute be wrapping you in a body bag."

Ignorance about park wildlife was more the rule than the exception. As that was the case, the chief intended to let the fellow off with a lecture. But when he got his wind back, rather than take the lesson, the tourist squawked about his rights, his taxes, and his contributions to Glenn's paycheck. He received a written citation to boot. Many did not understand the park's laws. Rules and regs existed, generally, to protect people from their own ignorance. They were often violated out of that same ignorance. It was all black and white to Glenn Merrill; no shades of gray. There was nothing gray about ignorance or stupidity. Press hard, sir, six copies.

It was the year nineteen hundred and ninety-six.

For thirty-three years, President John Fitzgerald Kennedy lay moldering in his tomb; placed there by a bullet from the gun of Lee Harvey Oswald. Four years past, Operation Desert Storm had been fought and won in twenty-eight days, allowing the United States to strut its modern warfare technology. South Los Angeles had exploded in riots two years before, as the rusted chains of slavery were replaced by the gleaming chains of prejudice; fettering men of all colors. Newt Gingrich, despite lying to an Ethics Committee, had been re-elected House Speaker. Slick Willie Clinton, despite lying to everybody, had been re-elected President. Madonna, a pop singer, was the top news story in the country and the darling of the media for becoming a single mother. Computer technology was turning the world into a global community...

...and there was much pain in the ancient Stinking Country.

Yellowstone was the nation's first and largest national park. Its diversity and complexity was a wonder and fascination to most everyone who happened across its threshold. Its land mass was a mosaic of mountain habitats stretching across 2.2 million acres; sagebrush flats, high plains prairie, lodgepole, spruce and fir forests, lakes, rivers and streams, snowcapped granite peaks and valleys spewing forth the scalding steam and the hellish sulfur of the earth's inner core.

Amid that landscape, part Hell, part Eden, lived as great a diversity of wildlife. Sprawling herds of elk and bison roamed the countryside along with moose, mule deer, antelope, bighorn sheep, mountain goat, and lesser creatures too numerable to count. There were also predators: the wolves, mountain lion, black bear, and the great grizzly. Mankind rounded out the massive Yellowstone community. Tucked away in the far northwest corner of Wyoming, Yellowstone was more than a national park. It was a multinational city encompassing some of the most rugged, beautiful, and awe-inspiring natural wonders of the North American.continent. The complexity of the place, and his position in it, filled Glenn's thoughts as he drove toward Mary Bay on Yellowstone Lake.

A shakeup in the Park Service two years earlier had created many administrative changes in Yellowstone. Now, nearly everyone in authority, including him, was of a younger, more aggressive breed. Glenn was proud of his position as chief ranger, but the adjustment from being out on the streets to jockeying a desk had not been an easy one to make. On the day of his promotion, a retiring ranger had told Glenn, "The Niagara River is just as calm below the falls as above... but the transition can kill you."

"That it can," Glenn said, remembering those wise words. He realized he was talking to himself and laughed. "Just don't start answering." He drove past the substation next to Roosevelt Lodge and waved at the ranger just starting his morning shift. At times Glenn missed patrol work, particularly when administrative paper shuffling got heavy. Then he would take a reality check in his patrol vehicle. But not today. Today would be no joy ride.

Glenn thought of the dead bear awaiting him near Mary Bay. His staff had already been scrambled in response and he knew they were capable of doing their jobs effectively. Franklin, one of his best rangers, would be in charge of the initial investigation. Still, Glenn wanted to be there. Grizzly bear was on the Endangered Species list and that might draw a lot of bad press. Besides, capturing poachers was one of Chief Merrill's personal priorities. He fed the carburetor extra juice.

In nine years with the Park Service, Glenn had seen all there was of human decadence, but he hated poaching most of all. His job was handling humans in a predatory world. But poachers were a different animal altogether; a detestable species. There were four lower classifications; those who poached animals for meat, those who poached for the heads and hides as trophies, those who killed for commerce, and the despicable fourth variety that merely relished death. The first two were simple criminals; too lazy and self-important to secure their meat and trophies through legal channels. The fourth was completely beyond his understanding. How anyone could kill a creature as majestic and beautiful as the grizzly simply to watch it die was, to Glenn, unforgivable and insane. The third type of poacher, the man who killed for money, the human animal empowered by need and greed, was in a sad way understandable. An Asiatic market for natural aphrodisiacs made elk and black bear an especially common target. Antlers and gall bladders, too, drew big dollars from overseas. The men meeting these wants were vicious and cold-hearted, but rational; they were the most dangerous poachers of all.

A bear had been poached at Mary Bay, but what kind of a poacher was responsible? That question churned in Glenn's head and heart as he rounded the curve at Tower Falls and started south on the long pitched climb toward Dunraven Pass.

*

Ranger Franklin was a young go-getter who always started his patrol shift early. He was on the road and ready to respond when he received the call. Within fifteen minutes he had crossed Fishing Bridge and was looking for the site of the bear kill. It was not hard to find. Six cars and two trucks with campers had already converged on the spot. The anxious tourists mingled, taking photographs and chatting about how such a thing could happen. Morbid situations attracted people like flies to putrid meat, a fact that burned Franklin to no end. Why didn't they just go see Old Faithful, he wondered.

He parked his white Blazer on the shoulder of the road, called dispatch for help with traffic control, and began dispersing the crowd. Although it was still early in the morning, the traffic from Cody through the east gate made it clear it was going to be another busy day in Yellowstone.

*

A young couple at the trailhead on Dunraven Pass flagged Glenn down. They were planning a day-hike around the upper elevations of Mount Washburn and wanted information on the conditions on top.

"There is always the chance for unexpected storms this late in the year," Glenn told them. "It's been a good year so far, but lightning can be a hazard up high. Watch the weather."

Dunraven had been opened late that spring, owing to a heavy winter snow that the cool summer had melted very slowly. Though it was the end of summer in the valleys, it was pushing toward winter again in the high country. He gave them the customary advice on rock slide dangers and unstable soils during rainstorms, told them to stick to designated trails, then wished them good luck and a good day.

Starting down the opposite slope, south toward Mary Bay, Glenn noted the abnormal temperature. A cold spell was settling into the area. He made a mental note to give notice to the troops at roll call; they'd need to keep a special eye on the rivers and creeks. The waterways were another dynamic of the wild that tourists were unable to comprehend; as inviting as the wildlife and just as dangerous. They were running high that fall throughout the park, and any heavy rains could mean his troops spending time fishing for drowning victims.

Glenn decided to make what he could of the poaching situation by breaking in one of the park's new staff members. They had yet to meet, but he understood the new biologist did good work. He grabbed the radio mic. "Dispatch, One-oh-one."

"One-oh-one," came the metallic voice from beneath the dash. "Go ahead."

"That new biologist," Glenn said. "I think they call him J.D., is he on today?"

"Ten-four," dispatched answered.

Glenn could have sworn he heard laughter in the background. "Send him down to Mary Bay. It should be good experience. I'll meet him there."

"Ten-four, chief."

Again the laughter. He would have to talk to them about screwing around on the radio. A lot of visitors carried scanners and it didn't sound good. Glenn parked his white Suburban behind Franklin's Blazer and stepped out into a cold wind coming off the wide expanse of Yellowstone Lake. Fall was beautiful, Glenn thought as he buttoned his jacket, but the first breath of winter already had a bite.

Franklin seemed to have things well in hand. The poaching site had already been cordoned off with yellow crime scene tape and two rangers were carefully scouring the interior for evidence. Patrol vehicles were stationed on the road, both east and west of the site, directing the bottle-necked traffic. As each visitor's car passed the site, they slowed to a crawl and strained for a glimpse of whatever had caused the excitement. Glenn felt like stopping each and every one. It would do them good to see how some people treated the park's resources.

Franklin was bent over the grizzly's carcass taking notes, as Glenn stepped up. The bear lay sprawled, a dark mass of lifeless fur and muscle. The light colored tips of its hairs proclaimed that the bruin had paid his dues and survived a lot of tough years. The coat was still damp, apparently from a recent bath in the lake, though it could have been a nearby river or a creek. Having rolled on the ground while fighting for his life, the wet fur had been coated in a thick layer of dirt and mud. Blood permeated the fur of one shoulder, coloring the mud a dull maroon. Part of the skull was missing, leaving a large stain in a halo around what was left of his scarred and time-worn face.

"Morning, Frankie," Glenn said. "What's the scoop?"

"Morning, chief," Franklin said, standing. "This is Bear #113; a real old patriarch. It looks from the surrounding sign like he'd been scrounging for a meal across the road and along the lake shore. He was making a break for the tree line when someone plugged him. More than likely they drove up to watch the bear, he dashed, and they shot him from the window of their vehicle."

Glenn grimaced as if he'd been jabbed in the gut.

"That isn't the worst, chief," Franklin said. "It looks like the bear wasn't killed with the first shot. I'd guess it broke his shoulder. You see how the vegetation is torn up around the body? He fell and was rolling around when the trigger man stepped out of the vehicle, walked over to about there, and put a second bullet into old #113's brain. We found remnants of the slug buried in the dirt under the bear's head. It must have made a nasty mess on the inside because there isn't much left of it."

"Anything to go on?" Glenn asked, disgusted at the picture Franklin had drawn.

"Well, yeah," Franklin said. "When the poacher chambered his second round, he did it right there. The first casing was left behind. They apparently spent some time admiring their work, too, because we found two empty beer cans. I've got that stuff bagged and ready to send off for analysis."

"Good work," Glenn said, shaking his head. "I'm going to nose around a little. Keep at it and see what else you can find."

Glenn crossed the road to the edge of Yellowstone Lake. Bear tracks decorated the shoreline. He stared off toward Stevenson Island, as if the lonely clump of lodgepole pines in the middle of the slate blue water held answers to his questions. The chief was thankful people like Franklin kept coming into the ranks. Once you'd been in the business awhile, you lost faith in your ability to make a difference. New blood always helped. Glenn remembered the early days when he, like Franklin, had been ten foot tall and bulletproof. He'd come out of college with all the answers, and then from the academy with all the weapons, ready to save the world. A lot of water had passed under the bridge since then. Franklin would soon learn you solved a lot fewer of these cases than you'd care to remember, but it was a lesson he'd have to learn on his own. Glenn's job was to keep the rangers motivated and working.

He lifted a rounded stone and threw it far out into the lake. Maybe we'll get lucky this time, Glenn thought. Looking out across the great expanse of water, he noticed the thunderheads building over West Thumb; a storm brewing and headed their way. He thought of the couple on Dunraven Pass and hoped they heeded his advice about watching the weather.

He turned toward the road as another Park Service rig pulled up behind his own. Glenn came out of his sullen mood as he watched the petite young woman jump down from the government pickup. She was five-foot-four maybe, blonde, and pixie-ish. She couldn't have weighed a hundred pounds, he thought, with rocks filling the pockets of her drab green coveralls. His first impression, that she looked like a child's doll, burst as she slammed her truck door, turned, and strode to the scene of the bear kill like a three hundred pound wrestler crossing the ring. Curious, to say the least, Glenn headed over to meet the new face.

"Chief Merrill," Franklin said. "Meet Jennifer Davies, wildlife biologist."

"I prefer J.D.," she said, extending a hand. Glenn looked as if someone had hit him in the head with a ball bat. "Is there a problem, ranger?" J.D. asked in mild irritation.

Glenn smiled, realizing the joke was on him. "No problem at all. Glenn Merrill. And that's chief ranger, little lady." His hand swallowed hers.

J.D. shook it stiffly, but there was no greeting in her greeting. "I am a woman. And small," she said with controlled menace. "But 'little lady' isn't going to cut it, chief." She added his title at the end as if it was a sneeze.

Franklin turned, hiding a laugh.

"No harm intended," said Glenn. "My apologies."

16

"No blood, no foul," J.D. said. "Now, can I ask why I'm here? This is a law enforcement problem and I've got a lot of my own work to do."

Glenn paused to collect his thoughts. Miss Davies didn't waste any time and that was good, but this first meeting was not going as he'd intended. "I understand your workload," he said, choosing his words. "But you'll find soon enough that there will always be more work than time in Yellowstone." He offered a smile that was not returned. As being friendly seemed to be getting him nowhere, Glenn decided instead to just be in charge. "I asked you here," he said, "because it will help you to better comprehend the big picture. None of us work in a vacuum and, unfortunately, this is a side of wildlife management, too." He pointed. "That's a bear. You're a bear biologist. Maybe you can teach us a few things. Maybe you'll learn something yourself. At worst you'll get a break from the routine."

J.D. nodded curtly then returned her attention to the other ranger. "So what do we have here?"

Franklin gave J.D. the rundown, almost word for word as he had to Glenn. The chief stood quietly by, sizing up this new biologist and cursing the political correctness that made working relationships so complicated.

A honking horn diverted Glenn's attention. He turned to the road where the line of gawkers continued passing slowly by. Four vehicles back in line, laying on the horn of his monster travel trailer, sat the obvious malcontent. The heavyset, middle-aged man pounded his steering wheel, gesticulating wildly like a frantic mime behind the huge windshield. The driver's side window soon came down and the man began shouting at the overtaxed ranger directing traffic on the road.

Glenn sighed, shook his head and, like the sky to the south, clouded over dark. Why did they always have to be in such a hurry? The vehicle, bearing Texas plates and pulling an expensive SUV on a car caddie behind, passed with its horn still splitting the air. It was just another visitor with more dollars than sense.

17

J.D. knelt to examine the carcass. "Does this happen here regularly?"

"Not often with grizzly," Glenn said, returning his attention to the scene. "But name any animal in the park and I can take you to a spot where we've had one poached. Some years you'd think we were operating a shooting gallery. It's a real problem."

"What are the chances of catching this guy?"

"Unless we come up with a good eye witness," Glenn answered. "Slim to none."

"Why?"

"For starters," he said. "Our list of suspects include any one of three million visitors, none of whom live here. Most visit for less than a day and a half. A large percentage of those don't live in the United States. We have locals from as far away as three hundred miles. Then there are seasonal employees, not only for the park, but for the concessionaire; they come from all over the world. On top of that, we've got one rifle casing and two beer cans as evidence. It's hardly an open and shut case."

"Welcome to Yellowstone," Franklin added.

For the next hour and a half, J.D. watched the rangers work. She was glad the chief had asked for her. She hated the fact a bear had died senselessly, but she was definitely learning a few things. They found two witnesses but their usefulness was questionable. The elderly couple, staying in the Fishing Bridge Campground, thought they saw a suspicious vehicle. Of course, the gentleman added, they lived on a farm outside of a small town in Kansas. Most everybody seemed suspicious to them. They thought they'd heard shots. The old man had wanted to investigate but "mother" wouldn't hear of it. Their statements were taken for the reports and, "Yes, ma'am," if they needed anything else they'd contact them. The scene of the kill was searched, searched again, photographed, and searched once more for good measure. That finished, it was time to remove the bear.

Glenn found J.D. sitting on the shore of Yellowstone Lake, with her back to the ant farm activity of the crime scene. "You're going to freeze out here," he said, approaching the biologist. "It might only be September but the wind off the lake can still make a believer out of you."

"The air feels good," she said. "Believer in what?"

"The raw power of this country," Glenn said, remembering yet another reason he loved it there. "You okay?"

J.D. turned to the chief ranger, failing to hide her mild surprise. He actually sounded like he cared. Maybe he wasn't as big a jerk as she'd first imagined. "I'll be all right," she said. "I just find it hard to believe this kind of thing happens."

"People will always be people. When it gets to you, just remember: if you take the time to let it, Yellowstone will help you cope." Though he'd delivered it like reading a fortune cookie, J.D. appreciated the sentiment and nodded her understanding.

Meanwhile, Glenn dropped his tone to that of somber business. "Say, the boys need your pickup to transport the bear. Can I give you a lift back to Mammoth?"

"Sure," J.D. said, rising. "Just let me get my pack from the truck."

*

The bear was unceremoniously hefted into the pickup. It would be packaged and sent to a lab in Oregon to be necropsied. Once the pathologists had finished poking, prodding and examining each minute portion of the bear's body, the animal would probably be stuffed and donated to a museum or put on display in a traveling Stop Poaching exhibit. The great leviathan of the mountains, soon to be reduced to the role of a sideshow freak.

The rangers in charge of traffic control were the last to leave the scene. Get the vehicles moving, restore the traffic flow, and then off to the next problem. And then there were none. In ten minutes the roadway was clear, save for the usual progression of tourists on their way to Old Faithful and parts beyond. They'd have a big day ahead of them. They would watch the geyser spout, buy a T-shirt for the

19

kids, grab a bite to eat and a bumper sticker for the car as proof they'd gone "back to nature." Then they would drive like there was no tomorrow toward the closest exit. They were on vacation and there would be no time to waste.

Bear #113 had simply become another statistic.

Chapter 3

The carcass of Bear #113 was in good hands for shipping, and the collected evidence had been properly stored. Glenn and J.D. climbed into the Suburban and drove out of the parking lot of the Lake Village substation. They headed north, with Mary Bay shrinking in the distance behind and silence filling the cab.

"I apologize," Glenn said, breaking the icy quiet, "for the way we got started back there."

"Forget it," she said, looking out the passenger's window.

"You caught me by surprise. I thought you were going to be a guy."

"Story of my life," J.D. said. "So did my father."

Ouch, Glenn thought; that hurt. Okay, it was going to be a challenge. He was the boss. The boss meets his challenges. "I'm Glenn Merrill," he said, extending a hand. "The little people call me chief but I will answer to Glenn under certain circumstances."

She eyed him suspiciously, then smiled. "Jennifer Davies," she said. "People call me J.D."

"I'm pleased to meet you, J.D. And looking forward to working with you."

She shook the hand and studied the face of the smiling chief ranger with serious eyes.

The Park Service vehicle continued on to the Canyon Village junction. Glenn turned right at the same time that an old, green bus pulled from the gas station lot on his left. The chief ranger locked up his brakes in time to keep from hitting the other broadside. The bus continued across the road and into the Canyon Village complex, oblivious of Glenn and J.D. Glenn eased his Suburban behind the bus and started to pass when a small pre-teen boy peered through the rear window, below a Cub Scout Troop banner, and stuck out his tongue. The chief drove on; that guy had trouble enough.

*

Aboard the bus, the harried driver, Scout leader, baby-sitter, big brother and surrogate dad, Rob Jones, was about out of steam. He'd accidentally cut off a Suburban at the last interchange, a park policeman no less. Thank goodness the ranger at the wheel had been alert, or he'd have had no choice but to broadside them. Wouldn't that have been a sweet halftime event in their park tour? Jones needed a break. Who wouldn't, five days into a ten-day trip with this bunch of hooligans? Strike that, Jones thought, checking his attitude. This group, twelve total, of excited and energetic 10 year-olds. A dozen fourth and fifth graders, uniformed in blue, beneath a bold banner reading Webelos Pack #182, in a rented green bus and, after a long morning ride, ready to explode. He parked in an elongated space at the back of the lot, among the oversized motor homes and vehicles with trailers. Then he took a deep breath and faced the screeching heads, poking above the bench seats like shooting gallery targets.

"Listen up." Nobody did, of course. "Hey," Jones called, "quiet down a minute." Half of his contingent obeyed. He raised the volume again for the remaining half. "Hey, you guys, quiet!"

As the last of the rumble died and the bobbing heads became stationary, a small figure burst into the center aisle. He dashed forward and slapped a larger boy on the back of the head.

"James," Jones yelled. "That's enough!"

As quickly as he'd come, James returned to his seat. With the face of an angel and the heart and mind of an imp, he lowered his blonde head to hide his smile.

"What's the Scout Slogan?" Jones asked.

"Do a Good Turn Daily!" James replied.

"Think about that."

James nodded solemnly. He'd been pinched, but that was okay. He'd managed to collect a debt with Greg, the bully of the bunch, first.

"Greg," Jones warned, "Retribution is not on the list of attributes in the Scout Law. Got it?"

The bigger boy nodded too, but he was wearing a frown.

Jones decided to let it go and hope for the best. "Listen up, everybody," he told his scouts. "You guys have thirty minutes before we move on. Be back on the bus on time. As you off-load, come by single file and I'll dole out ten dollars each from your fun money."

Cheers, and high fives, erupted.

"All right," Jones said with a sigh. "Spend it any way you like but remember, you guys have five more days on this trip and you have to make it stretch. And behave yourselves. You are not only representing yourselves, but also this Webelos Troop and your families back in Pocatello. Have fun and be back on the bus in thirty minutes."

Eleven of the twelve blue-clad bodies exploded from their seats, grabbed their cash, and scattered like wind-blown leaves throughout the complex. James waited until Greg was well gone, and then eased out the bus door.

"Mr. Jones," he said, "can I buy anything I want?"

"Anything ten dollars will get you."

"All right," James shouted, heading for the gift shop.

Jones smiled. James was a good kid but, seriously, he was going to get killed messing with Greg. He shook his head and stepped back onto the bus for thirty minutes of well-deserved peace and quiet. Jones fell into his seat, gratefully closed his eyes, and just missed seeing a pickup truck the color of sunbaked red primer pull from a parking stall without any regard. Had James not jumped to the side, he'd have been a goner. The truck, driven by a mean-looking twenty-something kid in a faded blue Chicago Cubs ball cap, continued out of the lot without slowing.

*

"Mr Jones. Mr. Jones!"

Rob Jones had no clue how long he'd been out. It felt like seconds but, for all he knew, had been hours. He was still in the driver's seat of the bus; literally, asleep at the wheel. One of his scouts was excitedly trying to wake him.

There was trouble in the gift shop, he was told, and it didn't take a rocket scientist to figure out the likely problem had two first names, Greg and James. Sure enough, upon arrival he found the dynamic duo, James looking sheepish, Greg defiant, standing beside a post card rack that looked blasted to smithereens, in the presence of a scowling middle-aged shop clerk who looked ready to do some blasting herself. "What happened?" the alarmed, and still slightly comatose, Jones asked.

"I heard them arguing, all the way from the front counter," the clerk said. "When I got back here they were shoving each other and the display looked like this."

This was a disaster. This was every card that had been in the rack, pulled out and thrown down on the floor; scattered to kingdom come. Every card save one, that is. One stack. Each card in that stack featuring the same image. That one post card remained front and center in the rack; a picture of a four-legged, white-coated creature in the wild. Exactly which animal was not immediately apparent, for each and every one of the remaining cards had been ripped in half, with the hind portions of the pictures left in the rack and the head portions missing. Where they'd gone, the clerk had no idea, as they were not among the littered mess on the floor.

"Why Cub Scouts, of all people, would want to do something like this is beyond me," she declared indignantly.

"I didn't do it," Greg said.

"I didn't either," James insisted.

"You were going at it tooth and nail when I got back here," the clerk barked. "Don't deny it. I saw you. I told you to quit."

"We were arguing," James told Mr. Jones. "I am sorry for that. But we didn't do this." He pointed at the floor and shook his head. "Honest!"

"Well, there was nothing wrong with the rack this morning. I opened. I ought to know." Her mouth was a thin, angry line. "In fact," she said, pointing at the rack. "I know there was nothing wrong just a short while ago. Hasn't been twenty, twenty-five minutes ago I sold one of these very post cards. The white elk. Sold it to a young man, along with a counter full of groceries and camp supplies. He most certainly would have said something if the rack had been damaged then."

She didn't add that that young man had been memorable himself. He'd given off what she could only describe as a creepy vibe the whole time she'd dealt with him. Just struck her as wrong. But then, some folks did that. You couldn't get along with everybody. And it had nothing to do with the matter at hand. Fact was, creepy or not, he'd bought a post card, that post card, and hadn't mentioned any problem with the rack. Clearly these boys had destroyed the display in their fight.

The boys held fast to their denial. The clerk remained unmoved and insisted that, once the rack was restored, the damaged cards be paid for. Jones saw clearly what needed to be done. The boys soon had the mess cleaned up. The clerk had rung up a bill of sale. Jones had split the damage three ways. He would pay a third for failing to supervise them, and Greg and James would each pay a third, if not for damaging the display, for causing a scene in the store in the first place; a charge for which both were clearly guilty. "It isn't fair!" Both scouts complained together.

"No," Jones agreed. "Many things in life aren't."

With that day's fun money devoured by the ugly incident, Greg and Mr. Jones both left the store empty-handed. James, on the other hand, insisted on being allowed to take part of his purchase with him. He left the gift shop with one of the cards, the huge, white, headless elk tucked neatly in his shirt pocket. The first post card he'd ever bought.

*

For Glenn it had been a long, long morning. The early drive south, the sad hours at Mary Bay with Bear #113, the rough start with J.D. (the park's new bear biologist silent there in the seat beside him), the long road all the way back north again. With Lake Village, Canyon Village, and Tower-Roosevelt behind them, Glenn decided he needed some air. "Have you seen much of the park?" he asked J.D.

"No. I haven't had time to breathe since coming down here. This is a busy place."

"Just wait. You don't know the half of it," he said. "Would you care to make a stop?"

J.D. groaned. "I've had all the tourists I can take for one day."

Glenn laughed. "I agree completely. This is different. This is my anti-tourist spot."

They crossed Blacktail Plateau, chatting only occasionally but much more amicably like two strangers after a war discovering they were in fact wearing the same uniform. Suddenly, and quite without warning, smiling like a naughty boy with a secret, Glenn applied the brakes and made a U-turn. He pull the Suburban to the right edge of the road and parked beside a sign she'd missed seeing on the way past, and couldn't read now for the angle. She inspected her surroundings out the windows and, other than the usual grandeur of northern Wyoming, couldn't for the life of her see anything in particular the sign might be pointing out. Dropping her voice to the deep and silly range, she turned and asked the chief ranger, "Y-es?"

In answer, he climbed from the vehicle. She followed and met him on the shoulder of the road. "This is it," Glenn said. He swept his arm before them to the south. "Apparition Lake."

What lay before them was a fifty acre depression in the ground, resembling nothing so much as a massive oblong salad bowl complete with salad. The bed looked like a hay field with the long brown grasses of fall mixed with the last of the summer's green growth overwashed with ten inches of muddy standing water. The green-brown matte swayed as a breeze rippled the puddle.

"This is a joke, right?"

"No joke," Glenn said. "This is a temporal lake. It appears and disappears seasonally based upon the amount of precipitation. The last couple of years haven't seen any water in it at all. Other years it fills up nicely. With all the snow we had this last winter it gathered some moisture, and the cool summer left a lot of it behind. It's not very dramatic now, but it is a hint of what it might look like during another of its ghostly appearances."

"A phantom lake?"

"Apparition Lake," Glenn said.

"Weird."

"Yeah," Glenn said with a laugh. "A few years ago, I was patrolling out this way and saw a guy planted on the bank under those lodgepole pines." He pointed into the distance. "On the other side. He was fishing."

J.D. did a take and laughed. "Bet he wasn't having much luck!"

"That's just it. I was going to be a nice guy and tell him; explain the situation. I suggested he try one of the other lakes in the park because, being seasonal, Apparition Lake was dead. No fish."

"What did he say?"

"Well, the guy said, 'I'm not going anywhere, and you can't make me. I can fish here if I want to.' So, stupid me, I'm still trying to help out. I said, 'Sir, I don't have any intention of making you do anything. I'm just trying to tell you, there are no fish in this lake.'" Glenn turned to J.D. looking gob-smacked. "This guy stood, stepped up, put his face in mine and said, 'You're a liar. I know there's fish in here. I've caught them here before.'"

J.D. laughed. How could she not, picturing the chief ranger being barked at by an irate tourist. "So what did you do?"

"I took a deep breath," Glenn said. "I smiled, wished him good luck, and told him to have a nice day. Then I walked off and left him to his fishing."

J.D. cupped her hand over her brow and scanned the distance. "Do you think he's still here?"

"I hope so," Glenn said making a point not to look. "Nothing but a skeleton scratching his skull, holding a fishing pole, and wondering why they aren't biting." They laughed together, gently, wearily, letting the tensions of the morning drain away.

Suddenly J.D. stopped as, out of nowhere, an icy shiver ran up her back and vibrated her slight frame. She hugged herself and groaned, chilled by a cold breeze coming across the low water. "Wow," she said, zipping her jacket. "I don't mean to be critical, but your phantom lake is suddenly a little creepy."

"What do you mean?"

"I don't know exactly." J.D. was still laughing but the joy had gone from her voice. Now it was an embarrassed and nervous laugh; a fearful laugh. "Who knows? Maybe it's the skeleton. All at once I feel something, I don't know... eerie. Maybe it's just the name? You don't happen to keep apparitions at Apparition Lake, do you?"

Glenn hesitated, turning from J.D. to the lake. "Not that I... know of." Suddenly he was feeling it too. It was a coldness, a darkness that seemed to well up within him. He'd visited Apparition Lake a hundred times, passed it hundreds more, and had never felt that way before.

It wasn't a foot race back to their vehicle, not exactly, but neither of them wasted any time getting there. Glenn wasted no time in pulling away.

Had they stayed, the two would have seen a subtle change take shape over the water. Despite the bright sunlight and moderate temperature of the morning, a gray mist began to form over the lake. It moved up and out, swirling and changing with the breeze, settling finally into a strange blanket of fog broken only by green and brown shoots of foliage cutting through from below. Beneath the fog the dead waters of Apparition Lake began to whirl of their own accord.

Chapter 4

A small step back in time will show that the Yellowstone rangers were not the only ones having a rough day. Early that same morning, Glenda Ewing sat alone in a cozy little booth with a window that opened toward the Shoshone National Forest. It was a tiny café; across the street from the motel room they'd occupied the night before on the western edge of Cody, Wyoming. She admired the glow of the sun as it lit up the eastern slopes of the mountains in front of her, but was nonetheless disappointed. Glenda had wanted to be up in those mountains when the sun came up. As it was, she sat quietly, sipping hot tea and waiting on her husband.

Jason Ewing had been his usual mulish self when she'd roused him that morning. He had told her to leave him be for a few minutes; he'd be right along. That had been an hour ago. Glenda still loved Jason, but he certainly had become hard to live with over the past thirty years.

The waitress had been by several times to check on her, and was headed her way again as Jason strode through the door. In the race to the table it was a tie between the waitress and Jason's booming voice. "Mornin', good lookin'." Jason arrived a few seconds later, ignoring his wife. "How about a big ol' cup of coffee?"

"Yes, sir."

"Ah, shoot. You don't have to call me sir. Name's Jason," he bellowed, broadcasting to all of Cody. "'Course my friends call me Stubby. You can call me Stubby too, darlin'."

The waitress made an abrupt about-face then, unseen, made a face, rolling her eyes as she headed into the kitchen.

Glenda's pink embarrassment quickly turned to red frustration. "I don't know why you insist on being so... so flamboyant."

"Talk English, woman," Stubby grunted as he sat across from her. "Or don't talk at all."

"Where have you been?" Glenda asked. "You knew I wanted to see the sunrise this morning."

"Well fer cryin' out loud, Glenda. Look out the window already," Stubby hollered. "The sun's arisin' while you jabber on." Then, as his mind wandered back, in a satisfied tone he said. "I got tied up. I was talking to an associate about a... plumbing situation. Geothermal plumbing, that is. Besides, they was doin' a special on the Cowboys on that mornin' talk show."

Born and raised in Dallas, Texas, there were only two things in Stubby's life worth consideration; commercial energy and the Dallas Cowboys. Energy, because that was how he'd earned his fortune, and the Cowboys, because of those cheerleaders.

Glenda had little interest in either. "I don't understand how you ever expect to get away with tapping into the park's..."

"The park's... nothin'," he barked, cutting her off. "Mother Nature give it to us to use as we see fit. Now stop goin' on about something you know diddly-squat about, cause I ain't half in the mood for none of your whinin' about the poor bunnies and antelopes."

The waitress returned with Stubby's coffee and more hot water for Glenda's tea. "Will there be anything else?"

"You betcha," Stubby said, eying the poor girl into her own embarrassment.

"Jason, I'd really like to get going," Glenda pleaded.

"Horse pucky! I'm gonna have me some breakfast first. What's the hurry, fer cryin' out loud, sun's up already." He turned to the waitress.

"Make that biscuits and gravy, couple eggs sunny, some crisp bacon, why don't you throw a short stack on the side, and if you need help carrying it, darlin', you just give ol' Stubby a whistle."

*

Breakfast had taken entirely too long to suit Glenda's tastes, but finally they were on the road and her anticipation and excitement climbed with the terrain; up Sylvan Pass and into Yellowstone National Park. The Ewing's had never been to Yellowstone before but, of course, Stubby was certain he'd already been everywhere that was important.

Glenda considered it the trip of a lifetime. Stubby thought it might be a good way to try out his new toy. The motor home was the size of a commercial bus, with most of the comforts of his home and far more than the homes of most working men. Glenda didn't understand why they bought the thing in the first place, because they never stayed in it. Stubby always insisted on the best hotels. She figured he'd picked it out just to drive around. He was so ostentatious. The SUV on the caddie behind was another example. She didn't think Stubby even knew how to put it into four-wheel drive.

The trip was pleasant enough, until they got inside the park and started down toward Yellowstone Lake. The view was gorgeous and took Glenda's breath away. Stubby couldn't have cared less. His temper, spurred on by the traffic congestion, rose like an elevator and reached the top floor when they were stopped by a traffic jam along the lakeside. A park ranger stood in the road, directing traffic through the congested area around Mary Bay. Stubby pulled alongside, honked his horn, and barked out the window. "What's the problem?"

"Sorry for the delay, sir," the ranger said. "We've had a grizzly bear poached along the road. We'll move you through as quickly as possible."

"Fer cryin' out loud, boy," Stubby shouted. "If I wanted to sit in a traffic jam I'd 'ave stayed in Dallas!" The ranger stared blankly.

As the traffic began to move, the park official waved Stubby on and then shook his head as the Texan pulled away. On Stubby's side of it, he didn't know the traffic cop, or Glenn, J.D., Franklin, or any of the other park employees working the scene that morning, and couldn't have cared less. He drove off, honking his horn and waving his arms at those still ahead of him.

Stubby's mood hadn't improved any when, two hours later, he sat on a bench along the boardwalk at Old Faithful, waiting for the famous geyser to put on its show. The area had been nearly deserted when they first sat down but as the clock counted down the time until the geyser's next eruption, the benches and the boardwalk filled and overflowed with anxious tourists. Bored with the entire ordeal, Stubby tossed chunks of sweet roll onto the ground at the edge of the boardwalk. Yellow-bellied marmots in mangy coats stood below and snatched each morsel, as if it were manna from Heaven.

"Jason," Glenda said. "The sign says not to feed the animals."

"Fer cryin' out loud, woman," Stubby snapped. "Leave me be. Besides, the stuff they sell here ain't fit fer human consumption. Least ways the gophers oughta benefit."

Glenda just shook her head.

A murmur started in the crowd as Old Faithful began spitting and sputtering in the first act of its performance. "Look, Jason," Glenda exclaimed. "It's starting!"

"Yeah," Stubby said absently. He tossed the last of his roll to a brave marmot that had climbed onto the boards at his feet. There certainly wasn't anything spectacular about water shooting out of some hole in the ground. Even oilfield gushers didn't hold the magic for Stubby that they once did. Except, of course, for all the paper they supplied; forest green paper, lots of it; each decorated with the face of a dead president. On the other hand, the blonde to his left was sure worthy of a second look.

The great geyser's spout grew higher and higher into the sky to the scattered "Ooooohhs" and "Aaaahhs" of the crowd. It reached its pinnacle to their shared applause, the pop of flashbulbs, and whir of their automatic cameras. The blonde on Stubby's left clapped and bounced up and down. Her ample chest responded accordingly and the Texan felt like clapping too. The act ended with Old Faithful taking a bow in the form of a sputter and final belch of steam. Its cloud evaporated. So did the crowd, wandering off to other adventures. Great show, thought Stubby, as the blonde departed. "Can we go now?" he asked Glenda.

It seemed every tourist in Yellowstone decided to leave the Visitor's Center at the same time. Stubby guided his mountainous motor home from the parking lot and into the fray, growing angrier by the moment. Glenda hid her face as the traffic forced Stubby into the wrong lane and he had to make a second circle around the confusing route to find the exit. As he screamed and cussed at the idiots in his parade, Glenda tried to remember why she'd married him in the first place. Finally, taking the exit ramp onto the loop road north, Stubby glanced at his watch and found his smile again. The bars would be open by the time they rolled into West Yellowstone. He eased his grip on the steering wheel. Glenda noticed the change in his demeanor and relaxed too. Maybe the rest of the trip wouldn't be so bad after all.

*

It was the middle of nowhere; south of Yellowstone, southwest of Tie Hack Ranch, on the unpaved, virtually unknown, Grassy Lake Road. The absolute middle of nowhere. But the mean young man in the baseball cap had found it just where the old man said it would be, looking as alone and forgotten as the overgrown road that brought him.

When settlers first emigrated to this portion of the country, what they brought with them had to be carried on their backs, on those of their horses and oxen, or in their meager wagons. Their homes and outbuildings were small and functional. The materials were cut from the raw lumber growing wherever they planted their families to start new lives, without luxuries like power tools. But what they built was meant to last.

The barn on this long-abandoned homestead ranch was no different. The hand-hewn logs from which it had been constructed had been pounded by decades of rain, snow, woodpecker beaks, and the savage Wyoming sun. Taken from this very spot, the logs matched their surroundings as if they had never been felled, and rarely did anyone so much as see it if they didn't already know it was there.

The old man was waiting for him, waiting and watching. He must have been because, as the kid maneuvered the sunbaked pickup along the two-track and up to the barn, the door come unhitched and there he was, gray beard to his chest, green and brown camouflage from neck to ankles, worn jump boots on his feet and a weathered brown Stetson atop his head, pushing from the inside and walking it open. "You finally got here," the old heathen said, waving him in. The boy pulled the truck into the barn. The old man pulled the door closed. From outside, the place was abandoned and lonely again.

Inside, along the west wall, up on pole brackets, was a rear-entrance camper topper, all ready for when the time was right. Just back the pickup under it, lower the camper on the bed, and go. To the other side, along the east wall was a big ol' unhitched, but ready for hitching, horse trailer complete with license plate that, if he knew the old man at all, was as hot as a Yuma noon but taken so discretely it wouldn't be reported stolen 'til after the October centerfold had unveiled her pumpkins. To the north, the rear of the barn had been fenced off with on-end pallets nailed to posts creating a handy, temporary stable for what looked like five good horses; two for riding and three for packing.

The old man, Gerry Meeks by name, had tied the door closed again and was coming up on the truck. "Took you long enough," he said. "Expected you two hours ago."

The boy, Bass Donnelly, jumped from the cab wearing a baby-eating grin. "Well, let me tell you, Gerry," he called out. "I have had me a morning."

"Ain't surprised," the old man said, peering into the bed of the truck, wondering after the supplies, reaching in to paw the bags brung from the village stores. "You usually have you a morning. Question is did you have us a morning? Did you get the grub? The camp supplies?"

"You see 'em, don't you," the young one hollered, already around the cab and opening the passenger side door like the whole world depended on it. It was easy getting mad at the codger, pushy as he was. "You're already running your dirty hands through 'em." Then, knowing better than to light a fire he couldn't put out, he backed off some. "I been to the stores."

Donnelly had only seen Meeks truly lose his temper one time, early on after they'd met. They'd been talking business at Meeks' place when the old man got up to take a leak. Nosing around to kill time, the kid had found an envelope from the Social Security Administration addressed to the codger; addressed, as God was his witness, to Geronimo Meeks. The kid near laughed his head off and couldn't wait for the old man to come back into the room so's he could, at the first opportunity, call him by that freight train of a legal name. And he did.

In a flash, the old man pulled a knife from his boot and stuck it in the kid's face. "You ever call me that again," he said in a voice Satan would have envied, "I'll gut you like a fish."

Bass Donnelly knew, more than likely, that he could take the old boy if need be. But with that glinting blade two inches from his wide and staring eyeball, the risk just didn't seem worth taking. If Geronimo Meeks preferred to be called Gerry, it was no skin off his nose.

"Did you get what we need?" Meeks hollered, drawing the kid back from his memory of that early day. The old man had two sacks out of the truck bed and was carrying them to a rickety table on the south end of the barn, on the camper side. Behind the table was the cold-camp gear; a small tent, bedrolls, and one lantern. The table groaned as he put the bags down. "Did you get what I told ya'?"

"That," Donnelly said, "and a whole lot more." He had a cooler chest out of the truck and was hurrying around with it, the ice thunking and rattling inside. He lowered the tailgate, and then moved the chest to rest there. He grinned like the Cheshire cat. "Blink them old eyes of yours; get 'em good and moist." He nodded at the cooler. "Then you just take a look in there."

Laughing again, Donnelly sunk his hands in his pockets, hunting for the sugar cubes he'd stored there, and started for the corral at the back of the barn.

Meeks, his curiosity as piqued as it was ever likely to be, ran his hands through his beard, once, twice, three times for good measure, and moved to the back of the truck. He took a breath and opened the cooler. Then he took a deeper breath and unwrapped the blood stained cloth inside. "Well, I will be." He reached in and lifted out the open package, showing off a bloody but otherwise black-looking, tear drop-shaped hunk of meat. There was no mistaking a cooled bear gall bladder. He didn't know, and wouldn't have cared to know, that it was the gall bladder of Bear #113. When he asked, "Where did you get that?" what he meant was, "Were you seen taking that?"

Inside his own head, at the corral in the back of the barn, Donnelly didn't hear either question. He was feeding sugar to the horses over the rail. One of them missed his turn, whinnied a complaint, and shook itself out.

"Bass, don't get those horses riled. I told you before, we need to keep quiet out here."

"There's nobody around for miles and miles."

"You don't know that," the old boy barked, "and you better always assume the opposite. Especially when we get up in that park." The kid frowned and dropped down on a bale of hay. Meeks was frowning himself as he slid the gall bladder into a plastic bag. "You didn't answer my question. Where did you take the bear?"

"Sign said Beach Springs. And you don't gotta worry; there wasn't a soul around. Just me and the bear." He told the story, taking careful aim all over again when he mimed a replay of the money shot. He ended the tale beaming with pride. "That old bear popping up, Gerry, that was a slice of luck, I give you that. But I took him without help and, if you ask me, you ought to be grateful."

"I am. I ain't sayin' otherwise." The old poacher lifted the bagged trophy, waving it triumphantly in the air. "You done good. This is worth a pretty penny to the folks we're already dealing with. Yessir-ree." He placed the bag back in the chest and set the works with the rest of the gear. No sooner was he done then his smile turned into a sneer. "But don't you get it into your head we'll be doing this again. We ain't hunting bear. And we ain't hunting anything on the side of the gol-darned road."

The kid ignored him and pulled a bent post card from his pocket. He'd bought it just that morning, right after he'd knocked blue hell out of the rack upon which it had been displayed. He stared at the card, studying the image of a huge white bull elk. His mind was drifting.

"Elk antlers," Meeks said, still lecturing. "That's what we're here for."

"I know what we're here for. I scouted the Lewis River on the way down, just like you told me. There's elk there, and plenty of 'em, just waiting to hand us their antlers."

"There you go," Meeks said with satisfaction. "Elk; that's the game plan. Get off the game plan once too often, you'll get caught sure as water is wet. I got no plans on gettin' caught."

The kid stood and hung the post card on a bent nail like he was decorating his living room back home.

"Are you listening to me?"

"Don't worry about it," Donnelly snapped back. He rubbed a dirty finger across the huge white animal in the picture. "I got nothing on my mind but elk. Nothing at all."

"Instead of wastin' your money on pretty pictures, you should have bought yourself a decent hat," Meeks growled. "Nobody gives a hoot about the Cubs out here. You need to get rid of that bright cap and get something that goes with the country and the weather. You stick out like a whore in church."

*

Stubby Ewing may as well have been made of stone. He drove on, acutely aware of the steaming hot pots and pools in the Upper Geyser Basin, like few could be, but oblivious to their beauty and color. He was unimpressed with the regal elk gathered along the banks of the Little Firehole River near Sapphire Pool, and less than interested in the small but stately herd of bison grazing near Midway Geyser Basin. He had no time for that crap. There was business on his mind and a cold beer waiting somewhere in West Yellowstone with his name on it. Besides, the cable sports channel had coverage of the Cowboys' last game coming up right after lunch.

Glenda, on the other hand, had given herself over to her surroundings. Never in her life had she imagined the beauty and the diversity of life to be found in the wonderland called Yellowstone. She wanted so much to get closer to it all.

They passed a sign reading: Firehole Lake Drive. The name alone struck a chord of mystery and intrigue inside her that would not be denied. "Jason," she said excitedly. "Firehole Lake! Let's stop and see."

"Fer cryin' out loud, woman," Stubby howled.

"Jason, please!"

He shook his head in disgust. "I wouldn't mind so much if you knew what you were looking at. But all you see are pretty holes filled with hot water."

"Just one more. Then we can go to West Yellowstone. Please. I promise."

"Oh fer cryin' out loud. One more and that's it. I'm thirsty." Resigned, but still grumbling, Stubby turned onto Firehole Lake Drive.

Glenda marveled at the beautiful purple stalks of elephant's head blossoms that gave way to sparse pines, their trunks turning white as the minerals in the swampy soil fossilized them even as they lived. The timber grew thicker as they rose slightly above the flat plateau, then thinned again as they dropped down, following the winding arc of the drive. They parked at the edge of the wooden walks encircling the area.

Glenda led the way. Stubby followed as sullen as a six-year-old dragged from the Toy Department by a mother headed for Women's Lingerie. "It's hard to believe," Glenda exclaimed as she started out onto the boardwalk, "that something can be so pretty and yet smell so awful. It's just like rotten eggs."

"That," he whispered to her emphatically, "is the smell of geothermal money."

"How is it money to you?"

"Lord, she has eyes but cannot see." Stubby couldn't help himself; he was shaking his head again. "Why do you think I've been buying all that land around this so-called park? Do you have any idea what a few wells sunk into Yellowstone's thermal plumbing will do for the relationship 'tween me and my banker?"

"Jason, you can't drill there. It's against the law, isn't it?"

"You're forgettin' the Golden Rule. He who has the gold... makes the rules."

Glenda frowned, decided there was nothing to be gained by arguing with her husband, and gazed out over the lake, turning her attention to the wonders around her. Stubby was intent only on getting done and getting out. Just ahead, a long haired photographer blocked their way with his tripod set up smack-dab in the middle of the boardwalk. Glenda wished him a good morning as she slipped by. Then Stubby jockeyed around, doing the fellow the unearned favor of not knocking either him or his camera into the lake. Safely on the other side, he tugged up on his belt and barked, "Excuse you." He finished under his breath with, "Hippie."

Over his shoulder, Stubby spied the object of the photographer's attention; a sun-bleached bison skull in the shallow waters of Black Warrior Lake. The vapors rising off the heated pool swirled around the skull, causing it to vanish and reappear like a spectre. Stubby paused to ensure his eyes weren't playing tricks on him.

Glenda, in the lead and oblivious to Stubby's new interest, kept walking. When she finally realized he'd fallen behind she turned and spotted him by the young cameraman. Something had their attention. She followed their gaze out into the mists. Glenda's eyes grew wide. She gasped. Then she screamed and threw her hands in front of her face.

The photographer, focused minutely on the skull in a close-up through his lens, jerked his head up to peer over the camera. Then he saw what Glenda saw and shouted, "Oh, my God!" He grabbed his tripod and scrambled back away.

Stubby remained motionless as his bowels gave out.

A huge grizzly bear, as monstrous as anything Stubby had ever imagined, appeared out of the mist above the bison skull and the lake. A fearsome roar escaped its massive, towering head. Piercing steel-gray eyes stared angrily above a gaping maw and a flash of fangs. Then the beast charged; through the heavy, swirling mists, straight at Stubby Ewing with the speed of a bullet and the bulk of a battleship.

Ignorant of the mess in his pants, Stubby turned to run and fell off the narrow boardwalk. The Texan bellowed in pain as his forehead slammed into the ground. He scrambled awkwardly, trying to regain his feet, when his legs broke through the thin gray crust covering the boiling waters beneath.

Stubby screamed; fear, frustration, and pain contributing to the tune. His pants accepted a new stain as his shins bled from the cuts opened by the sharp mineral crust. His ankles burned from the touch of the scalding waters. Stubby crawled from the broken hole and hobbled out into the stinking swirl rising from the earthen kettle. He tried to stand and was hit by a new pain... in his chest. It was sudden and excruciating, acute and crushing, as if somebody had parked his fancy motor home on top of him. With the speed of an electric arc, the pain expanded to his shoulder and shot down the length of his left arm.

He couldn't talk. He couldn't breathe. Sweat burst from the pores of his clammy forehead like water from a sprinkler. He'd forgotten his bleeding shins; forgotten his blistered ankles. But even with the compression in his chest he had not forgotten about the bear. Stubby managed a look over his shoulder and saw that the demon in dark fur had renewed its charge. The Texan let out a soft whimper, grabbed at his aching chest, and toppled into the bubbling cauldron.

Glenda looked on in horror as the monstrous bear ran over top of her husband. With a final roar, it vanished into the heavy fog beyond. Glenda screamed again. The photographer, numbed into silence, instinctively snapped photo after photo as the Firehole mists closed in upon themselves.

CHAPTER 5

Michael Stanton knew some of his staff called him the "Boy Super-intendent" behind his back. The name didn't bother him so much as the fact that, on days like this, it probably fit. He had always marveled at how his people seemed to have a finger on the pulse of the park. It was a trick he had never been able to master. Of course, that had nothing to do with his capabilities. It was simply that up-wardly mobile people like him did not have the time for the details that got you inside individual events. That was for the worker bee. Climbing the ladder of authority in the Park Service, like ascending any corporate or political structure, required less attention to detail and far more general viciousness. You had to claw at those above, kick at those below, and pray to whatever god was currently on the throne that you didn't fall off. It went without saying that you never paused to enjoy the view. Now, only eighteen months into the most prestigious superintendent's position in the National Park Service system, Stanton wished for those days of old when he could hop into a patrol vehicle, simply do his job, and leave the administrative headaches to somebody else.

The buzzing intercom interrupted his self-indulgent pouting. He turned from his office window already aware of what his secretary wanted. The rain storm on the outside of the glass was getting worse and it mirrored his mood. "Yes, Althea?"

45

"Mr. Stanton, your 7:30 appointment is here." He sighed. Why did the problem children always have to be the first of the day?

Yellowstone Forever promised to be a regular on Stanton's calendar for a while. As the newest environmental activist group in the Greater Yellowstone Area, they were already stepping knee deep in every issue that crossed his desk. It wasn't that he minded hearing from environmental groups, they often had bona fide concerns and occasionally offered real solutions. But radical groups within the movement often created headaches just for the sake of the headache. It was too early to judge, but experience told Stanton that Yellowstone Forever might well be radicals. "Send them in."

Althea knocked softly, opened the door, and ushered in three guests. Stanton circled his desk, put on that winning pretty-boy smile for which he was renown, and extended his hand to the first of the trio. "Nice to see you again, Nelson," he said. "How are you?"

Nelson Princep shook with a boney hand, grinned with a skeletal face, and looked every minute of his sixty-years. His stringy gray hair clung to the top of his head, as if combed with a squeegee but hung straight to the collar of his pinstriped suit coat; long for an executive. "I'm fine, Michael, thank you," Princep said with a click of his dental plate. He gestured. "May I introduce my associates, Priscilla Wentworth and Todd Muncey? Priscilla, Todd; Mr. Michael Stanton, Superintendent of Yellowstone National Park."

Cordial greetings were exchanged and a third overstuffed armchair slid up to join the two already in front of Stanton's desk. The superintendent slid into his own high-backed chair, clasped his hands atop the polished uncluttered surface, and grinned as if he were Jimmy Carter about to address his "fellow 'mericans" protected only by his teeth.

He stole a good look at Princep's associates. Wentworth was all that her name implied; schooled, spoiled, and with all the snottiness money could buy. She may have been attractive but, dressed like the headmistress of a horror film boarding school, was doing her best to keep it from the peasants. She'd settled back comfortably, Queen of the realm, wearing a humorless expression. Glenn was going to love this one, Stanton thought. Even he, as politically correct as his office forced him to be, saw no reason to pick Priscilla for his stick ball team. Muncey, on the other hand, looked another story entirely. A conservatively dressed, athletically built black man of, probably, twenty-five years. Muncey looked anything but comfortable. Perched on the edge of his chair as if he'd rather have been anywhere else, Stanton would have bet real money this was the young man's first encounter with the government. He couldn't help but wonder what in the name of creation he was doing with these other two stiffs.

"I assume," Princep said, raising a single brow, "that you received word from Senator Conrad's office."

"Yes," Stanton said, his voice cracking. Calm down, he told himself. Give the little worm the idea you're on the run and your troubles are just beginning. He cleared his throat. "I spoke with the Senator last evening. How, exactly, would you like to proceed?"

Yellowstone Forever wanted free rein in his park, Stanton knew; and they had a know-nothing Senator on their side. A thin tightrope lay directly ahead and he had been given no choice but to walk it. To keep his job, he would have to oblige these greens and humor the Senator. But Stanton also knew there were unspoken intentions in the room and he wasn't going to be a floor mat. He would not jeopardize the park and would draw a line in the sand if and when it became necessary.

"We have definite plans for fixing this park's problems," Wentworth stated plainly. "To properly formulate an action plan, however, we need to analyze your operations in the field."

Stanton bit his lip. The witch didn't mess around. Princep saw the superintendent's reaction, apparently read his mind, and glared at Wentworth. The look was little more than a flash, but Stanton saw it. A silence settled.

"What Priscilla is getting at," Princep said more graciously. "Is that we would like to offer suggestions for amending the park's position on a number of environmental and operational issues. Before we can do that, we need to get a closer look at what you actually do; meet your staff, see them at work, perhaps get our hands dirty along with them, I'm sure you understand."

Stanton understood perfectly. Yellowstone was the new cause and Yellowstone Forever was spearheading the assault. He was expected, out of political expedience, to go along to the slaughter without kicking or screaming. Stanton stood and gazed out his window. Two cow elk were hunkered down under a huge pine along the sidewalk leading to the building. A bison bull grazed nearby, oblivious to the battering wind and pummeling rain. Little bothered those impressive beasts. Oh, Stanton thought, to be a bison.

He sighed and turned to face his guests. "I am willing to cooperate with your organization, Nelson," he said. "The Senator was clear in his request. But there will be ground rules. I cannot give your people unrestricted access to this facility." He returned to the window, buying time, searching for the right words. With no intention of budging from beneath their natural umbrella, the elk pointed their ears and eyes down the walk where the object of their attention, Glenn Merrill, was approaching the entrance. Stanton nearly cheered. The cavalry had arrived.

"My chief ranger is just coming in," he told Princep. "Let me just slip out and have a word with him and we'll see what we can do."

"Certainly," Princep replied nodding with a wry smile.

*

A dead bear and a dead tourist had made for a long yesterday. No sleep had made it a longer night. Receiving a "Get up and get in here!" phone call from the superintendent's office in place of his alarm was not exactly what Glenn considered the perfect start to a perfect new day.

It wasn't that he and Stanton didn't get along, far from it. They had served together on Glenn's first assignment, working the monuments in Washington D.C. The chief ranger remembered how the two of them had spent a week one night in one of the more burly drinking establishments near Capital Square. They chased too many beers with too many shots of bourbon and, before the night was over, crossed paths with a gang of hoods unimpressed with their All-American looks. To this day, Glenn was amazed how well they fought together, even when staggering drunken.

Stanton had been a good ranger and a better friend for the two years Glenn was in D.C. Then they parted company, professionally and socially, until Mike was promoted to Yellowstone. That was a year and a half ago. They still liked each other but the pecking order prevented them from fraternizing anymore.

The chief ranger and the superintendent shared the understanding that crap rolled down hill. Glenn had gotten fairly adept at getting out of the way, while Stanton was a wiz at giving gravity a helping hand. Even as a ranger, Mike had never failed to shake the hand, lead the tour, nod the right number of times, and otherwise kiss the butt of whatever passing authority could best butter his bread. Glenn was a ranger and Stanton was a climber. That was how it was.

More power to him, Glenn thought. Appointed positions came and went with appointers and kings, for better or for worse, always lost their thrones. He would eat the garbage passed down by Stanton, knowing his boss would eat the garbage passed down from Washington. The chief had the joy of knowing the Boy Superintendent had a bigger plate.

Glenn entered the secretary's reception area, Stanton's barricade against the world, and was greeted with a warm, "Good morning." Althea, one of those bright ageless women who liked everybody and whom everybody liked, was Moneypenny to his bedraggled Bond. He hung up his rain gear and hat seeing, by the crowded coat rack, that he was already late to Stanton's early morning party.

Behind Althea, Stanton suddenly appeared with his back against his office door as if something inside had frightened him out. It was not a good sign. Glenn tried to ignore him, savoring Althea's smile for what it probably was, the single pleasant moment of the day before him.

"I'm glad you're here," Stanton told the chief, refusing to be ignored. "I hope you slept well?"

Recognizing his diplomacy for what it was, the lead up to war, Glenn decided not to have any. "Frankly, I didn't sleep. And, from the look on your face, things are not destined to improve."

"Nonsense," Stanton said. "Just some people you need to meet."

Glenn gave Althea the look. She turned away not to laugh, got her face under control, and then turned back to issue the chief ranger a warning with her eyes, 'Hold on. The manure is being delivered in an end loader this time.' Stanton, opening the door and leading the way, missed it all.

Glenn would plead guilty to the charge of being a cynic in any court in the land. He'd practically invented the attitude. Regardless, he spotted the three occupants waiting within and forced his eyes to the floor to avoid rolling them up into his head. No doubt carefully selected, to exacting diverse standards; age, race, and gender (check, check, and check), to appeal on a subconscious emotional level to 63.4 percent of those they'd been sent to annoy, the chief couldn't help but wonder which p.c. organization they represented, and what any of them had to do with him?

Stanton waved his arm as if introducing royalty. "This is. . ."

"Nelson Princep," the oldest of the three said, interrupting him. The fellow was emaciated, and Glenn wanted nothing more than to make the poor guy a sandwich. He bit his lip taking a tip from Althea on curbing his amusement.

"These are my associates," Princep said, introducing each. There followed a round robin of warm handshakes and Glenn felt a tinge of guilt wondering if he hadn't misjudged. "We represent an organization known as Yellowstone Forever."

"My pleasure," Glenn said, smiling, not at meeting them but in the pleasure of discovering he'd been right in the first place. They were greens; his instincts were sharp as ever.

Stanton's discussion with Glenn had taken place only in his mind. He'd made his decision in the time it had taken to cross from his desk to the outer office. The easiest way to deal with these people would be to pass them down the line like secondhand clothes. To that end, he spoke now with lots of authority and a dash of goodwill. "Glenn, I'd like you to see that these folks are well cared for here in the park for the next couple of weeks. They're researching our operations. Show them what we do, and how and why we do it."

Glenn's jaw twitched as a train of adult words raced through his head. He bit his tongue in case one of the cars stopped at his mouth.

Stanton was still talking. "And, of course, listen to what these folks have to say. Maybe they'll have some suggestions we can apply here." No sooner did he get the words out than Stanton realized he might have poked the wrong lion.

"Yes, sir," Glenn said from behind clenched teeth. He was picturing himself leaving Stanton behind in that stink-hole bar back in D.C.

Princep, a long-time veteran of the political game, recognized the exchange between the chief and his superior for what it was. He knew the next year was going to be difficult enough on them without his organization, let alone with. There was no sense in stirring the pot too soon. In his most diplomatic tone, he said, "Chief Merrill, we haven't had breakfast yet. If you don't mind, we'll go remedy that while you and Michael work out the ground rules." He gestured toward the door and his associates started out. "Would an hour be all right?"

"Perfect," Glenn said in a tone resembling the low distant rumble of thunder.

The trio rose, vacated the office, and pulled the door closed without Glenn seeing them. His eyes were locked on the red face of his former partner (now backstabbing politician). "Just what is going on here?"

"Don't use that tone with me, Glenn." His nervous expression belied his authoritative words.

"What tone do you expect? Come on, Mike, with that bear poaching and the Texan's death, my rangers are stretched to the limit; not to mention this rain storm. There are potential flash flood dangers all over the park. I'm even working the road to try to stay ahead. Now you want me to baby-sit a bunch of greens? Have you lost your mind?"

"No, I haven't," Stanton barked. "Sit down a minute and calm yourself, will you?"

Glenn threw his arms in the air and dropped into one of the vacated chairs.

Stanton frowned and turned to stare out his window again. The bison had moved off toward the post office building looking for cover and the superintendent couldn't help but think, we're all fighting some kind of storm. "Look, Glenn, you know I don't make all the decisions around here. We go back a long way. I respect your opinion and trust your judgment. But this time neither one of us has a choice." He took his seat behind the desk, leaned back, and took in a chest full of air. "These people are fanatics. They basically want to put a hurricane fence around the whole park, keep the people out and the wild in. You and I both know it isn't practical, or possible, but this group is also connected."

Glenn stared.

"Do you remember Senator Conrad?"

"Yeah. The psycho who thinks we should raise wolves and grizzly together so they can live like brothers of the earth, instead of the competing predators they are."

"That's him. He is now this group's favorite contact in Washington. I don't know if you're aware of it, Glenn, but Conrad is also on the Senate Appropriations Committee. He holds our purse strings."

The chief stiffened in the chair, glowering. "What's that have to do with me?"

"Don't be naïve. He's on my back. They're on my back. And it all rolls downhill. You will take the representatives of this organization out for a reasonable look at what we do. Show them around; make them feel like we're cooperating until I can figure something else out. And, whatever you do, keep them out of trouble."

"You're the boss," Glenn said, not because he respected the notion, merely as a statement of fact. He left the super's office without another word. Althea recognized a gale when she saw one and let the chief pass without interruption.

For his part, Glenn had a single purpose; to get to his own office sanctuary before he said something regrettable. He was halfway there when a twenty-something halfwit in a cheap suit blocked his path. "Chief Merrill," the man said. "I'm Howard Lark of the Billings Reporter."

Glenn nodded but kept moving, thumbing behind him. "The superintendent's secretary has a Press Release for the media. Right down the hall."

"I've seen it," Lark said. "Identity withheld? Cause of Death undetermined? Come on, chief, I'm no fashion critic but the emperor is buck naked. Can't you give us a few threads?"

Already annoyed, Glenn paused. "A park guest died yesterday near Firehole Lake. There's nothing I can add to that at the moment, Mr...?"

"Lark. Howard Lark. All right. How about the incident at Mary Bay? Your Press Release gives us nothing on that at all."

"What incident?" Glenn asked, caught off guard. It dawned immediately and he recovered. "You're talking about the bear? We compile statistics on incidents of that kind for annual reports. They don't figure in Press Releases."

"I'm surprised you don't take it more seriously. Doesn't that policy devalue the animal... and the hunter, for that matter?"

"We take what happened at Mary Bay very seriously, I assure you. And we're not talking about a hunter; we're talking about a poacher."

"Ta-may-toe, ta-mah-toe," the reporter said with a smirk.

"I'd love to help untwist your perspective, Mr. Lark. Unfortunately, I haven't the time. If you'll excuse me." Glenn walked away leaving the bemused reporter behind. Already surly, that little interview had not improved his mood and the chief ranger's outlook was positively overcast when he turned the corner and saw his office door ajar. Like the weather outside, he entered ready to blow.

Glenn's office occupied the northeast corner of the administration building. Its two picture windows opened out onto the ridge running from Mammoth down toward the Gardiner River and the steep slopes on the opposite side in the Gallatin National Forest. Glenn loved the view but that morning there was nothing to see but a wall of falling water. He wasn't interested in views, at any rate, and the windows might just as well have been bricked over.

Two men sat in overstuffed chairs by a coffee table inside his office door. One was Pete Lincoln, an old-timer with more years as a Yellowstone ranger than anyone – ever. He'd been offered the chief's position several times and had always turned it down. He was good at what he did and had no interest in office politics or administrative wrangling. Glenn valued his boundless knowledge and, even more, his common sense. Lincoln stood as Glenn came into the room. "Morning, chief."

"More good news?" Glenn asked, heading for his desk. He plopped into his chair before realizing the man still seated was not on his staff. Definitely not. He was a stranger and looked like a mountain man; shoulder length brown hair and a scraggly beard ripe for nesting in. "I'm sorry," Glenn said, standing again and rounding the desk. "I'm afraid the day didn't start on solid ground."

"Dave Lambro," the stranger said, introducing himself. "I don't imagine we're going to improve your footing any."

"Chief," Lincoln said. "Mr. Lambro is the photographer who was on-scene at Black Warrior Lake when the visitor from Texas died."

"Please, sit down." Glenn grabbed a third chair and joined them at the coffee table.

"We developed and returned most of Mr. Lambro's roll," Lincoln said, laying down a manila folder. "But I thought you ought to see these."

"Let's take a look." Glenn opened the folder and examined, in detail, the 8x10 color photographs. Halfway through the stack he looked to Lincoln with a befuddled expression. "Where is it?"

"The bear?" Lincoln asked.

"Yes, the bear. Where is it?"

54

"It's not there, chief."

"I can see that," Glenn said. He leafed through the photos again, dropped them to the table, and frowned in Lambro's direction.

"I know what you're thinking," the photographer said defensively. "But I also know what I saw, Chief Merrill."

Nuts, Glenn thought. Right back to square one.

"Look," Lambro said, his voice rising in desperation. "You guys have got to believe me. I shoot images for a living and I make a good living doing it. I've worked in fog, rain, snow, any weather condition you can imagine. I'm no stranger to bear in close situations and I know what I saw."

"So how do you explain these?" Glenn asked.

"I can't. This isn't possible." The three men stared silently down at the photograph atop the heap. There in vivid color was the image of Stubby Ewing preserved forever. The Texan was on all fours trying to escape his position on the boardwalk. He was looking over his left shoulder, in utter terror, at... nothing. Lambro tapped the image. "The man was attacked by a bear," he insisted. "And it was charging from right there when I took this photograph."

There was nothing under Lambro's finger but a cloud of swirling fog and rolling mist.

Chapter 6

Psychologically speaking, where you were in Yellowstone depended upon where you'd come from. Some folks might have been on Interstate 89, others on US Highway 287, but the tourists aboard that particular bus, out of Jackson, Wyoming (sixty miles to the south), and Rock Springs the day before, to their way of thinking, were on US 191. It was all the same road headed through the park from the south entrance. The driver eased the bus to a stop along the shoulder, just west of the Lewis River.

A uniformed guide stood beside the driver, turned to the back, and looked over the sea of balding heads and beehives of white, silver, and blue hair. He grabbed a microphone, to be heard over the sound of the slapping windshield wipers, and cleared his throat. "Our schedule allows no time for detours and little time to stop," he told his charges. "But we will pause here for just a moment. To the right of the bus is the Lewis River and, beautiful as it is, that tends to grab everyone's' attention. But, just now, if you look out the left side of the bus, onto the slope above... I know it's a little hard with the rain but it's worth the eye strain. You'll see a sight even more beautiful, I think; one of the herd of elk that graze throughout Yellowstone. I envy those of you with binoculars because this is a rare sight for most citizens of the United States."

The passengers, some with field glasses, crowded the windows for a glimpse. Two hundred yards from the roadway and on the edge of a clearing on the timbered slope rising above them grazed thirty-five cow elk, yearlings and calves of the year. Though beyond the tourists' hearing, the elk mewed and chirped to one another, conversing as they milled about, too preoccupied with filling themselves on the last meals of fall to be concerned with the rain that soaked the ground beneath their hooves.

Three bull elk, carrying small sets of antlers and little experience, circled the herd. While the intent was passing their hereditary seed to any cow coming into the breeding cycle, they were too intimidated by the mature bull that patrolled his harem's perimeter to chance an encounter. Like moons orbiting a planet, they remained just far enough away to avoid confrontation while waiting on a young lass to escape through a bedroom window. As a simple reminder of the butt-whooping that awaited brave upstarts, the herd bull periodically uttered a loud, piercing bugle and guttural grunts – the male elk version of 'I dare you to step across this line.'

Sadly, there were other magnifying optics trained on the elk. From the thick timber on that same slope and a hundred yards further from the road, a single lens found its mark. The soft focus of the searching rifle scope settled in on the master of the herd; shoulders set, neck-muscles bulging as he sparred with a small pine, the massive dark antlers stripping bark and breaking branches in a display of fighting acumen. The focus hardened and became crystal clear as Bass Donnelly's eyes adjusted to the magnification. The image cleared and a well-defined set of black crosshairs settled over the sweet-spot on the regal animal.

The air brakes on the tour bus were released. The engine revved. The tour group was on its way. First, a picnic lunch at Lewis Lake. Then souvenir gathering at the Grant Village shops. Of course, the elk were a topic of conversation aboard the bus, and would be for another three or four minutes.

From within the timber, now disappearing behind the exhaust fumes of the bus, echoed a single report from the rifle. None would recognize the abrupt percussion beneath the patter of the rain and the rumble and belch of the laboring bus's engine. The body of the herd briefly scattered, kicking up divots in their momentary panic, but the majestic bull remained in place. His shoulders and back hunched upward as the projectile found its mark. His front legs kicked as his heart exploded and his lungs ruptured. The wapiti king dropped to the ground. A single involuntary kick was the last movement and the words deadly silence had optimum meaning.

"Well, looky there," Donnelly crowed. He lowered the rifle and looked to his mentor for approval.

Ten yards away, Meeks spit a gob of chaw, wiped his mouth with his sleeve, turned to the boy and winked with pride. That was one fine shot for his first commercial hunt, not counting that gol-darned bear, of course. Yup. That was an impressive shot.

*

The confluence of Miller Creek and the Lamar River lay in a lush valley to the northwest of Saddle Mountain, deep in the heart of Yellowstone's backcountry. To Glenn, the place represented the closest thing to Heaven on Earth. To Bear #264, it represented the Siberian Steppes. The backcountry was where nuisance grizzlies were sentenced when they got into trouble elsewhere.

Bear #264, as far as the United States Forest Service was concerned, had become a nuisance. A three-year-old male, Bear #264 had turned south when his mother decided he was old enough to fend for himself. The grizzly version of "get out and get a job, you bum." An inexperienced wilderness vagrant, he wandered throughout an impressive portion of the millions of acres available to him in four National Forests and two National Parks in Wyoming, Montana, and Idaho. Finally, Bear #264 ended his search by taking up housekeeping along Pacific Creek in the Bridger-Teton National Forest.

*

Mr. and Mrs. Stanley Grabonski of Ames, Iowa thoroughly enjoyed their day of touring in Jackson, Wyoming. They had visited every shop Stanley could possibly endure; at least a dozen, he swore, were carbon copies of one another. They each had picture postcards of jackalope, toy bows and arrows, rubber tomahawks made in Taiwan, cheap shot glasses made in Japan with elk and deer tattooed on their sides and, of course, sweatshirts and t-shirts with glorious renditions of snowcapped mountains and pristine lakes hand-printed in Mexico.

The galleries were more to Stanley's liking. Such beautiful depictions of the western way of life, and wildlife, he had never before seen. When the Misses found a bronze that was perfect for their living room, Stanley nearly fainted at the ten thousand dollar price tag. "Mother," he told her. "Corn prices have never been that good."

They took each other's picture in front of the famous elk antler arches on the Town Square and the Missus asked another passing tourist, an elderly Asian gentleman, to take a picture of them together. Though his English was poor at best, the message was finally conveyed and he gladly snapped their photo. The Grabonskis remained an additional thirty minutes paying back the gesture by taking pictures of the old fellow and half of his tour group.

They watched a delightful wildlife film at the museum. They looked out over the most impressive National Elk Refuge where, too bad, the elk had yet to gather. They headed north again, among the parade of vehicles from every state in the Union, to "Ooohhh" and "Aaahhh" at the magnificent vista afforded them along the drive flanking the Teton Range.

At the Grand Teton National Park Visitor's Center in Moose, Mrs. Grabonski asked a ranger where they might find a less crowded place to park their camper for the evening. Although they had certainly enjoyed the tourist attractions, she explained, they really wanted to commune with nature in a rustic setting. The ranger understood and, wishing more folks would take that approach, offered directions to a location few visitors would find without the inside tip. Pacific Creek, she said, was the perfect place to get a real taste of the wild while still enjoying the comforts of trailer camping.

Mrs. Grabonski was delighted with the helpful lady ranger and repeatedly told her husband so as they made the drive up the unpaved road; first through sagebrush, then beautiful green and white aspen stands and, finally, thick lodgepole pine forests. She was so excited by the trip she forbade Stanley's stopping to read another of those tourist kiosks along the road. At her insistence, he passed the next board without giving it a second look. It was information outlining proper Clean Camp procedures while visiting in bear-country.

As the lodgepole ceded to cottonwood trees, and Pacific Creek's running waters came into view along the right side of their camper, Mrs. Grabonski chose the perfect site for their night's stay. She cooked like a great chef of Europe (one of the reasons Stanley had married her in the first place). After dining on one of her better efforts, Mrs. Grabonski produced a fresh pitcher of lemonade and the happy couple sat and talked of their day's adventure, until both were too tired to bother with the dishes.

"Leave them until morning," Stanley said. "They'll keep."

*

Bear #264 was hungry.

It had been a hard day for him, what with trying to earn a decent living in unfamiliar country. While traveling along the west bank of Pacific Creek, just after sundown, his supersensitive nose picked up a most delicious and inviting smell.

Had they discussed it, Bear #264 would have certainly told Stanley his wife was a most amazing cook. As events unfolded, however, there had been little time for a discussion. The Grabonski's night of communing with nature was cut short when Bear #264 entered their camp and scared three years of life out of the Missus. Stanley, still in his boxers, grabbed the little woman, fired up the old camper, and beat a hasty retreat back to Moose. They left the dishes, their camp chairs, and a half pitcher of homemade lemonade behind. Those items, along with their portable folding table, were spread hither and yon by their uninvited guest.

The friendly raid on the Grabonski's camp had been strike one for Bear #264. As in America's favorite pastime, bears were allowed three strikes before they too were called out. Three strikes meant they were dangerous to visitors and when that became the case there was no choice but to either send them to an animal holding facility, like a zoo, or put a bullet into their head. Few zoos were in need of bears.

The unfortunate part about Bear #264's first strike was that he had been rewarded with human food; that wonderful combination of sweetness and salt that can only be found in places people frequent. Such delicacies were not natural in the wild. Having had a taste, Bear #264 would surely return for seconds if not removed from the area. To keep him in the ball game, it was decided he would be relocated away from human contact. It was the Steppes for Bear #264.

*

The torrential rains had ceased for the moment, and the ride arranged for Bear #264 could finally get airborne. The tops of the pine trees bowed respectfully as the U.S. Fish and Wildlife's converted Huey was eased vertically into position over the drop site. Below the helicopter a box trap, and the nuisance bear it held, depended from an umbilical line that slowly swayed with the last winds of the passing storm and the downdraft of the metallic bird.

An anxious trio waited at the side of a temporarily marked target area set up on a level spot along the east bank of the Lamar River. The group shared a great deal of excitement and no small amount of apprehension.

J.D. was there to attach a radio collar to Bear #264. Although many creatures were adorned in a similar manner, nuisance bears in particular wore the bulky jewelry in order to allow wildlife biologists to track their whereabouts and their behavior. It was a procedure J.D. had participated in many times while working her internship in Alaska. This, however, was her first outing as a lead biologist. She held it together on the outside but inside her nerves rolled like spaghetti in a boiling pot.

Nelson Princep, present as the official observer for Yellowstone Forever, did his best just to stand in place. The downdraft from the copter blades threatened to toss his skinny frame, dress jacket and all, into the fast and foamy current of the Lamar. But he held his ground. Regardless of how ill at ease he felt, he had every intention of protecting the rights of the bear during the operation. It was vitally important the animal be treated fairly in its relocation. Yellowstone Forever knew what was best for grizzly bears. He would see they got what they deserved.

Glenn rounded out the trio as the gun bearer; carrying a 12-gauge Remington pump loaded with slugs. The idea of having to shoot a grizzly appalled him but, if for any reason something went wrong, it was preferable to zipping one of his team members into a body bag.

The last time Glenn administered first aid to a mauling victim, he'd had nightmares for two days. And he'd been on vacation. The victim, a Casper, Wyoming elk hunter, had left his party and gone off on his own in the backcountry of the Bridger-Teton National Forest not far from Togwotee Pass. He'd been sneaking through the woods, like the round-headed hunter in the Warner Brothers' cartoons, and had accidentally come upon, and startled, a grizzly. As was its nature, the bear charged the hunter. That was when the guy really screwed up.

Had the hunter stood still, the bear would most likely have recognized he was not being threatened and halted his charge. At the worst, had he played dead when attacked, he'd have probably gotten off with a couple bruises, a few superficial bites, and one heck of a scare. The hunter chose, instead, to try to scare it away. Already threatened, the bear felt no relief in seeing a screaming, contorted creature bounding around in its territory. Consequently, it continued its charge. The animal closed to within eight feet before the hunter decided to shoot.

There was no doubt, the hunter was packing knockdown power. He had a .375 H&H bolt-action, the heavy-duty artillery used by outfitters to kill bears in Alaska. But bears are faster than most would believe. That fellow had left himself a fraction of a second to draw a bead and fire. Whether or not he hit the bear was never determined. He failed to kill it immediately, guaranteeing his being creamed by nearly a half-ton of enraged wildlife.

The animal had been left without a choice. He lunged, taking the hunter by the left arm and driving him into the hard ground. The bear then released him, considered his options and jumped back aboard, sinking his teeth into the hunter's head. Several critical facial bones gave way under the pressure and one of his eyes vacated its socket. When the hunter quit moving, the bear released him.

Amazingly, the guy survived. Following the bruin's departure, he managed to fire his weapon to attract the attention of his hunting buddies. Glenn and a lady friend, with whom he'd been hiking, arrived on the scene shortly after. The elk hunter was evacuated by helicopter and treated to three hours in a surgery theater at the Casper Medical Center to help him remember the backcountry rules.

Now, Glenn and his team waited in silence as the chopper lowered the trap. When the crate was safely on the ground, J.D. disconnected the umbilical line. The flight crew reeled the line back in, gave a thumbs up when it was secured, and lifted their craft vertically. The bird banked right, to the north, and disappeared down the length of the Lamar leaving them in quiet save for the roaring river and the whistling wind.

Bear #264 lay prone on the floor of the trap, conscious but in a stupor from the sedative he'd been given twenty-five minutes before. J.D. unhinged the door on the short end of the box and Glenn sidled in alongside to help pull the animal free. The going was tough as the bear outweighed them both by at least a hundred pounds. "You're supposed to pull the bear," J.D. snapped. "Not ride the thing."

Glenn grinned. "Too much to handle, little lady?"

J.D. flushed red. She reached in, got hold of the bear's front leg, then grunted like a free-lift contestant at the Olympics while she pulled. With Glenn on the opposite leg, the bear slid forward and plopped out on the ground. With her fists on her hips in triumph, J.D. locked her jaw and stared Glenn down. The chief ranger laughed enjoying a triumph of his own. Her expression softened, turned reluctantly up at the corners and, finally, broke into laughter too.

"Shall we finish?" Glenn asked.

There were no parades, speeches, or keys to the city, but Bear #264 was home. Belly down in the high grass with his head resting sideways atop his front legs, the paralyzed bruin watched his captors with lethargic eyes. Glenn glanced into the sad brown orbs, sorry for the discomfort the bear felt, but knowing that here he would have a new lease on life, far from uninformed and inconsiderate people.

Glenn also realized time was against them. The bear was showing signs of recovery and the drug would soon wear off. J.D. hurried to wrap the radio collar around the animal's neck.

Dragging the bear across the smooth surface of the trap had been one thing but supporting the dead weight of its head, protecting the creature from injury in the process, and securing a bulky radio collar all at once was more than one small wildlife biologist could reasonably accomplish. Short arms didn't help. "Can I get a hand here?"

Glenn turned the 12-gauge, offering the butt to Princep. "Hold this a minute."

"I don't want that," the green leader said, refusing the weapon.

"Would you rather Ms. Davies and I get mauled?" Glenn asked.

Princep hated guns. Their invention had been nothing more or less than an earth-shattering symbol of man's barbaric tendency toward, and love of, violence. Making no effort to disguise his displeasure, he took the shotgun. He held it at arms-length, as if handling a poisonous snake.

Though too groggy to lift it, the bear rolled its head to the side. It fell awkwardly off his legs and onto the soggy grass. "We'd better hurry with this," Glenn said. "He won't be out much longer."

Princep wiped the sweat from his forehead nearly dropping the shotgun in the process. He hadn't realized what bear observation really meant. Without realizing it, he pulled the gun into his chest, gripped the stock as if it were trying to escape, and fingered the trigger.

J.D. continued to fight the collar. In an effort to help, the chief straddled the bear next to the biologist trying to reach underneath. "Glenn," J.D. griped, "get on the other side and lift."

"Relax. I'll slip it around his head. You grab the pliers."

J.D. released the collar and hurried to the field kit. Glenn jumped to the spot she'd vacated. Bear #264 jerked his head up and around, drawing his shoulders off the ground. Regaining some muscle control, the animal released a halfhearted growl and nipped at the ranger. "Whoa!" Glenn cried as he jerked away. Startled, Princep swung the shotgun down to his hip and inadvertently pulled the trigger. Glenn screamed, "No!" The environmentalist simply screamed. The 12-gauge issued a terrifying report. All three sounds merged into one unintelligible echo that bounced down through the valley.

Bear #264's forehead exploded in a crimson arc as the slug disappeared into his skull just to the left of his right eye. His body twitched violently, then lay still, surrounded by a deafening silence.

Chapter 7

The drive from Mammoth down to the little town of Crowheart took hours but Glenn considered it time well spent, the cheapest therapy west of the Mississippi. From the moment his Suburban cleared the south entrance of the park, Glenn felt the muscles in his neck and shoulders unwinding. It had been a nasty week and he needed a few days away from the grind to put things back into perspective. The chief loved his job, and Yellowstone, but the last several days had just been too much. He needed someone to talk with, someone who actually knew how to listen. He needed Johnny Two Ravens.

Glenn passed through the small community of Dubois, heading steadily southeast and marveling at how the country changed so quickly in the western states. The lodgepole forests he spent so much time in gave way to unending miles of open country covered with sagebrush.

He'd heard many tourists call it ugly country. and Glenn could understand that point of view coming from the uninitiated. At first glance, it did seem to be little more than interminable flat barrenness speckled with dry bushes looking more dead than alive. A closer look, however, revealed something magic and wonderful about the land. The country spread before him like a hand-woven Native American blanket; more complicated and beautiful than the casual observer could know. The land was not flat. It was, to those who took the time to really see it, an unending vista of softly rolling hills fractured and framed by jagged washes carved maze-like into the sandstone by the torrential rains of fall and the run-off of melting snow in spring from the surrounding mountain peaks. Throughout the seeming desolation thrived herds of mule deer; feeding on grasses, forbs and sagebrush to replenish body fat lost during the hard winter on the wind-blown side of the rugged, distant rock buttes. On those distant peaks lived bighorn sheep and elk. There was not a square inch of the wilderness that Mother Nature didn't fill with productive life. Little was as it appeared in the west.

As he crossed the boundary into the Wind River Indian Reservation, that final thought frustrated the chief ranger. There was something about the recent events in Yellowstone; they were not as they appeared. Glenn felt like a tourist seeing only the surface. He was missing something. But what?

"Relax," he said aloud. "You're on a mini-vacation." He'd been talking to himself too much of late. He laughed, then yelled, "Help me, Johnny Two Ravens!"

Two Ravens was the closest thing to a best friend a man in the wild could have. He was honest, too much for his own good, and had a sense of humor as sharp as a Bowie knife. Not to mention he drank his whiskey straight. Glenn and Two Ravens had polished off many a black and white labeled bottle over the years. They made quite a team; fishing, fighting, carousing.

Two Ravens was a full-blooded Shoshone; the son of a tribal sub-chief named Oscar Eagle Feather. Glenn remembered the night Two Ravens had enlightened him to that fact. He had confessed, in his own way, that he didn't know Indians still had chiefs "and all that jazz."

Two Ravens had simply stared back at him, wearing his trademark emotionless expression. "It isn't jazz," he said. "And I could write a book about what you don't know." Glenn was having too much fun at the time to pursue the issue. He'd let the discussion drop with every intention of picking it up again one day.

Two Ravens owned an outdoors shop and outfitting business. If you met his healthy price, he'd take you anywhere in the greater Yellowstone area or Wyoming. His regular clients knew they would find game and fish aplenty, they'd have a good time and Two Ravens would get them back in one piece. His reputation was his best advertisement and he made a fair living at what he did.

Glenn respected the man for more than his business sense. Two Ravens had a good ear, which Glenn troubled sparingly. He didn't spout nonsense and he wouldn't listen to it. His friend was just the medicine Glenn needed. He'd had all the nonsense one man could stand.

The beauty of the reservation countryside was upstaged and tarnished as Glenn entered Crowheart. The snowcapped peaks of the Wind River Mountains towered in the background to the west, making midgets of men. The sky was just as stunningly blue and free of clouds, the air just as sparkling clean. Yet from the moment he passed the bent, bullet hole ridden government sign declaring he'd entered Crowheart, the only descriptive word that came to the chief ranger's mind was bleak.

The highway Glenn traveled was maintained for the sole purpose of transporting tourists to and from the great parks on the opposite side of the Continental Divide. The highway, therefore, was as beautiful as asphalt could be. Were it not for tourists, however, that same roadway would have been neglected long ago.

Neglect was the rule of the day once you exited that two-lane strip of yellow brick road. It was the only asphalt in the community, a dividing line that nearly split the reservation down the middle, and at once proved unequivocally that maintaining the place was always somebody else's problem. It had apparently never been decided just who, exactly, that somebody might be.

The Lunkers Galore Trout Farm was the first place of business encountered as Glenn motored into the reservation town. Serviced by a dirt lane intersecting the pavement, the farm consisted of a barn on the left that served as the fish rearing facility for the trout pond and a small single story house nearly as old as the town. The residence was a tiny version of the barn and its first coat of paint had probably been its last. The pond was a two-acre puddle set back in the sagebrush with a half dozen weathered picnic tables dotting its sparse shoreline.

Tommy Two Fists was the owner and sole operator of Lunkers Galore, and a more cantankerous old geezer Glenn had never met. He would argue about the color of the sky. There must have been something to Indian mysticism that Two Fists' parents were able to pick a name for him that wore like a tailored suit. That or he must have been a bilious grouch screaming at all of creation as he slid out of the birth canal.

Two Fists made his living charging white tourists an exorbitant fee to rent a pole and catch trout from his pond. There was little challenge to the affair, particularly since Two Fists fed the fish only enough to keep them sufficiently active to bite the baited hooks offered by the saps he graciously called clients. Idiot folks from Chicago and New York were more interested in a guaranteed catch, complete with a victory photograph, than they were of seeking out a stream somewhere in the backcountry and actually going to the trouble of doing it the right way. That was fine with Two Fists. It provided him with day old bread and a bottle of his favorite-colored liquid. Two Fists was nowhere in sight as the ranger passed. It was just as well.

Ramshackle housing in stereo made up the remainder of the first block of Washakie Street, which was the only entrance to the town. The street was named after the Shoshone's greatest chief; and Crowheart after one of Washakie's greatest victories.

It was near that spot in 1859 the Shoshone and Crow Indians, bitter enemies, met in a decisive battle. Big Robber, the chief of the Crow, had taunted Washakie, calling him a "squaw" and "an old woman." He proclaimed the Shoshone chief too cowardly to fight. The ensuing battle lasted three days before culminating in a duel between the chiefs. Washakie killed Big Robber, cut out his heart and ate a portion of it. What remained of the organ, he impaled upon his lance and carried during their victory War Dance. Thus was born Crowheart.

Teetering picket fences seemed to bow as Glenn passed. That imagined graciousness, coupled with the serenading of mutt dogs from several of the yards, was the only outward greeting he would receive from the residents of the sleepy settlement. At that, he was never sure whether the dogs were giving him a welcome or telling him to get out. The message from the people on the street was subtler. White people, in general, were a necessary evil to the Indian population. Few were liked, none were trusted, but their tourist dollars bought food and clothes. Shopkeepers offered them fake smiles, plastic beads, and rubber tomahawks in exchange for their money. Indians on the street simply stared as they passed wondering to themselves what the whites wanted now. As a whole, the community would have preferred to put a turn lane at the town's entrance, with an arrow pointing into a basket, and a sign reading: Put your money here and get out! Unfortunately, it didn't work that way and they knew it.

Every time Glenn entered the town, he was greeted by hollow stares. At times like that he wished he were any other color because of what his 'white' government had done to the once proud Native Americans. Glenn did not, however, feel sorry for them. He didn't feel sorry for anyone.

The American continent had hundreds of varied Indian Tribes stretching to its four corners. Crowheart had two, Shoshone and Arapaho. In truth, however, Glenn had come to realize that now there were really only two kinds of Indians regardless of tribal affiliation: the traditional and the BIA.

By far, the majority were BIA; that is, they worked and lived under the governing rule of the United States Bureau of Indian Affairs. Their ancestors had, for the most part, come to the reservation over a century before under treaty with the white Union government. Realizing all things change, they'd chosen peace instead of war and believed the promises made to them. They'd signed away their freedom, their history, and their way of life to get along. They'd signed away their spirits.

Hundreds of broken promises later, all on the part of the government, the BIA's who were once a proud people were now a clan of burned-out drunks living in squalor and hopelessness. They had nowhere to go, nothing to do, and nobody to care about their plight, least of all themselves. It was easier to give the Bureau total control of their lives – and their destiny. Glenn felt no remorse for a people who had surrendered their very souls.

The traditional Indians were another matter entirely. As far as the government was concerned they were red devils. They were uncooperative, stubborn, single-minded ingrates who didn't know a good thing when they held it in their hands. They were given everything and appreciated nothing. The government's stand on traditional Indians was simple; they were troublemakers. Glenn liked them.

Two Ravens was a traditional Indian and Glenn was proud to call him a friend.

The Crowheart business district stood much like that of any other small town but overshadowed by the shabbiness of the worn and weary reservation. The town's one small liquor store and lounge sat opposite the post office. White painted wooden letters were nailed above its single picture window, which faced the street and announced to the world its unimaginative name, The Crowheart Bar.

The heavy front door stood wide open, as was customary. The solitary patron inside was enjoying the comfort of air-conditioning in true reservation style. Over the front of the building hung a dilapidated shake-shingle roof, supported by ageless burled pine timbers. Between them hung a bright orange banner, a harbinger of the season, reading WELCOME HUNTERS. If the truth were known, anybody with a spare quarter was more than welcome at The Crowheart Bar.

A transplanted Nez Perce Indian named Smohalla owned the place. With the trade slightly off of late he was also behind the bar whenever the doors were open. Not unfriendly, Smohalla was nonetheless quiet and seemed to frown deeper with each drink he sold. The community had lost more than its share of bright, young Indians thanks to alcoholism and suicide. Glenn often wondered if Smohalla seemed so sad because he felt responsible.

Down the street and opposite stood the Tomahawk Motel. Gray and vacant, it resembled the monoliths of rock found just outside of town in the sagebrush. Mrs. Boinaiv, the owner, had lost her husband seven years before. He'd been shot in a bar brawl and the old woman had run the place on her own since. She teetered slowly back and forth in an old rocking chair on the wide front porch, as colorless and empty as her motel. Mrs. Boinaiv wore a glazed expression, lost in a distant place and a better time, and seemed not to notice Glenn's passing.

Joe White inflated a child's rear bicycle tire with the rusted air compressor on the south side of his filling station. He waved to Glenn as the ranger passed, smiling as if the world could not have been a better place. Joe was a jolly fellow, by reservation standards, and only the good Lord knew why. Other than tourists, few cars needed filling. Joe's wife had gone east years before and had never returned. The details he kept to himself. His only son, Ed, was a first class hellion on a first name basis with law enforcement agencies throughout the area.

Faded signs in the dirty windows advertised oil and transmission fluid. A vintage gas pump, with a glass globe top, sat at the side of the building. It would have been worth a fortune, had the globe not been shattered years before. A scratched soda machine designed to dispense bottles, and still sporting a price of fifteen cents on its front, guarded the space between the yawning front door and the open overhead. An Out of Order sign hung over its coin slot, and had for months.

Joe finished with the little girl's bike. She tried to offer him money but Joe simply waved her off with a smile. The repair stall was empty, so happy-go-lucky Joe wandered over to a lawn chair in the shade alongside the building and sat down with a magazine.

An F&E Grocery store stood watch over the far end of the main drag. Within, BIA's traded food stamps for overpriced staples; without, two old codgers told lies on a wooden sidewalk bench. They paused as Glenn passed, eying him from behind weathered copper faces, showing neither friendliness nor malice but simply bland stares. Framed in his rear view mirror they took up where they'd left off.

Across from the grocery sat the brightest, newest building in town, the Wind River Taxidermy Studio. Its red brick seemed on fire in comparison to the sad nothingness of the rest of the block. A stuffed black bear towered at the entrance, greeting visitors with its frozen glare. Antler racks hung from the upper corners of the front window and a lifeless beaver, its tail aloft like a cricket bat, grinned over a chiseled log beneath.

Glenn turned off Washakie Street, just past the Taxidermist's, following the dirt side street a stone's throw to Two Ravens' place. He pulled to a stop and stepped out in a cloud of dust.

Johnny Two Ravens' Outdoors Shop lacked the modern brightness of the stuffed animal joint up the road. He could ill afford brick walls or petrified bears. What his place did have was pride. A freshly painted exterior of robin's egg blue called travelers and tourists in from the street and a wooden porch, erected with Glenn's help the previous fall, welcomed those who answered the call.

The ranger was up the steps and across the porch in four long strides. He ignored the CLOSED sign dangling from a hook on the door and entered to the jingling of bells. He scanned the shadowy front room and called out his usual greeting. "Hey, Tonto, where are you?"

Two Ravens appeared in the doorway to the back room silhouetted by dim lamplight. His weathered black cowboy hat enhanced the dark shadows over his eyes. His jaw locked in a chiseled grimace; he extended the hunting knife in his right hand. "You need something, Ranger Rick?"

Glenn threw his hands up in mock surrender. "I give."

Two Ravens smiled and drove the knife blade into the counter top. "Since when? All you white boys ever do is take."

Glenn eased into a knowing smile. The Indian was quick-witted and, at times, brutal in the game they played.

"You know, I don't mean to complain," Two Ravens said. "But one day you're going to come in here spouting that "Tonto" garbage and there's going to be some old Indian in here packing iron and absent my sense of humor."

The ranger grunted.

Two Ravens laughed. It was a low, friendly laugh that made a liar of his stern features. His long, straight hair, as black as Wyoming oil, draped in the traditional manner from beneath his worn hat.

Glenn had never seen his friend without that hat. Few had. The chief had, however, discovered Two Ravens didn't appreciate wise remarks about his headgear. Once, when asked about it, Two Ravens replied, "It keeps my hair in place, keeps the rain and snow off my neck, and the sun out of my eyes." He thought about it a moment, then added, "Besides, it sets me apart from eastern tourists."

"Yes," Glenn agreed. "The downside is it makes you look like an Indian."

Two Ravens immediately, without malice of forethought, whipped Glenn's hind end; a feat that took some effort. With his ranger friend face down in the dirt, he refused to let him up until he said, "Native American," three times – with respect. Half laughing, half crying, the ranger managed it, getting his reddened arm back as a reward. Glenn, of course, got in the final word. "No, really," he said dusting himself off. "It looks good on you." It was the last time he'd mentioned the hat.

The Indian examined his friend standing wearily in the doorway of his shop. "What kind of week have you had?" Two Ravens asked.

"Messed up."

"So says the gossip. Come on back, I've got a bottle with our names on it."

Two Ravens' living quarters reflected their owner, clashing images of the ancient and the new. The room was dimly lit by a floor lamp adjacent to an overstuffed chair and a smaller one atop an end table by the couch on the opposite side of the room. Two windows covered by drab beige drapes allowed some natural light to enter. The only other illumination came from above the fireplace where an artist's lamp cast a glow on two pipes on display. A peace pipe adorned with the white-tipped tail feathers of a bald eagle and colored beads hung in a place of honor to the left. To the right hung a more intricately detailed medicine pipe. Glenn understood neither their significances nor their differences but clearly the pipes were important to Two Ravens. The medicine pipe in particular. It had a polished wood shaft, wrapped in leather thongs from which hung beads and feathers of brilliant colors, and featured a stunning bowl carved from a block of elk antler into the shape of a raven's head. In hushed tones, Two Ravens had explained that the raven was his guiding spirit animal. The spirit stuff was beyond Glenn's comprehension but the pipe was the most beautiful artwork he had ever seen. Woven blankets, baskets, and beadwork lay scattered throughout, adding color to the otherwise brown and green room.

Two Ravens was a traditional Shoshone; the pipes, feathers, and stones had meaning for him and were displayed with great care. Still he was a man of the 20th century. In the far corner stood a table of leathering tools and, beside it, an old sawhorse splattered in old paint. Atop the sawhorse rested a saddle Two Ravens had been restoring. It too was a superb piece of workmanship. Johnny had made it clear that no tourist's butt would ever overshadow the gracefully curving seat. It was his saddle. Its leather glistened while the pungent odor of neat's-foot oil permeated the room.

A rolled tent and sleeping bags occupied another corner, along with lanterns, backpacks, fishing poles, and tackle boxes. On the wall above was a handmade gun rack adorned with two rifles and a shotgun, meticulously cleaned and oiled. Beside it hung another rack, containing a traditional longbow and quiver of handmade arrows. And beside that hung several wet suits before a cabinet of diving equipment; expensive foreign toys to Glenn. Though the room was large, it felt cramped with the Indian world on display and the new world crammed into the cracks out of necessity. A colored television and stereo occupied an entertainment center on the far wall, a high-tech testimony that not all modern conveniences were bad news. At the moment, however, the gentle rhythm of Native American flute music floated through the air.

Glenn rolled his eyes in mock disdain.

Two Ravens laughed and turned the CD player off. On his return trip, he removed a pink bathrobe from the back of a door and tossed it into the next room. Left by a recent guest, the robe told another part of Two Ravens' personal story. He was single and liked it that way.

"Big or little?" the outfitter asked, fingering glasses in the cupboard above his sink.

"Go heavy or go home," Glenn muttered.

He grabbed a tumbler and liberally poured the red-gold whiskey. "Want some water with that?" Two Ravens asked, renewing another ritual as old as their friendship.

Glenn looked at him as if he were stupid and responded with the ritual answer. "Water? Do you know what fish do in water?" They shared a laugh and the ranger was already feeling better.

Two Ravens handed the glass over then poured his own. Reclining on the opposite sofa, he took a slug of the potent liquor, exhaled at the hot burst in his chest, and crossed his feet atop a pile of hunting magazines. "Talk to me, bwana."

Glenn did. He let it all come out, recounting the events of the week; the grizzly poached by the highway, the Texas visitor who died during a bear attack near Firehole Lake, the freak thunderstorm that threatened to wash away half the park, and the horrible accident during the relocation of Bear #264. "This guy, Princep, was there to protect the interests of the bear and he's the one who killed it," Glenn said in disgust. "These green groups are a pain in the neck."

"They have their purpose, Glenn," Two Ravens said. "If we all took more care with our world, and our heritage, we wouldn't need the environmentalists."

"I understand that. The problem is these people get so caught up in their causes they forget their purpose. How many times have we seen them do more damage than good? How often do they work so hard to protect something that they end up destroying it?"

Two Ravens considered the question, nodded at an unspoken thought, reached for the remote and turned on his fancy television. He found the news and, for several long minutes allowed the talking head anchor to overwhelm them both with violence and crisis. Finally, he said, "It is man's nature to do more damage than good. Not only to nature but to each other." He tossed the remote on the table and headed for the bottle.

On the television screen, apparently finished for the moment spreading doom and gloom, the news anchor stuck his nose into the weather, schmoozing with the station's chief meteorologist. Glenn wearily motor-boated his lips, remembering a simpler time, with less bull and self-importance, when he was just a ranger and she would have been just a weather girl. The motorboat turned into a full-on raspberry when she couldn't explain the origins of the most intense storm they'd seen in decades, and which seemed to restrict itself just to Yellowstone National Park.

"So," the talking head said, "between the mud slide warnings and the potential for additional rain, it sounds like the Department of the Interior might want to get started building an Ark?"

"I wouldn't go that far," little Susie Storm replied, with a smidge of laughter and a lot of teeth. "But, were I them, I wouldn't put the boots away just yet, either."

"Great," Glenn said, reaching for the remote. "How's that for the cherry on top of the crap Sundae this day has been?"

Winding down the homey mirth, the anchor thanked "Jen," the weather girl. Then, before Glenn could cut him off, the news reader went all in earnest giving the ranger pause. "Now," the anchor said, "for those in our viewing audience that missed it earlier, here is a replay of tonight's guest editorial by the new park correspondent and columnist for the Billings Reporter, Howard Lark."

Glenn stayed his hand, lowered the remote, and then glared as Lark appeared on Two Ravens' big color screen, every bit as smug and self-satisfied as the chief ranger remembered him.

"Yellowstone's tourist season is in high gear," the reporter started in, "and, while all appears normal, one has to ask, 'Is everything all right in Yellowstone National Park?' To this reporter's mind, questions of safety are being met with precious few answers. Is Park Superintendent Michael Stanton aware of recent events in our nation's oldest playground? Or is Chief Ranger Glenn Merrill, famed for his Walking Tall approach to law enforcement, keeping certain facts to himself? Questions about recent elk and bear poaching incidents have been brushed away. But Merrill's office, when pressed, has confirmed two separate incidents resulting in the deaths of two grizzly bears. The grizzly is on the Endangered Species List. Additionally, a tourist recently died in the park, but rangers have steadfastly refused to give any details. Why? One of this reporter's sources indicates the visitor died during a bear attack. Is there a connection? Why, Chief Merrill, if everything is all right, have you canceled your rangers' 'leave time'? Why are all rangers working overtime? It's no secret that the top Yellowstone ranger carries a big stick. But isn't it about time, either softly or not, he begin speaking?"

The news anchor reappeared looking, it would be fair to say, a little shocked. He cleared his throat and started the standard disclaimer, "The views expressed..."

"Nice," Two Ravens said returning. He reclaimed his remote and shut the television off. "Glad we didn't miss that, huh?"

"Better and better," Glenn agreed. "I'd like to take a big stick and... What did you say about doing damage?"

"Go for it," Two Ravens said with a laugh. "You could always plead 'the nature of man.'" Then both were laughing; and pouring more booze. "You came with a problem. Have you found the answer, my friend?"

"Apparently not, Johnny. I'm still crying." Glenn emptied his glass and reached for the bottle. "You're the one who understands Mother Earth and all that jazz. What do you think?"

"I think, if you call my beliefs jazz one more time," Two Ravens said with a smile, "I'll pound you into dust." He thought for a moment then continued in all sincerity. "Despite the Howard Larks of the world, we do need to live in harmony with Mother Earth. The best answer to all of our problems is to take care of each other. In doing so we'll ultimately take care of ourselves."

"What are the chances of that happening?" Glenn threw his head back, gulping the burning liquid.

"Better than my chances of having any leftover whiskey, white boy."

Chapter 8

Dan Fresno was a cowboy.

He wasn't the Hollywood type that always seemed to be fighting redskins or chasing desperadoes. Those weren't real cowboys. They were works of fiction meant to entertain and generate box office dollars. Dan Fresno dealt with cows – for a living.

Real cowboys slept on the ground at the edge of high mountain meadows or in ratty old bunkhouses amounting to little more than a roof with a wooden floor. They had bowed legs from straddling horses sixteen hours a day. Their skin was weathered and brown, aged beyond their years, thanks to endless weeks in scorching heat, freezing cold, rain, sleet, snow and whatever else Mother Nature decided to dump on them throughout their lives.

Real cowboys were loners because that was the only way they could do their jobs without going crazy. Riding the range might seem romantic to city slickers but being alone all day, every day, for years on end was not nearly as romantic as it was a hard way to earn a buck. Real cowboys packed guns, not for shoot-outs but to protect their herds from predators, to kill the occasional snake in camp or, God forbid, to humanely put their horse out of its misery if it took a bad fall and broke a leg in the backcountry.

Real cowboys helped cows deliver their calves when they couldn't do it on their own. They branded them when they were old enough but before they got too big to handle. They drove the herds into the mountains in the spring, moved them from one grazing area to another throughout the summer, and drove them back out again in the fall.

Real cowboys smelled like cow dung and horsehair. They dressed in denim because it was durable; wore wide-brimmed hats to keep the sun out of their eyes and the weather off the back of their necks; and chaps to protect their legs from thorns, brambles, and low hanging limbs they often rode through. They didn't dress for style. They dressed for comfort and utility.

Real cowboys were long and lean from too few home cooked meals and too many backbreaking, interminable days of work. Dan Fresno was a real cowboy.

Dan, like most folks, had a nickname. Colorful as nicknames tended to be, they were usually born of real life. In Dan's case, they called him "Beans." Dan loved beans, baked beans in particular. Ride into his camp on any summer evening, pull up a log and help yourself to a cup of coffee and a plate of beans. There might be a slice of bread to go with it, or the occasional slab of bacon, but if you didn't like beans you'd go hungry in Dan's camp.

Beans originally hailed from Texas as most cowboys did, especially in the early days of the frontier when that was where the cows came from. Cows needed cowboys to tend them, cows came from Texas, and cowboys came with them. Beans rode for the Cattlemen's Association. The stock he tended were not his, in the legal sense of the word, but he rode them – so they were his. Cows were Bean's business. Cows were Bean's life.

Not surprisingly, when a grizzly sow decided his beef was on the menu for her three cubs, Beans took it real personal. Grizzlies were considered 'Endangered' and were offered protection under the law. Cows were not endangered so the law didn't much care. Beans cared; forget the law.

After he'd come upon the remains of one of his cows, and the telltale signs indicating a bear as the culprit, Beans put most of his energy into looking for the interloper. It took several days but Beans found what he was looking for. He was riding the grazing allotment ten miles east of Jardine, Montana in the Gallatin National Forest. It was rough country, comprised of a long, deep valley where the Absaroka Mountains drained their heavy load of snowmelt in the form of swiftly moving streams. Many were seasonal, most unnamed. The rivulets started above the flight path of eagles, widening as they descended the steep slopes. They merged with like-streams and grew, gaining in size and increasing in power, until they reached the valley floor. There they joined to form Hellroaring Creek.

In dryer times, decades past, beaver had dammed Hellroaring Creek. They built their homes and raised their young on the resulting pond. The beaver had since moved on. Time and spring floods had since rerouted Hellroaring Creek. The pond had filled with sediment and vanished, leaving a lush green meadow with its passing. Moose fed in the willows on the banks of the new creek. Elk sustained themselves on the grasses farther back when the snow drove them from their high country haunts. Cattle, as well, grew fat on the bounty left long ago by the industrious beaver. Now the cattle were absent and it made Beans uncomfortable.

Riding a low ridge line overlooking the meadow, the cowboy spotted the problem. On the opposite side lay the remains of another cow and, at her side, the shredded hide of a yearling calf. Beans cussed and spurred his mount, cutting down the ridge and into the willows. He crossed the meadow, now marshland from the deluge of late-season rain, en route to examine the kill. Beans knew already that the bear had struck again.

His horse suddenly flared its nostrils, jumped sideways, and started to bolt. Beans tightened his leg hold on the animal's midsection, pulled slack from the reins and hung on, unaware his mount had their best interests at heart. An instant later, Beans understood the problem. The willows erupted with a ferocious roar and the blurred blonde shape of the subject of the cowboy's search.

A grizzly sow, sated for the moment on fattened beef, had been lying in the willows with her three cubs, resting and guarding their leftovers. Driven by her instinct to protect her progeny and their meal, she had no tolerance for intruders. The charge came so fast Beans could not react. His horse took the lead instead, nearly tossing him to the ground. Then she did what horses do; she ran like the wind. Too full to bother further with the fleeing pair, the angry sow roared a warning that the cowboy not come back, then she returned to her nap.

*

Bart Houser had been a friend to Beans for years. They first met when Beans, tired of the Texas desert and looking for new adventure, moved into Wyoming cow country. In those days, Houser worked a little on the ranches himself. He was a native of Montana. He loved the life of the cowboy and wanted to make it his career. Unfortunately, the price of beef wasn't what he thought it should be and Houser liked more expensive things than what a cowboy's salary could buy.

Instead Houser did what a lot of people did in that part of the country. He looked to the park for a better wage and a softer life. He went to school and, barely, earned his degree then went to work as a ranger. Getting in was tough. Like everyone else he started as a seasonal ranger. Full-time positions were hard to come by and some never made it at all. Houser was not there yet.

He'd been working the park for nearly five years, Memorial Day to Labor Day. The money wasn't bad and it would get better if he could ever get a full-time slot. In the meantime, he spent his winters working with Beans or helping out at the Gardiner Feed Store. Houser would, on occasion, bend the rules a little bit. There was good money in wild meat and hefty antlers. There were too many elk in the park anyway; even some environmentalists agreed on that. They wouldn't miss a few. Besides, if you asked Houser, the park owed him.

Beans had a thorn in his saddle and needed a hand removing it. The cowboy went to see the part-time ranger following his encounter on Hellroaring Creek. After all, Houser was his friend and he was connected. He agreed it would be more effective to shoot the things but he also realized that hiding a grizzly kill, let alone four, would not be an easy task. He preferred doing things the easy way.

"Let's give the problem to the park," Houser said. "Cows aren't worth much to the government but bears are. It shouldn't be hard to convince them the sow and cubs are a threat to human life and in danger themselves."

"How you going to do that?" Beans asked.

"Easy," Houser said with a grin. "I just tell them some irate rancher will end up shooting their precious bears unless they're relocated. If they have a choice between four bears in the wild and four bears in boxes, they'll move the bears."

*

That's what Bart Houser got for opening his big mouth.

Sure, Superintendent Stanton had said, we can trap the bears and move them out of the allotment. Unfortunately, his regular teams were all busy. Houser had been on bear relocation projects in the past and had done well. There was no reason, Stanton said, he couldn't take the plunge and run the operation himself.

So Houser had to move the bears and, man o' man, Beans was going to owe him.

Apparently, the chief ranger didn't think he'd been dumped on enough. On top of everything else, he'd ordered Houser to take two environmentalists along; a young fellow named Todd Muncey and a mean-looking broad named Priscilla Wentworth. "They need to observe our operations," Chief Merrill said. "Their extra hands might be useful." Yeah, Houser thought, useful as screen doors on a submarine. So there he was, misunderstood, under-appreciated, improperly rewarded Ranger Houser, saddled with two greens and in charge of relocating a grizzly sow and her three cubs. Life was not fair.

An aerial survey had been conducted the evening before to check the four culvert traps set and baited in the meadow on Hellroaring Creek. The helicopter pilot confirmed that at least one of the traps had been sprung. Eight o'clock in the morning brought that same helicopter, Houser and his team to a flat piece of real estate one-half mile south of the trap zone. The team consisted of five members, necessitating two trips between Mammoth and the target area. The team would hike into the area, verify bear capture and, in the event they'd been successful, call for an airlift. When the operation was completed the team would hike back to the drop zone to be lifted out. It was going to be a long day for Bart Houser.

The last of the team unloaded their gear. The chopper lifted off and disappeared beyond the Absarokas. Houser reviewed the operational plan with the group one last time to make sure they understood their responsibilities. He was in charge and everyone needed to understand that too. Art Sebastian, biologist and all-around nice guy, was responsible for darting any bear in the area that had not been trapped. He carried a specially designed rifle for that purpose. He would also evaluate the health of the animals and provide any special treatment needed before their relocation. Mark Montayne, another seasonal ranger, with three years of experience, stood as the team gun-bearer. He would keep them in one piece should Sebastian fail in immobilizing any immediate threat. Montayne carried the customary 12-gauge with slugs. As far as Houser was concerned, Muncey, one of the observers, might just as well make himself useful. The ranger heard, of course, about the chief's trouble with his green observer and Bear #264. That was Merrill's problem. Houser had four bears to deal with, so Muncey was given a 12-gauge to carry as well, end of story.

Muncey had no interest in shooting a bear but he was not a stranger to weapons. He'd used a 12-gauge before, pheasant hunting with his dad back in Illinois. Besides, he'd grown up in Chicago and had seen his share of chopped-barrels on the south side. He knew how to use a gun and would if given no other choice. Wentworth was told to assist Sebastian if the need arose. As far as Houser was concerned, she'd contribute plenty by just looking good in her designer jeans. If only she wasn't such an uppity snot.

With assignments confirmed, Houser started the hike toward the beaver pond turned half-flooded meadow on Hellroaring Creek. They cleared the final rise and closed to within forty yards from the traps when the ranger discovered he had his hands full. Two of the traps were sprung. One contained the sow, the other one of her cubs. The remaining pair, one hundred-pounds of thick fur and energy each, stood beside the sow's trap. Their mother was unhappy, to put it lightly, and letting the world hear her displeasure. One of the cubs spotted the group as they approached and made a dash for the willows to the right of the traps.

Sebastian had been there before. He raised the rifle and, with uncanny accuracy, fired a dart into the fleeing cub. Now he had a real problem on his hands. Not knowing what they'd find upon arrival, Sebastian had loaded the dart with dose enough for a full-grown grizzly. Coursing through the small cub's body, that heavy a dose would be lethal if not counteracted quickly. Even as the thought occurred, the cub collapsed at the edge of the willows. The second cub was on the move in the opposite direction.

Sebastian dropped to one knee and retrieved a second dart, color-coded as a smaller dose, from a carrier on his vest. He loaded and raised the rifle. The cub was moving fast, putting distance between it and the intruders. Sebastian aimed and fired. The dart caught the cub high on its left flank.

"Bart," Sebastian screamed. "I don't know if that will take."

The cub disappeared into the willows left of the traps. The sound of the two reports from the dart gun had the sow incensed. Roaring, she threw her body against the inside walls of the trap, making it clear they'd pay if she got out.

"I've got to get an antidote into that first cub," Sebastian yelled. "I don't have much time." He sprinted towards the downed animal with Montayne right behind. Halfway there, Sebastian hollered back, "Follow that second cub. We don't want to lose it."

Wentworth dashed after the second cub feeling an adrenaline rush she'd never experienced before. Houser, meanwhile, felt like he had lost control. His team had suddenly scattered like chaff in the wind. He heard the outraged bellows of the sow as she slammed into the sides of the box. He saw the lady green making tracks. He turned to Muncey and pointed in Wentworth's direction. "Stop her!"

Muncey's athleticism showed as he sprinted after her. He caught her from behind, grabbed her by the back of her jacket, and locked up the brakes. Wentworth's legs kept going but her upper body came to an abrupt halt. She dropped, screaming, to her butt on the soggy ground.

"I need you here," Houser shouted, catching up to the greens on the run. "If that old sow breaks loose, I need you two here."

"What about the cub?" Wentworth protested.

"Let it go." Houser's voice was nearly drowned out by the roar of the angry sow. He shouted louder, "We'll go after it later."

Refusing the assistance of either Houser or Muncey, Wentworth lifted herself to her feet. With her lips a pressed line and her nose in the air, she started back toward the other members of the team. Muncey and the ranger followed.

Sebastian knelt over the first cub. The antidote had already been injected but whether or not they'd been in time was a question the biologist couldn't answer. They struggled awkwardly with the bear's limp body as they carried it back to the trap area. Should the drug wear off and the bear revive, cub or not, one hundred pounds of fighting bruin was nothing to mess with. They placed the animal inside an open box and secured the door.

The sow was going crazy, rocking the trap and roaring in anger. Fearing for her health, Sebastian reloaded his gun, lifted a small hatchway in her trap and sedated the animal. A moment later, the sow dropped over in silence. The third cub paced its enclosure, wailing miserably for its family.

"What do we do now?" Houser asked Sebastian.

The biologist was embarrassed both for and by Bart Houser. He shook his head in disgust and turned to the rest of the group. "Let's find that last cub."

The team members were soaked from working in the swampy meadow. Their nerves had been stretched like guitar strings. Sebastian split them into two groups, with a gun-bearer in each, and led them into the thick willows where the small bear had vanished. Within fifteen minutes, Wentworth's high-pitched shout echoed across Hellroaring Creek and up through the tiny valley. "Over here," she cried. "Oh, God, over here!"

The team members raced in her direction. As each arrived at her side they became still, silently staring over the body of the last cub. The small animal had finally succumbed to the effects of the dart, which still protruded from its left flank. The bear had dropped on the run and lay with its muzzle submerged in an eight-inch pool of marshy water. The young grizzly had drowned in its sleep.

Houser lit a cigarette, inhaled deeply, and blew out a gray cloud of smoke and frustration. Just then, he'd admit to himself that he didn't know much. But he did know one thing for sure. His Stars and Stripes saluting, rule book toting chief ranger, Glenn Merrill, was not going to like this. Not one bit.

"Aren't we going to do something?" Wentworth demanded through a stream of tears.

"Do what?" Houser asked. "It's dead."

Muncey knelt beside the creature and lifted its head from the pool. He laid it to the side on the marshy grass then stood and placed his hand on Wentworth's shoulder.

One cub was captured, another dead, and a third near death. Their mother was deep in slumber; no doubt dreaming of tearing a whole lot of people to shreds. The unnatural silence along the saturated meadow near Hellroaring Creek was interrupted only by the quiet sobs of the lady green. And quite frankly, just then, she was getting on Houser's last nerve. He shook his head and barked, "It's a bear lady. Bears die." He toked the cigarette again. "Besides, coyotes gotta eat too."

Priscilla Wentworth reared back and slapped Houser across the face.

Chapter 9

To the uninitiated, the trip north from the Wind River Reservation to Tie Hack Ranch near the southern entrance of Yellowstone National Park was uneventful. To Johnny Two Ravens, it was everything but. How people were able to traverse that incredible land, seeing nothing but the changing white and yellow lines in the middle of the paved highway, was beyond the outfitter's understanding. Every summer tourists infested the area like mites on a dog; hustling from one commercial spot to another, snapping the same pictures without even glancing at the creation of the Great Spirit booming about them. The tall, elegant lodgepole pines gave Two Ravens comfort as he maneuvered his pickup truck and horse trailer through the winding mountain roads. Minute by minute he fought the urge to pull off the road, step out, and smoke a pipe beneath their towering splendor.

A second pickup driven by Ten Trees, the Indian cook he'd hired to feed his clients this trip, came and went in Two Ravens' rear view mirror with each twist of the road. Johnny wondered what the kid was thinking. Did Ten Trees appreciate where they were and what the land meant? Or was his radio blaring music to numb the senses and shrink the grandeur of their surroundings? The young were often blind to the futility of so many of the new ways. They'd forgotten or, sadly, never been taught the importance of the old. White men and their new ways; just like his present clients...

The painful memory of Two Ravens' first meeting with his new clients flooded back to him. Four days earlier, at precisely five in the evening, he was pushing the front door of his shop closed when a smarmy little man leapt the three steps to his porch and jammed his foot in the door. "Hold on there, chief," he'd shouted through gleaming capped teeth. "You can't close yet."

There could be no doubt, he was from The Big City with an expensive, brightly colored shirt, baggy khaki shorts, and sandals. His skin was bone white, as if he'd never seen the sun, and he wore a trimmed goatee like a French painter. In a failed attempt at fitting in he also wore a tall white cowboy hat no more than two or three days off the rack.

Two Ravens pulled the door back, irritated by both the lateness of the hour and the goatee's greeting. That's how the Shoshone outfitter thought of the guy already, just the goatee, who, like most of his kind was unable to say hello without being rude. "How can I help you?"

"We want to organize a fishing trip, chief. A couple of old braves downtown said you were the guy to take care of it for us."

Two Ravens winced. The guy was either a total jerk or ridiculously stupid; but which? As was his philosophy in times like these, he would wait and see. In the meantime, he offered the man silence and his shopkeeper's smile.

"Well?" the goatee asked. "What do you say, chief?" He posed the question slowly, and as if he was talking to an imbecile, then raised his hand, palm up, and looked Two Ravens in the eye. "You want to make some heap big money or not?"

"I'm not a chief," Two Ravens quietly and calmly answered. "And I speak English perfectly well. If you would like to arrange a backcountry fishing trip, we can do that. If you want to play cowboys and Indians, go somewhere else."

The city fellow's eyes opened wide and his bearded jaw went slack. "No offense, chi... eh, buddy. I was just trying to be friendly."

Two Ravens nodded, stepped inside, and made his way behind the counter. The man waved to a friend out by their SUV who quickly joined him. The two entered the shop, surveyed the surroundings, exchanged worried glances, and stepped to the counter taking care not to touch anything. It wasn't out of respect; they just didn't want to get dirty.

Two Ravens saw it and, though greatly amused, hid his smile. "What were you looking for?"

"You tell us," the new man said. He was white too, without a beard. That's where the description ended. To Two Ravens they all looked alike. "We want to get close to nature and catch some fish."

I'll bet you do. That was Two Ravens' thought. What he said was, "Just the two of you?"

"No," the goatee said. "There'll be three more. We're with Pennsylvania Shale." He paused, waiting. When the Indian failed to react to the revelation, the goatee arched a brow, cleared his throat, and repeated himself, condescending to throw a pearl before a pig. "Pennsylvania Shale. I'm the son of the owner."

The other stepped in. "We've just moved up to become the United States' third largest producer of shale petroleum products. That means a big-time bonus for each of us. So we thought we'd celebrate by reeling in some big-time fish."

Two Ravens ogled the two; important and powerful men, by their own admission, come to tame the wild. "When do the other three arrive?"

"They're flying in to Jackson tomorrow."

"Do you want to go right away?"

"Whatever works," number two said. Then to show he was a pal, he added, "Kimosabe."

That did it. "Look," Two Ravens said, slowly setting down his pen. "Giimoozaabi is an Ojibwe word that probably means "scout." I'm guessing, because in spite of your ludicrous white, guilt-ridden belief that those people, meaning me and my people, are all one big happy family of Native Americans, whatever the hell that's supposed to be, I am Shoshone and I don't speak fluent Ojibwe. To assuage your guilt at what you've done to the land and our people, while you continue to do it, incidentally, you have translated that word to mean "faithful friend" without once considering what those words mean in your own language."

"Hey, man," the goatee said, coming to his friend's rescue. "I'm sure he didn't... "

"I'm not done," Two Ravens said, cutting him off. "I am a guide and a good one. I am also, as you've clearly noted, an Indian. But get this, my being a proud American Indian has no bearing on our conversation or our business. You fellows want a fishing trip to the backcountry. I want your business. I'll guide your trip and you'll have the time of your lives. But I don't need your business."

The goatee, not used to being put in his place, rose up to his full five-foot-six-inches. "Maybe you don't understand who I am, buck. I'm Paul Hastings. Of the Philadelphia Hastings."

"At this moment," Two Ravens said. "All you are is two white boys surrounded by a town full of Indians." Then, fully aware of the sobering power of reflection, the outfitter just stared, letting silence do the rest. From the looks on their faces, it clearly did. With their discomfort making them pliable students, he offered one final lesson. "My name is Two Ravens, Johnny Two Ravens. I am the son of a Shoshone sub-chief and, like you, I pull my pants on one leg at a time. If either of you ever call me buck again, or take another swipe at my heritage, through ignorance or not, I'll show you exactly why this town is called Crowheart."

His potential clients got the message, stowed the nonsense, and became clients. The pair had secured lodging at Tie Hack Ranch. The remaining members of their party would fly in from Salt Lake City and arrive the next day at the Jackson airport.

"That should work out perfectly," Two Ravens told them. He would arrange for a cook and they would all meet at Tie Hack in four days. Two Ravens would supply the packhorses for the backcountry trip, the necessary gear, food, and tents for their camp. He would then lead them northeast to Heart Lake; a gorgeous, secluded spot a good distance off the beaten trail. If they wanted the best tasting trout in Wyoming, his plan would put them onto them there.

"We bought rods and stuff," the goatee said.

"We've got them with us," number two added. "Did you want them?"

"You can leave them with me," Two Ravens said. "Or you can keep them and pack them the morning we leave. It's up to you."

Over the next fifteen minutes the two hauled in and, in the center of his shop floor, dumped the largest pile of the most wildly diverse, expensive, and completely unnecessary fishing equipment the outfitter had ever seen. Glenn Merrill, Two Ravens' thought, would have laughed himself to death.

In the days that followed, Two Ravens fulfilled his part of the bargain. He secured the services of Ten Trees who, despite his youth, was one of the best trail cooks he knew. He rounded up ten horses, the gear, and the tack necessary to sustain five inexperienced and naïve clients, himself, and the cook for a five-night outing. They pulled into Tie Hack Ranch on schedule, met the additional members of their party, and began preparations to hit the trail. Two Ravens and his cook unloaded the animals from the trailers they'd driven up from the reservation.

Two Ravens would guide the group along the trail, offer advice and instruction on matters of fishing and local lore, and tend to the stock. Ten Trees would handle the kitchen, cook for the group, and do the chores; gathering firewood, hauling water, and keeping the camp clean. His favorite chore was setting up the latrine. Ten Trees delighted in watching the tourists' faces as he explained how a toilet in the wild worked. 'This is a branch. This is a shovel. Drop trou, sit over the branch, do your thing, then shovel.' Rich people had the widest eyes!

They unloaded the pickups moving the gear to the horses. They started, of course, with the tack; saddles and bridals. Once saddled, the animals were loaded down with gear. Ten Trees took care of the two kitchen panniers; large leather containers overstuffed with pots, pans, and cooking utensils. The packhorse's saddle featured a wooden attachment over which those were hung, and additional items were top-packed over them. Three horses carried the rest of the equipment, sleeping bags, and tents. A manny, "tarp" to the city slickers, was pulled down over each bundle to bind the gear.

The added clients were city boys too, but seemed decent enough in Two Ravens estimation. He helped them into their saddles and offered riding tips as needed. The goatee was another matter. Though it was obvious he'd never mounted up before, the representative of "the Philadelphia Hastings" refused to be taught anything by a commoner like Two Ravens. That was his choice, Johnny thought, standing back to watch. How Glenn would have said it, 'just another visitor with more dollars than sense.' Hastings struggled through three bad attempts before finally landing a seat in his saddle. Two Ravens enjoyed the show promising to feel guilty about it later.

With everyone safely, if humorously, aboard their mounts, they headed out from Tie Hack Ranch on what would be a half-day's ride to their final destination.

*

Heart Lake lay, beautiful and still, below Mount Sheridan and east of that stretch of backcountry known as the Red Mountains. Two Ravens set up camp south of the lake and escorted his clients to the south shore to fish for trout.

Before his released them, he gave his charges their warnings. "We had a lot of snow this past winter, especially in the high country, and extreme rains this last week. You have nothing to compare it too but I'm telling you the water is much higher than I prefer. You'll have to be on the lookout for submerged boulders along the edges and steep drop-offs hidden along the shoreline."

Not surprisingly, the group responded with disinterested nods and moved right on to the usual amateur questions, Is this the right lure?, Is this the right fly?, Where are the hot spots?, What time is dinner? Two Ravens answered each patiently and, satisfied, they trooped their armloads of equipment to the lake shore to fish.

Fishing had always been a favorite pass-time for Johnny Two Ravens. But, within minutes of his clients' attack on nature from the lake bank, the outfitter knew he'd never look at the sport the same again. In the hands of those five, it looked like a badly choreographed dance by over-dressed clowns. They had it all; chest waders, fancy vests with hundreds of dollars' worth of baits, lures, and flies in decorative boxes, new rods (two custom made for the socially conscious among them), wide brimmed felt hats, and expensive polarizing sun glasses. They'd even remembered the sun block and mosquito spray. But, despite the money, none had invested any time in gaining knowledge. Had he had the inner peace to light a pipe, in the time it would have taken Two Ravens to load the bowl, the white Philadelphia half-wits had engineered chaos; lines were tangled in low hanging branches, in high growing willows, and around one another. It was going to be a long five days.

Two Ravens found a boulder bathed in sunlight a short distance from the lake. He stripped off his shirt, lowered himself across its tabletop, and edged the brim of his hat over his eyes. Yuppies were easier to handle when you were unconscious. The last he saw of his clients, they were plowing through the shallow waters at the south end of the lake waddling like crippled ducks in their fancy waders. Two Ravens chuckled, reminded of an old saying among his people, Never trust the water downstream from a white man. It was a good thought to take with him to sleep.

*

Two Ravens had no clue how long he'd been asleep. Roused by Ten Trees dinner bell, an old metal triangle the cook beat with relish, he sat up and waved the others in. It wasn't until they duck-walked to shore that the outfitter realized he was short one goateed client. "Where is Paul Hastings?"

97

The remaining four shared vacant looks and 'I don't knows.' Neither did they have any idea how long their friend had been absent.

"That's just great," Two Ravens said, fuming. "I made it perfectly clear nobody was to leave the immediate area without me."

"What's the big deal," one of them said. It was good ol' number two who'd accompanied Hastings on that first day in the store. "He's probably taking a dump behind a tree somewhere."

"That doesn't narrow it much." Two Ravens pulled on his shirt. "You guys head up to the camp and let Ten Trees feed you. I'll go look for him."

*

Paul Hastings was lost. How it had happened, even he didn't have a clue, but what difference it made now was of little importance. It sucked, that's all he knew.

He'd grown tired of fishing; which was nothing new. Hastings hated fishing and always had. As a kid, his old man forced him to go crappie fishing in Fairmount Park. Endless hours of sitting on creek banks. It got so tiring that, whenever the old man looked the other way, he'd pull the worm off his hook and recast, doing everything he could not to catch one of those slimy creatures. He'd only come to Wyoming to make his father happy. When you were heir to the third largest producer of shale petroleum products in the United States, you made your old man happy. Big deal.

Of course, Hastings volunteered to organize the trip. It was his pleasure. Paul Hastings would strip and drag his junk over a mile of broken glass to be in his old man's good graces. He'd even go fishing.

Now he was lost.

Hastings had been wandering for what seemed hours. He suspected he'd gone in a complete circle twice. He'd fallen once over a dead tree and had gouged a chunk out of his elbow. He'd even gotten burrs in his beard. God, he hated the woods, hated the park, hated the outdoors. And, just then, he hated their uppity guide. That good-for-nothing Indian could have this nature crap, he thought; the red-faced, smart-mouthed, Iron Eyes Cody-looking creep. If Two Ravens was such a great guide, why hadn't the alcoholic, tax gobbling, son-of-a-whore found him by now? It was getting dark!

It was then, after Hastings realized the sun was headed to bed for the night, that he heard the first strange sound amid the lodgepole. It was a heavy snap, rustle, and thud as if someone had tripped over a high tree root or low branch. He knew; he'd already done both.

"Two Ravens, is that you?" A long and awkward silence followed. Hastings strained, nervously scanning his surrounding, and wasn't sure but thought he saw a mist in the air. A few minutes more and he was certain; a fog was settling over the underbrush. "Two Ravens."

Hastings shivered, sorry he'd left his coat back at camp; sorrier still he'd stepped wrong and soaked his jeans playing bass master down in the lake. He was freezing.

The fog was heavy now, swirling. Another snap sounded, another rustle of foliage, somewhere in the trees, somewhere in the mist to his right. "Two Ravens," he called out. "Ten Trees?"

A deep growl escaped the darkness. An instant later it became a roar that drained the fluid from Hastings' spine. Wood cracked and splintered. The thick brush exploded in front of him. A massive head shown first, as if no body were attached, then the body followed; a half ton of charging muscle wrapped in silver-tipped, glowing fur. Still roaring, its murderous eyes cut through the darkness like lightning bolts in a summer storm. Then came recognition; it was a bear!

The animal slammed into Hastings with the speed of an express train and mashed him to the ground as if he were a child's toy. His lungs collapsed as he puked their contents of air. A brown and gray hell descended upon him. For a fleeting moment he told himself it couldn't be happening. He was Paul Hastings of the Philadelphia Hastings. He had money, lots and lots of money, and lady friends to spend it on. He saw their lovely smiles. Then the image vanished, replaced by rows of yellowed, gleaming teeth beneath hard, steel-gray eyes. There followed intense pain; then darkness.

Chapter 10

Bart Houser left the administration office building at Mammoth Headquarters feeling half mad and half relieved. His meeting with Superintendent Stanton had gone better than he'd anticipated. Still, it hadn't been easy. There were tough questions about Hellroaring Creek but, under the circumstances, Houser thought he'd acquitted himself rather well. Stanton had expressed his thanks that the sow bear and two of her cubs had come through the ordeal, but he made it plain there would be an investigation into the drowning death of the third cub. That was standard operating procedure. It was not unheard of for an animal to die during a relocation effort and, as long as he had followed protocol, Stanton said, he wasn't going to lose his job over it.

The superintendent was livid, however, about the comment he'd made to that Wentworth woman. Livid barely covered it. "Coyotes have to eat, too," Stanton had screamed. "What kind of remark was that? What in the world were you even thinking? You weren't thinking. Shut up! We'll be lucky if Yellowstone Forever doesn't file suit against us." Houser thought the top of Stanton's head was going to blow off. And his boss had left no doubt about his feelings. "If I weren't so short-handed right now, your butt would be on suspension."

Suspension? For what, Houser wondered, for putting a runny-nosed green in her place? It didn't matter. With all the problems washing across Stanton's desk, he'd be forgotten in no time at all. With dead tourists on his hands, the super wasn't going to worry for long about an off-hand remark made by a part-time ranger in the heat of battle. The bears had gotten him into trouble and now they'd get him out. The worthless things might have a purpose after all.

Anyway, he'd survived it all in one piece. Because of the manpower problems and, no doubt, because Stanton didn't want to see his face, Houser had been reassigned to the night shift in one of the park's south districts. That was all right with him. Bosses didn't work the night shift.

*

Houser rolled out of his driveway at 10:30 pm. He was early (his shift started at midnight) but he found he couldn't sleep. Truth be told, the roaring and banging of the sow grizzly in that culvert trap still haunted him. He needed to shake it off and knew it. What was the point of dwelling on it? If 'ifs' and 'buts' were candy and nuts, we'd all have a merry Christmas.

Houser drove into Gardiner for a cup of coffee, had his thermos filled, bought a jumbo bag of Cheez Crunchies, and headed back into the park. It would be a long drive south to the geyser basins and Old Faithful; his assigned district for the night.

Two major responsibilities rested with the night shift officers; check to ensure all facilities were secure, and patrol the campgrounds for unattended fires and inappropriately stored food. The first task was, at the risk of a pun, a walk in the park. The second was simply an aggravation.

Tourists, in particular campers, were a constant pain. Untended fires and improperly stored food and garbage were deadly sins in the park. Rangers had strict orders, "Cut no slack for violations of clean camp regulations." Normally bears were not a problem in camping areas. But with all that had been happening in the park, and with Hellroaring Creek still fresh in his mind, Houser intended to give clean camps his special attention. After the relocation disaster he could just imagine what that sow grizzly would do to a tourist over a cupcake.

Houser passed the sign for Indian Creek Campground and, on the spur of the moment, pulled in. He had yet to go on duty and was still miles from his district, but he had an itch. The campground rested along the curving merge of Indian and Obsidian Creeks. A quiet meeting place, it nestled between lush high mountain meadows and thick pine forests. Visitors loved Indian Creek. Bears did too.

Houser crossed the Obsidian Creek Bridge and circled into the campground. He slowed to a snail's pace and scanned each side of the road for irregularities. Most of the campers had gone to sleep and the area appeared peaceful enough. Then, Houser heard the sharp cry of a young voice.

He hit the brakes and lowered his driver's side window. By then the cry had become laughter. The ranger edged around a bend at the rear of the campground and, almost immediately, located the source of the noise. Two young boys wrestled on the ground, locked in a death grip, while a raucous huddle of boys the same age cheered them on. As Houser parked, he saw a lanky adult male step from a nearby tent on a bee-line for the combatants.

Greg and James had been going at it in one way or another for the whole trip and their scout leader, Rob Jones, was growing weary of the skirmishes. The bigger Greg had, more than once, acted the bully, but James was not without sin. The pint-sized Cub Scout had taken every opportunity to strike back and, on occasion, strike out at the bigger boy. The grunts and groans of the fighters continued, but the cheers and prompting stopped the instant Jones entered the circle. The boys' stares followed the scout leader as he reached into the fray, took hold of one ear apiece, and brought the grapplers scrambling to their feet. They struggled to the tips of their toes to ease the pain but Jones raised his arms to limit their success.

The scouts spotted the park ranger and moved their circle back as he approached. Their shared expressions spoke volumes about the trouble they expected.

"Good evening, officer," Jones said, still holding the wincing puppets by their ears. "Sorry for the trouble."

Houser smiled. "It looks like you have the situation well in hand."

Jones nodded, turned to the peanut gallery, and growled, "Everybody, back to your tents."

The boys scrambled away leaving Greg and James to their fates. The scout leader lifted higher, holding ears but seeing only trouble. "Gentlemen," he said, confident he had their full attention. "The two of you will now sack out. We will discuss this in the morning." He released them.

The boys grabbed their throbbing ears and disappeared into tents at opposite ends of the camp.

"Looks like you've got your hands full," Houser said.

"You don't know the half of it," the scout leader said with a sigh. "They're supposed to be earning their Webelos Badges, but I think I'm going to have to civilize them first."

"If you need any backup," Houser said. "Just call 9-1-1." The ranger chuckled, disappeared into his vehicle, and then into the night.

Jones stood red with embarrassment and sagging in relief. He'd governed a lot of scouts and they were all rambunctious but where these guys got their energy he hadn't a clue. If they made it out of the park in one piece, Jones thought, he was going to request a merit badge of his own.

*

Jones' evening in the campground was finally drawing to a close. Bart Houser's had just begun.

No sooner had he made the next bend in the road than he spied a textbook unclean campsite. A brightly colored and expensive tent had been erected just off the drive and a black Mercedes, with Massachusetts tags, sat nearby. On the opposite side of the site a picnic table lay peppered with the remnants of the camper's supper; a half-eaten bag of chips, grilled hamburgers, and several kinds of salads left to the night air. The scene was lit in a flickering red-orange glow from a fire still blazing in the adjacent pit.

Houser parked and approached the campsite serenaded by an apneic snoring coming from inside the tent. The ranger drew his flashlight and tapped a tent pole near the zippered entrance. "Hey," Houser said, trying for authority without waking the campers on the adjoining lots. "Wake up in there."

A second chorus of taps from the ranger halted the snoring. Still there was no response. "Hey," Houser called again, louder this time. "Wake up in there."

"Go away." It was a man's voice, frog deep and groggy. "I'm sleeping."

"Not any more," Houser said. "I need to talk to you."

"Get lost."

"I'm a park ranger," Houser said, irritated.

"Don't care if you're the Lone Ranger," the voice said. "I told you, I'm sleeping."

Houser considered counting to ten as an anger avoidance mechanism, and then decided against it. "Either drag your hide out of that tent," he said, "or I'll come in and drag it out for you."

A pregnant pause followed during which, Houser imagined, the camper considered his choices. "All right. Give me a minute."

A moment later the tent flap came unzipped and a twentyish kid emerged, wearing nothing but a pair of white briefs and a bright pink Mohawk. Houser didn't know whether to laugh or brain the freak with his flashlight. And he's driving a Mercedes, Houser thought. Where did I go wrong?

"What's the crisis, man? Why ya gotta wake me up?" asked the Mohawk.

"You didn't clean your plate," Houser said. With his flashlight he pointed out the mess on the table. "Before you go back to bed, you will do the dishes." He turned the beam on the campfire. "And put out the light."

"You gotta be jokin', man."

"No, sir, I am not," Houser said, spitting out the 'sir' like a sour grape. "Apparently they don't teach you boys to read in the city. If your fire were to get out of control, thousands of acres of national parkland would be ashes by morning."

The Mohawk eyed the campfire dully.

"Secondly," Houser said. "This is bear country and you are in violation of our clean camp regulations."

"Man, I've been in this park two days and ain't seen no bears. Besides, man, I don't know nothin' bout no regulations."

"Well, while you're cleaning your dishes you can pass the time by reading the permanent notice that's nailed to the top of your picnic table." Houser slid his flashlight into the loop on his belt and, in its place, drew a citation booklet from his back pocket. "Let me see some ID," he demanded, having used up all the time he intended to on this numbskull. He finished the citation quickly, tore it from the book, and handed it to the Mohawk.

"What's that for?"

"Have somebody read it to you."

"What's this gonna cost me?"

"One hundred bucks." The ranger smiled. "Or I can dismiss it... if you send me that crap hairdo in a paper bag."

You've got money, kid, Houser thought as he strode away. But you've got no style. As he pulled back out onto the main loop road and headed south, Houser enjoyed his first good laugh of the day.

*

Lights still burned in the Museum of the National Park Ranger as Houser pulled into the lot and silenced his vehicle. The staff began leaving lights on a couple of years back after someone broke in and stole artifacts on display. Houser made his rounds of the old log structure, checking windows and rattling doors. He even paused to gaze at a few of the exhibits through the front picture windows. Life had been rugged and isolated for the old boys stationed there in the late 1800s. Then again, Houser thought, they hadn't had to deal with agitated greens and pink Mohawks.

Already hungry, Houser decided to skip the check on the Norris Campground for the time being and take a break. He drove the short distance to the parking lot above the geyser basin. He grabbed his thermos, snack, and flashlight and started down the steep grade leading to the basin below. Houser turned left down the boardwalk and stopped to shine his light toward Emerald Spring.

The stark, white light reflected off the rising steam from the basin, piercing rapidly changing pockets of visibility as a slight breeze swirled the fog. The light played on the green algae that thrived in the acidic waters and gave the spring its name. He moved on, passing Steamboat Geyser, then turned left at the tee in the pathway. Houser made his way toward a set of benches in the viewing area next to Echinus Geyser. He deposited his Crunchies and thermos on the bench, belted his flashlight, and leaned over the railing to watch the geyser, lit now only by moonlight showing through the rising fog.

Maybe I'll take a little trip up onto the Madison Plateau in a week or so, Houser thought, and do some scouting for elk. The word on the street was prices for antler this season were going to be sky-high. "Thank God for horny Asians," Houser said out loud. He laughed at his own joke.

It wasn't funny and he knew it. Some people in that part of the world were convinced antler powders were a super aphrodisiac. They paid through the nose to get it. It was a tidy black market that helped make up for the park's lack of appreciation, Houser thought. He might just as well get a jump on the rest of the poachers and bag a trophy or two.

Echinus Geyser interrupted his thoughts with a sudden explosion of water and steam, firing its contents fifty feet into the air. Startled at first, Houser laughed as his adrenalin rush came back under control.

He watched the force of nature's underground plumbing blast the white steam into the sky and a fine mist of warm water showered down on him.

Just as suddenly, the hair on the back of Houser's neck came to attention. Out of nowhere, the ranger was overwhelmed with the sensation of being watched. Houser darted his eyes first left, then right, surveying the dark surroundings without moving his head. There was nothing.

He turned slowly to look over his left shoulder. The sensation intensified and the ranger was suddenly afraid without knowing why. But there was nothing there, nothing but fog dancing on a slight breeze amid the darkness. He turned again, coming full around. He resisted the urge to call out who's there?, like some sap in a bad horror film, opting instead to study the silence. He jumped and turned when the Arch Steam Vent hissed at him. He laughed nervously. It didn't feel funny but his psychological defense mechanisms were kicking in. Yes, he'd admit it, he was suddenly afraid.

Beneath the moonlight, brighter now as the cloud cover broke, the night grew alive with the sights and sounds of bubbling, gurgling mud pots and lesser geysers. They chanted at him and spit water while assaulting his nostrils with their pungent odors of sulfur and acid. Houser stood by himself, in darkness, before angelic sights, amid hellish smells... But something told him he was not alone.

He drew his flashlight again, flicked it to life, and pierced the darkness. He passed it over the basin, then he froze. There, in the moving shroud of white mist, two tiny mirrors reflected the beam. The synapses in Houser's brain fired a message. An instant later his mind decoded it. He wasn't seeing mirrors. He was looking at a pair of eyes! The unearthly vapor swirled around the glowing orbs like a phantom rising; it hovered, congealed, took form. The mist became a gigantic bear.

Houser stared. He trembled. He screamed. He turned sharply, blindly, and rammed into the railing he'd been leaning against. The blow knocked the flashlight from his grip and sent it thumping onto the boardwalk. It rolled off the edge and into a geyser, taking its light with it.

In a full panic, Houser tried to climb the rail. Behind him came a roar and, instantly, his shoulder was on fire; the pain so intense the rest of his body felt numb. Something, dear God, the bear, had hold of him. He felt himself being lifted. His right arm no longer worked. With his left, screaming again, he grabbed for the top rail, trying to cling to the boardwalk, to hold on to life. He started over, but was jerked back and shaken. Another blow followed and a convulsion wracked his frame. Through the pain, Houser thought of the old throw rugs his mother shook over the porch banister. That was him, a dirty rug being beaten. He was slammed to the boardwalk. The air escaped him like a broken bellows. Gasping without relief, he was lifted and slammed down again. The boards cracked under his crashing weight. His legs shot out and his heels bounced. The rest of his body went limp as he went from rug to rag. Houser felt the prick of splinters from the weathered and broken lumber beneath him as he was dragged down the boardwalk.

Outside of the ranger's performance, Echinus Geyser continued its captivating display. The rising waters merged with the fog and danced in the darkness; a gorgeous hell. With the grip of fangs sunk deep in his shoulder, Houser went in and out of consciousness as his body trailed the beast down the boardwalk and into the sea of steam. He was a rag doll in the hands of an angry child. The dragging stopped and Houser felt his shoulders come suddenly free. He stole a desperately needed breath. Then the back of his head was smashed onto the boardwalk again. Blood flowed from his nose, trailed over his cheeks, and trickled into his mouth. The liquid tasted of salty copper but he knew it was iron. Everyone knew it was iron. It was warm and soothing. Houser languorously mouthed the sensations like a fish on the beach. His mind snapped, took flight, and left his body to its fate.

The great bruin hunched over the ranger. It slashed Houser's midsection with its mighty paw and opened his abdomen wide. It grabbed him by the skull, lifted him off the ground, and flipped him into the darkness. With an earth-shattering roar, the bear vanished.

Houser's intestines spilled from the open cavity, danced around his cartwheeling body, and wrapped it like a stripper's boa. With a splash and a hollow thud, his body landed in a spring. The pool of water recoiled from the crash, met its outer boundaries, and swirled back into place. It covered the ranger's torso and, finally, enveloped his head. His blood joined the beautiful blue waters, creating eerie deep green streaks that swam in spirals before settling toward the bottom. In his final moment, Ranger Bart Houser became one with Cistern Spring.

Chapter 11

The mood the following morning was set by the black and green thunder clouds that hung thick and heavy over the Mammoth Hot Springs basin tiers.

Inside the administration offices, Glenn and J.D. made their way through a river of reporters from Glenn's office to the conference room when, suddenly, up darted the chief's very own piranha, Howard Lark. "Hey, chief, is there anything animal, mineral, or vegetable that can stay alive in this park on your watch?"

Glenn stopped nearly causing a pile-up with his biologist. For J.D., it was just as well the chief was between them. She didn't know the reporter from Adam but, all the same, felt a sudden urge to collect a blood sample from his pointed nose. Glenn faced Lark directly, not stung as the reporter had clearly hoped but surprised and disappointed. "What kind of question is that?"

"An impolite one, I imagine," Lark said with a smirk. "But one that deserves an answer. How many dead bears now? And two dead guests? And last night a dead ranger? What's going on? Have you found the connection? Certainly the people deserve something more than, 'No comment'."

Glenn's stare turned icy. "Nobody here has ever told you, 'No comment.' You've been updated with everyone else as information has come available." The ranger started walking again. With her short legs, J.D. hustled to keep up. Lark, as lanky as he was smarmy, followed apace. Glenn was talking as he went. "Nothing, as yet, suggests these incidents you've casually bagged up together are in any way connected. All are still under investigation."

"What about the poachers?" Lark demanded. "The bear at Mary Bay? And those elk poachers... they're running free; Lewis River, Pitchstone, Firehole." His tone showed disgust but Glenn would have bet real money he saw a glint in the reporter's eye. "My sources say they're pretty much making a monkey out of you."

They arrived at the conference room – and none too soon. Glenn opened the door, let J.D. pass, then turned on the Billings reporter with menace. "Mr. Lark, you are an absurd man."

"Can I quote you on that?" Lark asked with a grin.

Before he said or did anything he would regret, Glenn followed J.D. through and closed the door in Lark's face. He felt like he'd traveled to Hell and back since sunrise. It was only nine in the morning; plenty of day to come.

The room looked like you'd expect; a long table, plenty of serviceable if not comfortable chairs, the Stars and Stripes, Wyoming, and Park Service flags, a furled movie screen and a pin board at the front of the room, and maps – lots of maps. The room also contained three rangers, Franklin, Simpson, and Lincoln. They were Glenn's top people and had more than earned their money that week. Grazing on Danish and coffee around a side table, their chatter suddenly stopped. They turned as one to the little blonde biologist and their chief.

"What?" Glenn asked, breaking the silence. "I showered today."

Franklin choked on the coffee, spitting a slurry of cream and sugar down the front of his uniform. The others roared. Franklin, still gagging, swiped at his mouth with his shirt sleeve. He realized what he was doing and cussed. "Easy, Frankie," Simpson said, laughing. "You'll end up needing mouth-to-mouth... and then you're going to die." Franklin grabbed a stack of napkins and, to the continued laughter, dabbed at the mess. The badge came clean, the tie could be saved, but the shirt was a goner.

"It's not always this way," Glenn told J.D. "Some days it's much worse." With the entertainment over, they took their seats around the table as the chief introduced her to the troops.

Gloria Simpson was thirty and thick, but as experienced a ranger as Glenn had in the Mammoth District. A peerless professional, she could laugh with the smallest child and match shouts with the largest man and never lose a step between. Glenn liked her the moment she arrived in the park.

Old Pete Lincoln came next and they nodded agreeably at one another.

"You already know Old Faithful here," Glenn said, pointing at Franklin and his egregiously stained shirt. "If you're done showing off, Frankie, we'll get started." Glenn walked to the pin board.

It featured a large map of Yellowstone National Park. Color photographs of the mauling victims were pinned to it, each in the general location in which they had died, with a variety of diagrams and note cards interspersed. Glenn absorbed the bloody horrors on display, took a deep breath, and turned to the group. "We've lost one of our own," he began. "We're clowning now because we're devastated and we don't know how to react. It hurts. We all want to find out what happened to Ranger Houser. But we cannot develop tunnel vision; we've got to keep our eyes on the big picture. We're in the middle of more than Houser's death. At least one of our guests is killing our animals and at least one of our animals is killing our guests." He paused for a sip of coffee. "We will review each incident so we're all up to speed. Hopefully, together, we can come up with some answers."

The rangers traded dubious looks across the table. Answers had, so far, seemed in short supply.

"Let's take this in chronological order," Glenn said. "Pete, what have you got?"

The others swiveled in their chairs to follow him as Ranger Lincoln stepped to the pin board. He grabbed a pointer from the table and nervously tapped his palm. "The first victim was Jason Ewing, a.k.a. Stubby Ewing, of Dallas, Texas. He and his wife were in the Firehole

Lake area; specifically, on the boardwalk at Black Warrior Lake."
Lincoln pointed to the west-central area of the park map and traced
Stubby's movements.

"He left the boardwalk here," Lincoln said. "And, ultimately, died
here. We have two witnesses, his wife and a photographer who was
working the area. They claim he was the victim of a bear attack. Both
report the animal charging from the fog on the lake and disappearing
back into it again. The coroner's report lists the cause of death as a
massive myocardial infarction, uh, a heart attack."

"On the lake," J.D. repeated. "Did you say 'On the lake'? The
bear came from the lake?"

"Uh, yeah." Lincoln looked to the chief and, again, began nervously
tapping the pointer on his palm. "And, uh, then the story really
starts to get hinky. I mean, there are some problems." Lincoln took
a deep breath. "There is absolutely no physical evidence to support
the eyewitness accounts. The victim broke through the travertine
crust here. But there was no sign a bear had broken through either
in Black Warrior Lake or anywhere near the body. As big as the
witnesses described that bear, you would think he'd have left tracks
or broken through himself. No such evidence."

"How about the body," Simpson asked. "Any bite marks?"

"None," Lincoln said. "Other than the expected cuts on his legs,
and the burns from the pools, there wasn't a scratch on the guy. You
saw the photos, chief." Lincoln retrieved a file from the table and
passed Lambro's glossy 8x10 prints around.

"The photographer, a pro, claims the bear was in every shot," Glenn
told the group.

"Right," Lincoln said. "But, as you can see, the photographic evidence doesn't support that claim; not hide nor hair. I'm telling you,
if it weren't for the witnesses, who as far as we know were complete
strangers, corroborating one-another, I'd have a hard time believing
there was ever a bear there."

"This Ewing," Glenn asked. "What do we know about him?"

Lincoln scratched his head. "The FBI has a file on him... they are not willing to discuss. But, off the record, I was told he'd recently been buying up truckloads of real estate on the park's perimeter."

"What for?" J.D. asked.

"Only guesses. But Ewing has ties to a number of Texas energy companies, including researches in geothermal power."

"Anything else, Pete?"

"Nothing," Lincoln said. "And no answers."

"Thank you. You're on, Frankie."

"I don't know how much more help I'm going to be," Franklin said, rising. "In the Heart Lake incident we are definitely dealing with a bear, but the situation is almost as weird as Pete's." Franklin pointed to the location of the campsite where the Shoshone outfitter had guided his fishermen, not far from Yellowstone's south entrance. "According to Johnny Two Ravens," Franklin said. "He chose this site, not only because the fishing ought to have been excellent but also for the lack of bear sign. The body of Paul Hastings, our second victim, was found only two hundred yards from their camp. We think he got lost in the woods. His trail actually circled the camp before he was killed."

"You said you know it was a bear," J.D. said. "How is that?"

"Because of the condition of the body." Franklin pointed to a photograph on the board. "Hastings had been eviscerated. There were numerous claw and bite marks that definitely indicate grizzly. But I'll tell you, from the size of those marks, this was one monster of a bear. I've never seen damage to equal. And the tooth spread was just plain scary."

Shared looks and shared gooseflesh raced around the table. Glenn saw it and tried to head it off. "Let's keep our feelings out of this for now. I just want facts. Other evidence?"

"Nothing."

"What do you mean, nothing?" Glenn asked irritably.

"Just that, chief. No tracks, no hair samples. No kidding, the pathologist wasn't even able to find any saliva in the bite wounds.

I've never seen anything like it. There was a bear at the scene but he must have been cleaned and combed out. He left nothing in the way of evidence." Franklin sighed heavily. Then, oddly, he chuckled. "Unless you want to count the feather?"

Glenn's eyes narrowed. "What feather?"

"The feather that I found at Heart Lake." Franklin reached to the side of his chair, grabbed and opened his attaché, and removed a feather flattened on angle in a large zip-lock bag. It was just over 14 inches long (an attached label read 36 cm), gold leaning to golden brown with white interruptions in a barred pattern. He laid it on the conference table. "From a golden eagle."

"You found it at Heart Lake?"

"Yeah. Yes, sir." Franklin paused and considered. "Well, not at the lake. I found it in the forest... near Hastings' body."

"It's not in your report."

"Well, no," Franklin replied awkwardly. "It's a feather."

Glenn ignored the general chuckle and reached for the package. Franklin handed it over. "You took the trouble to bag it up."

"Well... in the heavy tree-cover... it seemed out of place."

"That's because it was out of place," Glenn said plainly. "Your instincts were working even if your brain wasn't. It's evidence. I have no idea of what. But it is protected contraband, in unlikely habitat, at the scene of a visitor's death, and it is evidence. Congratulations on finding it. Please, amend your report."

A shade redder, Franklin cleared his throat. "Yes, sir."

"I'll, eh..." All eyes turned on Pete Lincoln; the source of the stammer. He was sitting forward in his chair, redder than Franklin, biting his lower lip. "I'll have to amend my report as well," he said.

Everyone was looking. Glenn was glaring – a question that didn't need to be voiced.

"There was," Pete said, "a feather... uh, like that one... just like that one... at Black Warrior Lake too. I didn't mention it. Eh, I didn't collect it. It never dawned on me it was evidence. I mean, the sky's wide open. I didn't think about it twice. But, for what it's worth, I did see it, the, uh, feather, I mean; there in the pool. It had floated up against..." He paused, considering the matter. A light came on in his eyes and he snapped his fingers. "The pictures." He pointed at the pile on the table. "There was a bison skull in the shallows and the feather..."

The conference became a standing huddle with Lambro's photographs again the center of attention. One by one they studied the images, ignoring the appearance and antics of the late Texan, eyes glued instead on the bison skull in the fog-shrouded lake behind. There was nothing to see, save the skull, until Stubby went down in the fourth frame. Then, seemingly out of nowhere, like a tiny raft on a great ocean, a golden feather appeared on the lake. Just appeared. In the following three frames it floated up against the bison skull and, in the last, lodged in one of the empty eye sockets, held there by the ripple.

"That's where I saw it," Lincoln said. "Sticking out of the skull. I didn't give it another thought."

Glenn ground his teeth, unsure if they were seeing a clue or an odd coincidence. Unsure even whether to be delighted or angry. For the moment he decided to skip it. "All right. Do we know anything about the visitor, Hastings, personally?"

Franklin shrugged. "Nothing that has any bearing on his death, I think. We know he worked for his daddy's strip mining company, that he would have owned it one day, had he lived, and that he had more money than God. That's about it."

"Is there any connection?" J.D. asked.

"Connection? To what?"

"To Ewing. Both made their fortunes providing energy."

"And, what?" Franklin asked. "The bears are working for the EPA?"

Friendly laughter took another lap around the table. It skipped the chief ranger. Glenn, leaning back, the tips of his fingers touching and pressed against his lips, was deep in contemplation. Finally, stirring, he asked, "How about you, Gloria. Can you shed any light for us?"

Simpson sat erect and cleared her throat. "First," she said, "I need to put myself on report. I not only failed to properly collect evidence at the scene of Bart Houser's death. I removed evidence and violated work regulations. I... also found the feather of a golden eagle, at Cistern Spring, within ten yards of the victim's body. I picked it up because it was pretty, laying in a pool of bloody ugliness, and I knew that the mineral water would destroy it. I put it in my truck. It's there now."

It was, to say the least, a no-no on every level. Glenn stared, first at Simpson, then at the others in their turns, silently, his mind trying desperately to decipher the shape of this odd problem. One of his best rangers had violated one of the park's most basic regulations. You do not remove anything from nature without permission. Two of them had been derelict in their duties, failing to collect crime scene evidence. All three had failed to record and report crime scene finds. True, the fact they were talking about a feather sounded ridiculous and unbelievable. Still it was what it was and he was damned mad. He was also thankful, more than he could express, that all three had been alert enough to be able to corroborate what was now clearly more than a coincidence. It was the strangest clue ever. For the moment, Glenn opened a file drawer in the back of his mind and shoved it all in.

"Let's all back out of the tunnel." He pointed to the pin board up front. "The Norris Geyser Basin. Gloria, what else did you find?"

"Not much." She reluctantly stood and stepped to the board. "The first thing that struck me about Houser's death was that it happened at all. He was hardly an ignorant visitor. I find it hard to believe he got himself into a dangerous situation without planning an escape. He was a ranger, chief. He knew better than to spook a bear. It honestly appears as if he was stalked."

"Stalked? How do you mean?"

"Houser was stationary," Simpson said. "It looks like he was taking a break. The attack came from behind. We found the railing at Echinus Geyser cracked and scratched. Houser had splinters in his palms and wood under his nails. It appears the bear pulled him off the railing,

118

broke the boardwalk using his body as a sledge hammer, and then dragged him to the pool where he was found."

"Any other evidence?"

"Massive bite marks on the head and shoulders, fractured skull, broken spine and numerous ribs, and the abdomen was opened wide. He wasn't eaten, so this was not motivated by hunger." Simpson paused. "Other than the vicious damage to the body, this scene matches the others. We have not been able to find a single hair, a drop of saliva, anything to indicate a bear or any other animal for that matter was there at all. As to Bart, personally..."

Glenn raised a curious brow. "Please, don't tell me he was building a nuke plant at Mineral Hot Springs." Laughter all around again. This time with the exception, Glenn noted, of Lincoln. The elder ranger seemed suddenly deep in thought.

"A nuke? Not as far as I know, chief," Simpson said. "Just a friend of the animals like all of us."

"Okay," Glenn said. "J.D. can you help us with the scientific perspective?"

"We've been doing aerial surveys since the first attack," she said. "Not a single bear has been noted in any of the attack areas. All radio-collared bears are accounted for. None of them fit these scenarios. There are no reports of rogue bear activity other than these three isolated incidents."

"Do you think... and I'm asking you, the scientist; the bear biologist. For the moment ignore the environmental conspiracies and Aquila plumage. Do you think these attacks are related?"

"I do. I can't believe they aren't," J.D. said. "But how do you analyze a lack of evidence? If it is a bear, he's huge. I never saw anything in Alaska that could produce a similar bite radius, and they're the biggest bears in North America." She thought for a moment. "It's hard enough to believe in one bear of these proportions, let alone more. It must be the same bear. But that leaves us with a new riddle."

"Distance." Glenn said matter-of-factly.

"Absolutely. In order to be in all these places, at these times, the creature would need wings. The distances are far too great. The bottom line is the collected evidence tells us two things for certain; one, that our perpetrator has to be a massive grizzly, and two, that it can't be. Now add a conspiracy and decorate it with eagle feathers. I honestly don't know what to think."

"All right," Glenn said. "That's what the animals are doing to the people. Let's talk about what the people are doing to the animals. Frankie, you handled Bear #113 at Mary Bay..."

"Oh, wait. Sorry, Franklin," J.D. interrupted excitedly. "On that. I just got this." She dug for a file folder. "There was something strange in the necropsy report. The bear was missing its gall bladder."

Franklin showed no surprise. "Nothing strange there, J.D. It means we're dealing with pros."

Glenn nodded his agreement. "The gall bladder is dried and ground up. The powder is sold in countries where the culture considers it an aphrodisiac. They do the same thing with elk antlers. The international market in animal parts is worth hundreds of millions. Every time we lose a critter we worry about professional poachers."

J.D. shook her head. "I've lived a sheltered life."

"You mentioned elk, chief," Franklin said. "It isn't common knowledge but for days we've been losing elk in a number of places in the park. I'm afraid we're going to lose a lot more."

"And I'm afraid it's about to become common knowledge," Glenn said. "That moron, Lark, from the Billings paper, already mentioned elk poaching on television and just now asked me about it. If our office has an information leak, I want it stopped up. I know that's enough said in this room, but spread the word."

There were silent nods around the table.

"All right, Pete," Glenn said eying the old-timer. "Time for experience to put in its two cents. Tell us about our poachers. Who are we looking for?"

Lincoln studied the ceiling. "At least two men; no more than three. One is older, a pro, with years of experience like yours truly. At least one is young; muscle to get the nasty work done quickly." He paused to consider further. "They're on horseback..."

"Then we've got 'em," Simpson chimed in. "All livestock are registered coming in. We'll have their names and the license number on their horse trailer."

"Whoa," Lincoln said. "Hold your horse trailer, Ranger Simpson. Experience takes its time but I'll get there. I was about to say, our poachers are on horseback – illegally, of course. They wouldn't have brought a trailer through a park entrance for just the reason you spelled out. They rode in, probably at night, definitely in the thick timber of the back country, with pack horses. If they have a trailer, it's outside the park waiting for their triumphant return. They're cold camping and either caching their take in a secluded hiding spot within the park or are packing it out the way they came."

"Not to interrupt," J.D. said. "But what is cold camping?"

"Basically," Franklin chimed in. "A cold camp is one where there's no fire; to make it harder to detect. They use a minimum of equipment for sleeping, no cooking supplies, easy to set up and easy to tear down. When they break camp, the pros that is, they leave little trace they were ever there."

"Because they're pros," Lincoln continued, "we're just a stop along the way. They're ruthless. They see wildlife as nothing more than dollar bills wrapped in fur and carrying headgear. They may be loners but, more than likely, they're working for a top predator on contract. Who knows, could be a ring through the Rocky Mountain Range. I'd check with the LEOs in Grand Teton Park, Rocky Mountain Park in Colorado, and Glacier in Montana, see if they've been losing elk, too."

"You said the backcountry?" J.D. interrupted again.

"Pros don't hunt near roads. That would be asking to get caught."

"Then I don't understand. If that's your theory, why did they kill the bear? Why near a road? Do we have more than one group of poachers?"

"It's certainly possible," Lincoln said.

"If you don't mind police science and psychology jumping in," Franklin said. "It could still be one set of poachers. If your theory is correct and there is a young guy among this group of murderers, he may not know the finer points of the business and may have made a boneheaded mistake."

"Bear #113 was the first animal killed in this current series," Glenn said.

"Right," Franklin said. "Junior was impulsive, excited; he capped the first creature he saw. And the old pro decided not to waste the shot. I mean, there lay a gall bladder for the taking. Maybe the young guy was trying to make a name for himself?"

"Sure, why not?" Pete said. "Either way, it's been elk from then on so I'd guess Mr. Experience made it plain to The Grunt that it wasn't going to happen again."

"Ranger Franklin," Glenn said. "I want you on these poachers full time. Step up backcountry horse patrols and put a chopper in the air. I want these guys stopped."

"Right, chief."

"Everyone," Glenn said, rising. "Without mentioning eagle feathers again, I suggest each and every one of you immediately bone up on the rules, regulations, and laws that govern this National Park, reread your manual of Standard Operating Procedures and, when you've flushed out your headgear, get back to work. Keep your eyes open. There will be no more dead rangers. That is an order."

The meeting broke up and the team funneled out of the room, with the exception of Lincoln, who nervously lingered. The ranger's loitering did not escape notice. He'd reacted oddly during the earlier discussion of Bart Houser, and the chief ranger was starting to get curious. "Pete," Glenn asked, "was there something else?"

"Chief," Lincoln said. "We need to talk."

Chapter 12

A misty rain quietly enveloped the sleepy little community of Gardiner, Montana. Tucked into a long, narrow valley between high mountain peaks at the far north entrance to Yellowstone, it was the idyllic old west town; an eclectic blend of old and new.

Most of the buildings were constructed before their present occupants were born, repaired and remodeled as necessity dictated, and none too fancy. Architectural facades hid flat roofs and bore the scars of ageless war against the harsh elements of the high country. The lack of pavement and paint gave the town an eerie resemblance to Lago before the drifter rode in.

There were a few new buildings; strangers in that secluded country. On the north bank of the Gardiner River, beside the only highway into town, sat the Gas & Go. Its stark white walls and neon lights made it stand out like a ten dollar gold piece in a beggar's cup. There, the tourists could buy the Billings Reporter, a cup of coffee, and a breakfast burrito while they fueled up for the trip to anywhere. No matter where you were headed, it was a long drive from Gardiner, Montana.

Farther to the north sat the big chain motel. The new construction crept in that direction, away from Main Street, with its cramped quarters and old time shops. The new motel had been inevitable, what with Big City folks wanting their hot tubs, exercise rooms,

FAX machines and, of course, continental breakfasts. Anywhere else in town you got a room with a bed and were mighty glad to have it.

North of the river, high on the hillside, stood the newer homes, retirement havens for the transplants with money. They'd fallen in love with the simple lifestyle and, even if they couldn't bear to live it themselves, wanted to be close to it. South of the river, closer to Main, were the homes for the laborers. Compact and simple housing was the order of the day with a car and a pickup in the drive or, lacking that, parked on the lawn. Fishing boats on rusted trailers rested between the weekends beside recently replenished stacks of cut and split firewood gathered in anticipation of the harsh months of winter soon to come.

Most folks, those that meant to stay, had adapted to the remote location and simple life. They did without conveniences in order to hold onto their independence, relied on each other when times were tough, and knew and trusted their neighbors. It was the only way to survive. Nobody worried about locking their trucks, or even their houses, in Gardiner, Montana. What each man owned was his, and God help the fellow who forgot that simple rule.

If the Old West still lived, it hung its hat in Gardiner.

Summer brought change. The heavy blanket of snow melted away, turned the Gardiner River to a stream of liquid chocolate, and was replaced by a ground cover of tourists. Dudes. Those demanding, irritating hordes from places so far and so different they might just as well have been from other worlds; New York, Chicago, Los Angeles, Germany, Japan, England. Like invading aliens, they came by the thousands, tens of thousands.

Spotting strangers was easy. They traveled in swarms; colorful swarms at that. The men wore Hawaiian shirts, baggy shorts. and black socks with sandals. They sported cheap cowboy hats with a dead pheasant's tail splattered above the front brim. If they had a hat, dog-gone-it, they were cowboys. The women hung on the arms of their men and dressed in long skirts, western blouses over-decorated in shiny Conchos, pink or blue cowgirl hats and enough make-up to give Tammy Faye Bakker fits of green envy. They strolled the sidewalks, cameras dangling from their necks like jewelry, hungry for a taste of the west as told by Zane Grey and Louis L'Amour.

Above all else, they came for the park. Thank the park. Yellowstone National Park was a godsend for merchants wanting to make an honest buck and a headache for everybody else. To the people of Gardiner, Montana, the park had moved in and taken over. They even owned Main Street.

Main Street was like most other streets except that it had only one sidewalk, on the north side of the street. Like any sidewalk, you could casually stroll along in front of old shops, buy picture postcards, cheap souvenirs and t-shirts to tell the world you'd been there. But Main Street was also a dividing line. Look to the south and you had a view of the north entrance to Yellowstone, the jewel of the National Park Service. Step down off the walk, into the street, and you were in Yellowstone.

The gutter divided Gardiner from the park. The park divided Gardiner.

There was an old joke, told only half in jest, among local bar patrons. If you fought outside the Main Street gin mill, a common occurrence on Friday nights, make sure you stayed on the sidewalk. Have a good time, knock yourself out, on the sidewalk. When you were done, Big Lou, the sheriff, would chew you out for being a public nuisance, take you home, and pour you into bed. Make the mistake of falling into the street and the rangers would show up. In the park, public intoxication was a federal offense. You'd find yourself in front of Judge Hardnose at Mammoth Headquarters, facing a fine you couldn't afford and time to dry out in a place you wouldn't like.

For precisely that reason, the Sagebrush Saloon was the favorite drinking establishment in town. It was a half block north of Main Street. Mike Tyson couldn't hit you hard enough to knock you into the park from there.

The Sagebrush was more than a bar. It was a social center, the social center. One of the first buildings hammered together in the early days of settlement; it held more reverence to some than the church on the hill. While early miners and trappers lived in wall tents or slept in the back of covered wagons, they could always warm their outsides, as well as their innards, at the Sagebrush Saloon.

To enter the saloon was to step back to a different time and place. The walls were weather-stained pine mostly in shadow as the sun stealing in from the lone front window couldn't reach the corners of the room. The few electric lights offered little help. The south wall was a mirror, fronted by stacked bottles, glasses, beer mugs, and a small hand-painted sign reading: Don't Spit on the Floor. Several feet out from the mirror, running the length of the room, stood the dark mahogany bar. Polished by years of beer soaked bar towels, dirty elbows, and the tears of heartsick patrons looking for advice from their favorite barkeep; the bar was the altar in Gardiner's church of life.

Long before the sun came up the Sagebrush coffee pot was on. The regulars rolled in early and helped themselves to a cup. They found their chairs around their tables. That is to say, their chair, the same chair, every morning, with the seat worn to fit the cheeks just so. It was a chair not available anywhere, for any price, in the outside world. The day would start when it got there. Until it did nothing happened without java.

Over biscuits and gravy, bacon and eggs, cakes and sausage and hot black coffee they talked; and only the names changed. Who was doing what, who shouldn't have been doing it, and how the poor fool's wife was going to react when she found out just exactly what it was he was doing. It was a friendly, relaxed group of neighbors. They spoke the same language and said the same things, day in and day out in Gardiner, Montana.

This day, however, was different. This day those same, usually relaxed, people were black hornet mad. They were deathly afraid and, it appeared, their troubles weren't going away anytime soon. The bar stools had been pulled out from the altar, all the chairs were taken, and people filled the corners. They milled about talking, drinking coffee, cold soda or, in the case of a few, their first beer of the day. Latecomers squeezed in where room allowed.

Silas Miller was the mayor of Gardiner. His family had settled there when the town was only a notion. There were few old-timers left and it was only fitting he should run it. He asked John, the owner of the Sagebrush Saloon, for a roofing hammer. It made a good gavel and got everybody's attention. He put it to use, pounding on a short chunk of 2x4 so as not to mar the surface of the bar. "Looks like most everybody is here," Silas said. "Let's get started."

"I've got something to say," came a shout.

Silas followed the booming voice to the back of the room. Then he frowned. "Dang it, Billy. Everybody's probably got something to say. Just rein it in a minute. I ain't ready to listen to you preach yet. I ain't had but one cup of coffee."

There were spotty chuckles throughout the room. Billy Walton reddened a shade and settled back into his chair. Billy was a rancher. His livestock bore the Bar 7 brand; one of the first registered in the Montana Territory before it had even earned statehood. His was a proud heritage and there weren't many people he'd take a tongue lashing from. Silas was one of the few. He respected Silas.

There were fewer still that would cross trails with Billy, even when inclined to do so. He was a monster of a man, over six feet tall and rock hard. Four decades of throwing hay bales and wrangling horses would do that to you. Age had added a hint of a gut but no more. He was mostly muscled and mostly mean. Ask anyone, Billy had the disposition of a mad dog.

Silas poured his second cup of coffee, set the pot down on the bar, and addressed the crowded room. "For those of you who ain't quite up to speed, we had another bear killin' yesterday. He was a ranger; one of our hometown boys."

The room grew silent as the severity of the situation settled on the minds of those present. Silas took a sip of coffee and surveyed the crowd. The people were depending upon him and he had to show some strength. He just wasn't sure he was up to it.

"Now," Silas said, searching for the words. "We got a total of three dead people from bear attacks and the park has three dead bears. The Billings Reporter is callin' Yellowstone a war zone. I'm sure I ain't the only one that's seen traffic fallin' off. We have to talk about what we're gonna do or how we're gonna make the park do somethin'."

Joe Caleb, the owner of the Gas & Go, stood with his hat in his hands. "Silas, have you talked to the park? What do they say?"

"I called the superintendent's office yesterday, after I heard about Bart," Silas said. "Mr. Stanton wasn't in but his secretary told me they were doin' everything they could."

"What does that mean," Joe's wife stood as she spoke. Joe sat down. "Everything they could?"

"Probably not a blasted thing." Billy was yelling again from the back of the room.

Silas ignored Billy. He reached for his coffee cup, spilled it across the bar, and muttered. Stan Harju waved Silas off and wiped the bar with the rag he carried in his back pocket for such occasions. Stan was one master bartender.

"I don't know what that means, Mary," Silas said feeling inadequate. "Mr. Stanton hasn't called me back yet. Obviously the man is busy." He immediately regretted defending the park superintendent. All indications were Stanton was in over his head, but that wasn't his problem. The people of Gardiner were his look out. "I'm expectin' him to call soon," Silas continued. "In the meantime, we need to decide what, if anything, we can do."

Mary Caleb, looking wholly unsatisfied with the answer she'd received, sat again.

"Silas, we've got to do something," Tiny Tim Turner said. His calm manner and mousy voice made a liar of his 385-pound body. "My tour business is going straight into the toilet. Those two kids I've got working for me are afraid to go into the park anymore. Nobody wants to be bear bait but I've got a mortgage to worry about. Isn't there something we can do?"

Jim Bashford owned a gift shop two doors down from the Sagebrush Saloon. An elderly gentleman living out his retirement with a small business, he was respected for his wisdom and easy manner. "I think that we should all avoid going into the hills alone," Jim said thoughtfully. "There is safety in numbers and we should take advantage of that."

"Numbers didn't give that yuppie no edge," Billy hollered. "Course, you can't expect much from yuppies." He beamed at his own wit. When nobody else smiled he went on. "The park needs to suck it up and get rid of that bear."

Janice Stapleton eyed Billy with contempt. Janice was new to Gardiner, a Florida artist moved to the mountains for inspiration. "Mr. Walton, it isn't the bear's fault. Killing it would be wrong. After all, they were here first."

"What a bunch of bull," Billy screamed. "Why don't you take your paint brushes and your high society attitude and move back where you came from."

"That's enough, Billy," Silas said. "We don't need to be arguin' amongst ourselves."

"Well, for Pete's sake, Silas. Didn't you hear what she said?" Billy's disgust had him pleading. "It ain't the bear's fault. Well, whose fault is it then? If it was me killing folks like they were jackrabbits, bet she wouldn't waste any time stringing me from some big 'ol tree!"

"She's entitled to her opinion, Billy," Mary Caleb said. "Whether you agree with it or not."

"Look, folks, can't we carry on like adults here?" Silas said. Tempers were getting too hot and he was feeling more like a referee than a mayor. "These are rough times but we've seen 'em before." He sounded lame and Silas knew it. Why should they listen when he didn't believe it himself?

"Can't we go see the superintendent?" Stan asked. "You know, a bunch of us, Silas, not just you. Then he'll know we mean business and that we expect to see some results. They've trapped bears before. There ain't no reason they can't catch this one, is there?"

"That's a good idea." The mayor laid his hand on the barkeep's shoulder. "We can put together some delegates and I'll set up a meeting."

Tim came out of his chair as fast as his large frame would allow. He lost his balance momentarily and caught himself against the chair in front. "Meetings are fine, Silas," he said. "But what am I supposed to do in the mean time? Isn't there something else we can do?"

"You bet there is," Billy hollered, no longer able to contain himself. "We can take care of this grizzly problem ourselves. Everybody knows them tree huggers out of Washington have Stanton's oysters tied up in knots. If he isn't man enough to handle the problem, we got real men living up here. I ain't afraid of no bear and them greens can go straight to hell."

"Just what, exactly, are you getting at?" Silas asked.

"What d'you think I'm gettin' at? Shoot, shovel, and shut up," Billy said. "That's what I'm gettin' at? Or do you boys all have your oysters tied up too?"

"Silas," Amy Johnston called out. She was a widowed mother of two young girls who'd already had all the grief a woman could stand. All she could think of just then were her girls playing in the yard with a murderous bear on the loose. "I think Mr. Walton might have a point."

A hushed whisper followed her comment around the room. "No, Amy," Silas said. "I understand your fear, I really do, but that's not the answer. We can't have everybody runnin' off half-cocked. Why, we'd end up shootin' each other every time somebody heard a creakin' stair or crackin' tree limb." He turned to the rancher. "Besides, Billy, you know good and well the rangers would be on us like ducks on a June bug if they thought we was goin' to hunt down that griz."

Billy stood towering over the crowd. Momentum was swinging to his side and he wasn't about to give up now. "First off," Billy said, "I ain't talking about everybody. We all know Silas couldn't shoot a rabid dog. But I've got cattle to protect. Them grizzly are gonna run out of tourists and then they'll be looking for beef. There's too many bears around here anyway."

Billy saw a few silent nods about the room and took encouragement.

"And I'll tell you right now," he continued, "I ain't afraid of them no-good rangers. All them boys are is politicians with badges; and I hate politicians. They care more about their bunnies and bears than they ever gave a hoot about us working folks. I've had enough, and I'm going to do something about it. Now who's with me?"

"Wait a minute," Silas said in desperation.

"No, you wait," Billy hollered. "My family settled in this country before there ever was a park. My granddaddy killed lots of griz, and lots of wolves, too, making it safe for everybody that followed after. We cut a life out of this valley and I ain't about to let some hoity-toity from Washington D.C. come in here and tell me that my cattle are any less important than some worthless bear. To hell with the park! And to hell is where I'm going to send that bear!"

Billy stomped out the door of the Sagebrush Saloon into the drizzling rain.

He was fuming. To hell with them too, he thought, I don't need their help. When Billy Walton kills that murdering bear they'll change their tunes all right. They'll see... They will see.

131

Chapter 13

Fort Washakie lay south of Crowheart and for the most part, passed its time as uneventfully as every other reservation town, with the exception of Tribal Council nights. On those occasions, Indians from communities throughout the Wind River Reservation gathered in Fort Washakie to discuss the problems of business, and the problems of life, as they were unique to the reservation.

In the center of the meager Fort Washakie business district stood the Community House. It was a large, single story, concrete block structure. Truth be told, it looked more like a bomb shelter than a community center. As with most government projects, its construction had been funded and then forgotten. Maintenance had never been budgeted and any care the building received was from a proud few. Dollars were short but the building was a central point of self-respect for those who still cared about such things. Eggshell white paint must have been the bargain because that was the color chosen for both the exterior and interior of the Community House. Though it had been a number of years since its last fresh coat, it was nonetheless kept clean and had a quiet air of respectability. The concrete walkway at the front of the building was swept clean, the weeds had been pulled from the cracking asphalt parking lot, and the debris and garbage always carried on the wind had been policed from the grounds. The building was presentable and ready for the evening's meeting.

Two sets of gray steel double doors were the only entrances to the structure; one set squarely in the middle front of the building, the other its mirror image at the rear. The only other openings through the solid walls of symmetrical concrete blocks were two small, sliding-glass windows, one on each side of the front doors. Function, not fancy, had been the order of the day when this brainstorm was conceived and architectural genius was certainly not a necessity in designing this gift to the reservation people.

Upon entering the front doors one was greeted by a single, huge room lit by harsh, fluorescent bulbs strategically and precisely placed on the ceiling to assault the sensibilities of anyone and everyone who entered. To the far left and back corner were separate doors for the two rest rooms while a small alcove took up the remaining space in the front left corner. In this space stood a tiny folding card table upon which lay a half-dozen paper plates of home baked goodies; cookies of three varieties, brownies, and cupcakes. On the air was the sweet, delightful odor of banana bread, compliments of the Tribal Elders' wives.

Beside the plates were two pitchers of fruit drink and a stack of paper cups, simple but satisfying. Those in attendance could ill afford the luxury of treats in their regular diets but Tribal Council nights were special. They were not merely business meetings they were social gatherings. One of the few occasions when the people met their extended neighbors and brethren on their own turf, in their own time, and for their own purpose.

A tapestry, woven by the ladies of the town, hung colorfully on the far right wall. Though other adornments were found throughout the room, the tapestry was the atmospheric centerpiece.

When the building had first been put up, the government brought in a well-meaning but none too bright decorator to make the setting pleasing for the Council meetings. In her ignorance, she'd hung a huge painting of the heroic white Governor, Caleb Lyon of the Idaho Territory, offering a reservation treaty to local Indians in 1866. Apparently she considered it fitting in a building meant to foster good relations with these people. She failed, however, to consider that she was not in Idaho, that the Indians in the painting were neither Shoshone nor Arapaho, that the treaty depicted had never been signed, and that the whites did not keep the treaties later signed. All in all, the local residents considered it a hollow, if not entirely insulting, gesture.

Somebody, probably a village youngster on a self-conceived medicine journey, renamed the painting Governor Lyon Lyin' with a can of black gloss enamel. Bureau officials removed the slightly altered work of art and an undersecretary of the undersecretary of the Secretary of the Interior wrote a letter of apology to the governing Council. The letter had been placed with most other documents initiated by the overseers of the reservation, in File 13.

The resulting blank wall stared over many Council meetings until finally, the village ladies took it upon themselves to brighten the atmosphere. The tapestry, actually a large blanket, featured a traditional and brightly colored banded design around its edge and a repeating pictorial motif of bighorn sheep across its body in honor of the early Shoshone way of life.

A long folding table with gray painted steel legs and a faux wood-paneled top sat below the ornamental blanket and, behind it, a row of chairs for the Council Chairmen and Tribal Elders.

Folding wooden chairs, that would have been antiques had they been cared for, were arranged in two sections separated by a center aisle which took up the middle of the room and faced the head table. The back of each chair screamed out in vivid, white-stenciled lettering: PROPERTY OF U.S. GOVERNMENT. Apparently, the Bureau didn't want any of their valuable furniture being absconded with for the purpose of decorating private residences.

To the right of the rear doors hung an oil painting of Chief Washakie in full ceremonial dress, brightly framed and surrounded by accouterments of the traditional way of Shoshone life; a peace pipe, a battle axe, a beaded headband and belt, all in brilliantly colored beads and multi-hued feathers. The few Arapaho that occasionally complained about it were routinely overruled. To the left of the same doors was a portrait of the President of the United States and nothing more. On the floor beneath the President's serious expression lay a cardboard box containing out-of-date magazines and adjacent to it a scratched and dented blue recycling bin, containing only dust. The two walls spoke of the battle carried out in the heart of each reservation Indian, the ancient versus the new, the eternal and the temporal. Decisions about their chosen way of life could not be made in this public forum; they were subtle and personal.

Each of the eighty chairs now held an anxious Indian, four times as many people as usually attended the Council. Dozens more filled the aisles, making short work of the space reserved as standing room only. The din was numbing.

Among the throng were most of the business owners from Crowheart. Tommy Two Fists had ventured off of his trout farm to attend. Smohalla, the Nez Perce Indian who ran the Crowheart Bar had a seat in the front row. Mrs. Boinaiv, who inherited the Tomahawk Motel, had ridden down with Joe White. The filling station owner stood glad-handing old friends as if he were running for office.

Of course, Two Ravens was there as well. But this was a different Johnny Two Ravens than anyone had seen before. Normally stoic, strong and wry, this Two Ravens was a shaken man.

He'd found his client, Paul Hastings, only two hundred yards from their fishing camp at Heart Lake and it was the most sickening sight he'd ever seen. There was no question Hastings was dead. His corpse had been mutilated, ripped wide open, with his innards tossed wildly around the heavy green foliage. He'd packed Hastings' companions out at first light, following a sleepless night of venomous comments and accusations. He'd contacted the park authorities from Tie Hack Ranch and immediately returned to the site of the killing with rangers in tow. The investigation interviews that followed left Two Ravens feeling hollow and empty. He'd slept little since.

Holding forth with his inimitable cool was William Shakespeare. A tribal elder, Shakespeare had chaired the Council meetings and represented the Shoshone for the last half decade. A newspaper writer and speaker, Shakespeare could talk with the government's Agency Supervisor like few on the reservation. He had an equally trustworthy relationship with the chiefs of both reservation tribes. Whether Shoshone or Arapaho, Indian problems went to their chiefs, reservation problems went to Shakespeare.

In deference to the old and out of reverence for the ancient, Shakespeare wore a handmade buckskin shirt. He removed his New York Yankee's ball cap, placing it on the floor for the duration of the meeting, then adjusted a pile of yellow legal pads on the table. He said something, barely audible in the din, to Running River, the Arapaho Councilman, then tapped the table with a wooden gavel. The talking throughout the room ebbed to a murmur, then turned quiet.

"If we're ready to start," Shakespeare said. "I'll ask Running River to read the minutes from our last Council."

"Forget that bull!" The shout had come from the back and not a soul in the room had a doubt as to who had uttered it. The group turned as one. Fred Black rocked from one foot to another; insufferably pleased with the way he'd drawn their attention.

Fred was not yet twenty-three years old. Still, in that short time, he'd earned the fear and loathing of nearly every resident of the reservation. He stood big as a mountain, with shoulder length, mouse brown hair framing a face that always seemed to be issuing a threat. Tattoos decorated both the meat of his folded arms and his hairless chest; "permanent war paint" he called it.

"We're going to conduct this meeting in an orderly fashion," Shakespeare said.

"Nobody cares about last month's minutes," Fred said. "We want to know what's being done about all those killings around Yellowstone."

Another murmur went up through the crowd. Fred cast his evil smile at William Jones, the young Indian at his side. Jones, like a shadow, was always at Fred's side. He walked where Fred walked, drank what Fred drank, and nodded when Fred spoke.

The rest of their motley crew was in attendance as well. Bull Tarken, wearing the worn yellow and brown jersey from his linebacker days at Wyoming. Ed White, Joe's son, leaned against the back wall with his girlfriend, Angel Adams, leaning back against him. He had one arm around her throat and the hand of the other tucked into a pocket of her jeans. Ed was known as a troublemaker, Angel a tramp; both descriptions were oversimplifications. The Crow brothers, whose parents had messed them up for life by naming one Lawrence and the other Larry, leaned on opposite walls in the corner, both dreadfully bored with the entire affair.

"Well," Fred demanded. "What's being done about it?"

Shakespeare exhaled forcefully. He'd hoped to hold that discussion off for a while but it wasn't to be. "I can't tell you what's being done," he said. "The Yellowstone official I spoke with was reluctant to discuss the situation with me. He said it was a matter for the National Park Service; unrelated to the Wind River Reservation."

"Unrelated?" Two Fists stood as if his chair was on fire. "The people being mauled to death up there are our customers. How is that of no concern to us?"

Shakespeare raised his hands as if fending off blows. "I'm telling you what I was told, Tommy."

"Ask John Two Ravens if it ain't an Indian problem."

The outfitter winced visibly. Images of Paul Hastings' torn flesh, as he lay in a pool of his own blood, flooded back to him. He saw again, with even more distinctness, the looks of anguish and anger on the faces of his fishing buddies.

"If I go out of business," Two Fists said. "That's a concern for me."

"Of course it is, Tommy," Shakespeare said. "But Yellowstone said they'll handle it."

"Yeah," Fred hollered. "Like they've handled it already. There are three people dead, three in one week, from grizzly attacks. That ain't natural. They say they're going to take care of it, but it ain't natural.

Obviously they've done something to create this problem in the first place and they ain't saying what it is."

A clamor went up throughout the room. Shakespeare hesitated, allowing for steam to be blown off, and then struck his gavel again. "Please, everybody." The room quieted. "Fred, you have nothing to base that on."

Sam Coyote, the proprietor of the bowling alley in Fort Washakie, rose to his feet. "I don't know if Fred knows what he's talking about; there's a first time for everything." Sporadic chuckles were scared off by Fred's glare. "But it seems to me that whatever's happening up in the white man's park is the white man's problem. Let them take care of it."

There was a spattering of applause.

Two Ravens stood. "Shakespeare, may I speak?"

The chairman smiled, grateful somebody remembered his place, and nodded.

"Sam Coyote is right. It is a white man's problem, but it is also our problem. I lost one of my charges..."

"You should have watched him closer," Fred said.

Two Ravens stared daggers to the back of the room. When it seemed Fred had no more to add, he continued. "I feel responsible and that makes it my problem. These killings have been happening all over the park, west, south, as near as Heart Lake where the incident with my client took place. It could be one bear but these are great distances apart."

"Are you saying its more than one bear?" Shakespeare asked.

"I am saying it could be more than one bear. If so, how far will they travel? Do we remain quiet until it becomes more of an Indian problem? Will we bring on trouble with inaction?"

"You're cowards," Fred hollered, heading for the door. "You're all cowards."

Like ducklings, the rest of Fred's gang followed after him. Joe White watched his son disappear with the Adams girl on his arm. He hung his head.

"I've never seen such a display," Running River said, as the room began to quiet again. "Arapaho tradition allows no one to walk out of Council except the medicine man."

"You know it is no different for us," Shakespeare said hoping he did not sound as defensive as he felt. "They have no respect for the old ways. No respect for our laws."

Two Ravens, still standing, placed his hands on Joe White's shoulders. "The young ones are no different than many of us. We are all forgetting the old ways." The room grew quiet again. "For Mother Earth, there is a balance to all things. All things happen in their time."

"Including these killings?" someone asked angrily.

The Tribal Council continued, carried by voices that alternated between curious, questioning, and angry. It ended with no consensus being reached. Two Ravens stepped from the Community House into the crisp fall air. The scattered, dim streetlights of Fort Washakie did little to hide the brilliance of the star-filled night sky.

Fred Black was an outlaw, Two Ravens truly believed, but the drunken, hateful young lout had said something that stuck with the outfitter. What was happening in Yellowstone was not natural. Fred's claim that the park authorities had done something to cause the killings was ridiculous. Yet he was right all the same. It wasn't natural.

*

A bright white light pierced the darkness as two human forms made their way into the open meadow on Madison Plateau. A heavy thud and vicious crack broke the silence as Gerry Meeks separated antlers and skull plate from the top of a bull elk's head with a keenly sharpened hand axe. As cleanliness had always been next to godliness, it was no surprise that Meeks was interested in neither. Quick and efficient were his only concerns.

Having taken what he wanted, he handed the massive set of antlers to Bass Donnelly.

"Put those with the others and let's get out of here. We've got a long ride ahead and I want this load out of the park before sun-up."

Without a word, Donnelly tied the rack onto the back of a pack horse with the rest of their load. It had been a good day, with more than four hundred pounds of prime antler gathered since daylight. That was going to translate to more than seven grand in hard cash. The young poacher was already spending his share in his head and kicking himself that he hadn't gotten into the business long ago.

With the load secure, Meeks extinguished the light. "Let your eyes fix," he whispered to his partner. "Then mount up. I'll lead. You stay in my hip pocket, ya hear?"

Donnelly replied with a grunt.

"Just give your horse his head. He knows a hell of a lot more about what he's doing up here in the dark than you do. When we get in the timber, cover your face with an arm so you don't lose an eye to some low-hanging limb."

Yup, Donnelly thought, seven grand. Seven thousand dollars on top of what they'd already collected. That crotchety old buzzard could talk all he wanted, treat him any way he wanted, say anything he pleased as long as, when the time came, he paid him his share.

The clouds had finally cleared and the combination of moonlight and acclimated eyes allowed them to situate their pack horses and get into the saddle. Meeks clicked his tongue and spurred his mount into a walk. The soft creaking of old leather and the nearly imperceptible hoof beats of four horses on damp earth mingled with the whispering wind. Their pack-train, in silhouette, made its way back across the small meadow and into the darkness of heavy timber, then disappeared.

*

As if the forces of nature were aware of their brutal crime and bitterly angered by their violation, thirty-five miles away, an otherworldly fog appeared on the surface of Apparition Lake. Beneath the eerie swirl, the dead waters began to churn.

Chapter 14

A shroud of dark clouds hung in heavy layers in the sky, blanching the color from the landscape; a silent, depressing storm that again covered the valley like a casket pall. Everything in the glen looked wet and gray. Winter always started first in the high country. The rains would come, followed by the first snow settling on the peaks up top. There might still be wildflowers and blue birds on the valley floor, but the cold never truly let go its hold where the air was thin. Snow could fall any time of year. Winter was truly king in the mountains.

Billy Walton heaved the last of the hay bales over the corral fence, finishing his chores for the morning. Though it had been hours since leaving the Sagebrush Saloon, he was still mad at the whole bunch of them. He gathered the bailing twine he'd scattered on the ground while feeding his horses and threw it with the rest of the clutter in the back of his dented pickup, and then leaned against the corral fence to light a smoke.

He could not understand what was wrong with those people. Had they gotten soft over the years? Too much reliance on tourist money, that was their problem. It made perfect sense to him; bear kills cattle, bear kills people, rancher kills bear. It didn't get any simpler than that. Bears were useless critters anyway; nothing but voracious eating machines. It was hard enough to feed your family these days, let alone having to share with a worthless hunk of insatiable grizzly hide. Granddaddy Walton would never have put up with it. Billy wouldn't either. It was settled; the bear had to go.

Billy looked up toward the high country encircling the Bar 7 and smiled. It had been a good year for hay. The thick clouds covered the peaks but, in his mind's eye, he could see them; snow-capped and majestic. They'd already had more moisture than he'd seen in a couple of years and there was plenty to come. He would have to remember to tell his rider to keep the cattle off the river for a couple of weeks. He couldn't afford to have any of the stock drown. Yes, sir, it had been a good year for hay. After I kill that godforsaken bear, Billy thought, it's going to be a good year for beef as well.

Billy dropped his cigarette at his feet and ground it into the dirt with the heel of his mud-caked boot. It was time. He reached into the cab and took his rifle down from the rack in the rear window. He checked to make sure it was loaded, though he already knew, and hid it beneath three broken bales of hay in the truck bed. Rangers or no, he was going hunting. Let them try to stop him.

He climbed into the pickup, started the engine and flipped on the radio. A local country-western station was playing Garth Brooks, Standing Outside the Fire. Billy hummed along with the tune, feeling lonely and not sure why. He reached down to the passenger's side and pulled his third beer of the day from a sack lying on the floorboard. He thought of the rangers. He thought of the folks at the Sagebrush. He thought about his Granddaddy.

"They'll see," Billy said aloud. "They'll all see."

*

The rain stopped but the clouds had settled in for the day. On Mount Schurz, the second highest point in Yellowstone, a low grumbling began just below the summit. Hundreds of inches of snow pack from the previous winter had saturated the ground, which never truly settled over the short, cool summer. The torrential rains from the freak storms had only added to the stress.

A section of unstable soils, already clinging precariously beneath the peak's steep north face, sloughed off under its own weight. The slope above, now without a supporting toe, began to slide. The rumble grew thunderous and, without warning, a section of mountain broke free. The loose section of soils and rock, nearly one hundred yards in width, started slowly downhill. As it moved, it gained speed and busted other slabs free. Like falling dominoes, the moving earth overwhelmed the mountainside in its descent.

Propelled by its own weight, pulled by gravity and roaring like a runaway freight train, the slide toppled downward at ever increasing speeds. It uprooted trees without hesitation and pushed boulders the size of small trucks as if they were marbles. In thirteen seconds, the slide denuded the mountainside and came to rest fifteen hundred feet below. A dark cloud of uplifted dirt, mixed with heavy fog, gave the impression there had been an explosion. The rumble ebbed and the cloud slowly settled. The silence that followed, in comparison, was deafening. Far from civilization, no one saw and no one heard nature spreading the weight of the weather's work. All things in the natural world were fighting for balance.

*

Billy pulled in behind a short line of vehicles at the north entrance station to the park. Two cars ahead, in a two-tone brown rental, an Asian child with his head out the rear window was making faces at a black couple in a blue Buick with Mississippi tags right behind. "Must all be lost," Billy said. He laughed at his own joke, as intolerant of people of other cultures and colors as he was of bears. He belched and dropped an empty beer can, his fourth of the day, behind the seat of the pickup. He slid the sack of full cans under the passenger's seat with his boot. No sense looking for trouble, he thought.

His turn, finally, Billy pulled up to the station shack where he was greeted by a familiar smiling face. Jill was a seasonal employee of the

Park Service and had been stationed at that entrance several weeks. "Hello, Mr. Walton. What brings you to the park today?"

"Had it out with the old lady," Billy said, lying. "Just needed to go for a drive. Want to come along?" He grinned, proud of the way he handled his nerves.

She shrugged helplessly. "Wish I could but somebody's got to hold down the fort."

"I imagine so," Billy said. "Can't blame a fellow for trying." He pressed the accelerator, heading through the gate. It was too bad she was a government employee. Otherwise, Billy thought, he might just show that little filly some western hospitality.

Rounding the curve, Billy looked into the rear view mirror to make sure he was out of sight of the entrance station. He reached under the seat and removed his fifth beer of the day. He popped the top, took a swig, and laughed. This was going to be fun, Billy thought.

Ten minutes later, his truck had climbed the nine hundred feet in elevation to the Mammoth Hot Springs complex. He parked in front of the gift shop and headed inside for a snack. Beer always made him hungry. Billy returned with an armload of munchies, tossed them onto the seat, and leaned against the pickup bed to light another cigarette.

A large green bus pulled noisily into the lot and parked at the base of the Main Terrace. Billy stared as the haggard-looking driver emerged from behind the sliding door. He jumped down quick and looked to the rancher, as if he was making an escape rather than just getting off. The reason was soon apparent as a flood of blue Scout uniforms followed. Billy didn't care for tourists but he had to admit this group was a hoot. That poor driver looked like he needed to kill somebody. The swarm of Cub Scouts raced from the Main Terrace, up the winding boardwalk trail, to the Upper Terrace of the Hot Springs. Like ghosts, the boys disappeared into the heavy bank of clouds hanging above the Mammoth complex. First they were there and then they were not. It was the strangest looking thing he'd ever seen. The hair stood up on Billy's arms and a chill worked its way up his spine.

"You silly fool," he told himself, trying to shake the feeling of unease. Billy flipped the cigarette into a puddle. He started his truck and roared from the parking lot and up the road. The incline took him up, around the Terrace, and into the same cloud. He too vanished like a phantom.

*

To step onto Roaring Mountain was to step back in time to a primordial world. The slope stood nearly barren. Its scorched volcanic surface, sparingly dotted with the dead and twisted remains of a few lodgepole pines, appeared to have suffered a huge conflagration. Natural steam vents, open pits to Hell, hissed a somber melody to underscore the bleakness.

Billy parked in the small turnout across the road from Roaring Mountain. The beer having taken its toll, he crossed to the base of the charcoal slope to drain his bladder in the fancy outhouse there. The park had found it necessary to spend his tax dollars because you couldn't have sissy tourists dropping their drawers behind just any old tree. Free of the beer, Billy stepped back outside and stopped dead in his tracks. He caught his breath so as not to make a sound and sidled up against the building. He stared and was just able to make out a dark figure in the fog before him. Then it was gone and all the remained was the mist.

Condensed moisture on the nearby tree limbs fell in heavy drops and thudded on the beds of scattered pine needles below; percussion to the harmonic releases of steam from the mountain vents. Billy tried to block out the sounds, listening instead for movement. He took a few steps; a few more. Steam rose from the bed of blackened earth and mingled with the low hanging clouds. He strained his bloodshot eyes. There, in the deep shroud, above and to his left, Billy again saw the eerie form. It towered over the rancher, black and awful, its arms outstretched.

147

Then the mists parted and the creature revealed itself to be a stunted lodgepole pine. The skeletal tree, bare of all but a couple of contorted limbs, stood forlornly in the boiling witch's cauldron that had killed it. Billy cussed, closed his eyes, and took a badly needed breath. Shaken, he returned to his truck. He removed the rifle from its hiding place beneath the hay and placed it in the cab beside him. Then he reached into the tattered bag under the seat, intent on steadying his nerves with his seventh beer of the day.

*

Norris Geyser Basin was closed. Following the recovery of Bart Houser's body, the rangers felt it only prudent to keep the public out of the area. There was still a bear on the loose and they didn't need any more incidents. Billy was glad to see it. Empty of tourists, he would attract no attention at all wandering the basin with a rifle slung over his shoulder.

The rancher slid his truck into a spot next to the little museum building across the main road from the basin area. He didn't want anyone snooping around his pickup any more than he wanted a confrontation out on the boardwalks. He grabbed his rifle and locked the truck. Confident he was alone; Billy darted across the road and into the lodgepole pines on the opposite side. He moved to the edge of the pines overlooking the basin below. The heavy fog, combined with the steam rising from the geysers, vents and fumaroles, gave him the sensation of standing at the edge of the world. Only the tips of scattered pines showing through the white blanket gave any indication there was a bottom to the pit. A fleeting thought of turning back passed through Billy's mind but his arrogance would have none of it. It was him or the bear. One of them, he knew, would not see the sun set.

Billy worked around the edge of the basin's upper rim to a wide meadow of knee-high grass, a remnant of the summer's healthy growth already turning brown. Crossing it, he would be in full view from the road, but it couldn't be helped. It was the only way to the

148

boardwalk. He dropped the rifle along his side, to hide it from view, and strolled toward the lodgepole on the opposite side.

He was near half-way there when someone shouted, "What are you doing out there?"

Startled, Billy turned to see a park ranger beside his patrol vehicle on the shoulder of the road. No, no, no, the rancher's mind was screaming; where did he come from? Billy eased the rifle down his leg to the ground. He smiled, waved, and headed in the ranger's direction.

As he neared the officer, Billy studied the man's face. His expression spoke of curiosity, even annoyance, but neither fear nor anger. He gave no indication he'd seen the weapon. The ranger was twenty-five, at most, blonde and muscled; a poster child for the National Park Service. Just a kid, the rancher thought. No sweat.

"What are you doing out there?" the ranger asked again as Billy closed the gap between them.

"Stopped over by the museum to stretch my legs and my dog run off. I was just looking for him."

"Well, you're going to have to move along," the ranger said. "The basin is closed. We had a bear mauling here and it isn't safe to be wandering around, especially in this weather."

"A bear mauling," Billy said in mock surprise. "Sorry, officer, I didn't know. Look, I'll just walk back up and get my truck. But if you don't mind, I want to stop down here just one more minute and see if that dog will come to call. Then I'll be on my way. Heck, that old mutt was never worth all the trouble anyway."

The ranger looked Billy over trying to decide if he was crazy or just stupid. "Yeah, okay," he said, opting for stupid. "But don't be long."

"Thanks, officer. I really appreciate your concern."

The ranger's vehicle headed down the road. Billy followed it with his eyes and, as it disappeared, with his benediction. "Ya' jack booted thug!"

In the short walk to the truck, Billy gave the situation some thought. He'd have to be more careful. If he got himself arrested, old Silas would never let him forget it. He retrieved his rifle from the meadow and decided to move to different hunting grounds for the time being. Billy poured the fuel to the carburetor, trying to remember where the other idiots had been killed. He grabbed his eighth beer of the day mulling the question over. Firehole Lake wasn't too far south. There'd been a killing there.

The rancher blew through the stop sign at Norris Junction and raced down the open roadway. He wasn't paying attention. He was too busy wishing that punk kiddy cop had given him a harder time. He laughed at the mental image, fuzzy as it was, turned up the radio, and finished his beer.

*

When Yellowstone blew up in smoke and flames in 1988, Gibbon Falls was right in the path. Below the falls, and above the banks of the Gibbon River, the trees still showed the scars of the massive wildfire. Bare and blackened pine boles, reminders of the merciless cycle of life, stood watch over the newly rejuvenated ground cover of thick vegetation. Amid the abundant growth stood three large bull elk, grazing on the nutritious salad at their feet. Large, dark-colored crowns adorned their heads, massive antlers to be used in the mating rituals and battles for dominance just starting.

Billy pulled his truck to the side of the road to admire the monarchs of the forest. He wasn't, by any stretch of the imagination, a naturalist. In fact, he pictured himself putting a bullet or two in the big hunk of venison in the middle. That elk would look good staring over his pool table in his basement, when he got a pool table in the basement. Forget it, he thought. That wall was reserved for a murdering bear. Maybe he'd have the missus fry him up some steaks while he drove around Gardiner showing off that dead bear all stretched out in his truck bed. Billy laughed and pulled back onto the road.

He made it as far as the Madison River Bridge, south of Madison Junction, when his bladder began screaming again. What was that

150

joke? You don't really buy beer, you just rent it. That last one had put him over the edge again. And he'd had enough now. He'd save the rest of his stash for the celebration trip home. Having to stop was wasting valuable hunting light.

He drove the winding road up the opposite slope and, near the top, made a turn onto Firehole Canyon Drive. There had to be a spot up there he could pull off and relieve himself. He wound his way down to the banks of the river where the road mirrored its course through the slot canyon. As the road dipped at its lowest point, then began to climb up through the walls of rock, Billy marveled at the amount of water rushing through. He'd never seen the Firehole River so high. A few more days of rain and the road would be under water.

The Firehole River was a force to be reckoned with. Through the centuries it had carved its way down through the canyon eliminating everything in its path. The multicolored rock walls, left behind as borders, towered over sixty feet above the sluice through which the river passed. Even with his senses dulled by alcohol Billy was captivated by the raw strength of nature's forces.

He drove on, maneuvering up the steep roadway until it leveled on the upper rim of the east canyon wall above Firehole Falls. He squinted through the windshield, admiring the crashing water as it followed a horseshoe course; westerly, then back to the north, and finally east through a narrow gap in the rock walls. There, it shot over the lip of the shelf and tumbled thirty feet below to smash its way into a churning pool.

Even with the truck closed up, the tumultuous thunder of millions of gallons of unbridled water filled his ears. Steering left, into the turnout for sightseers, Billy parked to shield himself from passing cars and stepped out. He stood inside the open door, looking out into the sea of fog and lodgepole pines, and peed on the parking lot pavement. The sound of the falls was ear splitting. Billy couldn't hear himself breathe. And he didn't hear the eruption from the trees in front of him.

The grizzly appeared suddenly, as if out of thin air, charging on all fours through the pines and straight at the rancher. Billy saw it and, slowly, his mind registering what it was. He saw the smaller trees and brush breaking in its path, but it seemed unreal as he heard only the sound of Firehole Falls smashing into the massive pool below.

Finally, he realized what was happening. But with his instincts dulled, by the time Billy grabbed the rifle from the truck cab and turned back, the bear had closed within yards. He dropped the gun to his hip. The barrel disappear into the chest of the biggest, meanest grizzly he had ever seen. He jerked the trigger and felt the rifle kick but, so deeply was the weapon buried in the monster's fur, he saw no muzzle flash. The report of exploding powder sounded like the pop of a single kernel of corn.

Billy's feet left the ground and, an instant later, an intense pain shot through his body as he bounced off the side of the truck bed. He crashed to the ground, feeling nothing at all. Billy lay supine on the pavement, his back broken and, even in his beer drenched haze, knew he was about to die. Only sissies cried and only babies soiled their pants. Billy wanted to go out like a man. The great bear's face appeared above his, staring down with steel-gray eyes. In them, he saw an intelligence and, beyond that, an intense hatred unlike any he'd ever experienced.

Paralyzed, he could do nothing. The giant bear lowered its face to within inches. It opened its jaws and released a low, demonic growl. Billy closed his eyes, overpowered by the heat and stench of the bear's breath. The grizzly clenched its powerful jaws around his neck. Billy Walton, of the Bar 7 Ranch, hoped without much hope that his granddaddy would be proud. Then the lights went out.

Chapter 15

Glenn had worked difficult cases before. Some had been perplexing, others nearly impossible, but this ordeal was something else. Even outlaws and murderers had rules, habits, and patterns. Suddenly the black and white process of investigation didn't seem to apply. Answers couldn't be found for the simplest questions. Glenn could not fathom the confusion created by the few facts he had. He could stand anything but confusion. He needed to talk the troubles, the gray areas, out. But he couldn't talk to anyone. Any one, that was, but Johnny Two Ravens.

By the time Glenn arrived in Crowheart, Two Ravens had already started on their usual bottle. He'd been guiding greenhorns into the mountains since he was old enough to drive. He knew his job and had never had so much as a severe client injury, let alone a fatality. When, this time, they met before the outfitter's lit fireplace, drinks in hand, both were deeply troubled men.

"Two visitors, a ranger, now a rancher," Glenn said, rehashing the killings; just part of the strange occurrences in the park. "It just doesn't make any sense. Nothing makes any sense." He gulped his drink. "And it isn't bad enough Houser is dead. Now I've got to ruin his reputation as well. Another of my rangers, Pete Lincoln, couldn't handle the guilty knowledge and spilled it. Houser couldn't make ends meet so he started shaking down visitors. He was even poaching small game. Like I don't have enough trouble with professional poachers. And the bear deaths. And what you went through. The whole world is standing on its head."

"Have you thought any more about the connection J.D. mentioned?" Two Ravens asked.

"What? That our bear is killing environmental rapists?"

"Has it occurred to you we could be dealing with something outside the norm?"

"Of course it's outside the norm," Glenn said. "Bear attacks just don't happen with this frequency or ferocity."

"I don't mean that. I'm not talking about statistical normality."

The chief eyed his friend watching the firelight flicker in his dark eyes and off of his stern features. "What are you talking about, Johnny?"

"Has it occurred to you we could be dealing with the supernatural?"

Glenn grunted a laugh. "You're drunk."

"I'm not remotely drunk," Two Ravens said. "And I'm not kidding either." Now they were both staring, wrestling with their eyes. "Think for a minute. People numbering in the millions pour into churches every week, sometimes twice a week, and spend every second of the rest of their waking lives ignoring, and even denying, the fact that there is a spiritual world."

"Come on, Johnny."

"Come on, what? As a species we are meant to be in touch with every facet of this world."

"You know I don't subscribe to organized religion," Glenn said. "The hypocrites outnumber the supplicants four to one."

"I'm not talking about organized religion. I'm talking about the spirit of the world; Mother Earth."

"Johnny, I love you like a brother. In fact I love you more than my brother, he's an idiot," Glenn said with a smile. "But as far as I'm concerned Indian mysticism is just another religion. It's all guilt with music. Yours just happens to have drums."

154

"How could you have spent seven years in these mountains without discovering they have a life of their own?"

"Of course there's life here. . ."

"No. I mean the mountains are alive," Two Ravens said. "The trees are alive. The rocks, the plants; they are all beings with life energy. They all have spirits."

"Okay." Glenn raised his hands in surrender. "They all have spirits. What does that have to do with what's happening in the park?"

"Maybe the bear cannot be found because it does not always exist."

Glenn lifted the bottle of amber liquid. "I'm not drunk enough for this," he said, pouring.

"I know how strange this must sound to you."

"No," the ranger said. He took a drink, felt the burn of the alcohol in his chest, and exhaled. "No, I really don't think you understand how truly, unmistakably, irretrievably strange it sounds."

"I'm just asking you to accept the possibility. . ."

"What possibility? You're telling me we're looking for Casper the unfriendly bear."

"Don't be so quick to judge," Two Ravens said. He poured himself another drink and settled back. "There is a legend among my people. It says that over one hundred years ago the white man was stealing into the Stinking Country. . ."

"The stinking country?"

"Yellowstone; the Stinking Country."

"Oh, yeah," Glenn said. "The sulfur from the geothermal areas. Got it, sorry. Go on."

Two Ravens nodded. "The white man was trespassing on Indian land and poaching the animals. The legend speaks of a great and powerful medicine man who led the ceremonial Bear Dance then, empowered by the Great Spirit, Duma Appah, left the reservation and headed out to face the white man; the taker. The holy man's name was Silverbear."

*

155

By the third day of his vision quest, Silverbear had seen many things and been told much by the Great Spirit. The magic of the bear fetish had proven itself. His return to the tribe would be a happy one for all things were working out in the Earth's time, as they had been told. The day before he had sat by the falling water in the Stinking Country, what the yellowlegs called Undine Falls. With the feathered pipe he had smoked the rich tobacco. Then he'd been visited by a golden eagle.

It had appeared from nowhere, sent by the Great Spirit, and had circled above him in wide and beautiful arcs that shrank with each pass. It lit on a rock in front of Silverbear, folded its tremendous wings of brown and gold next to its body and greeted the Shoshone holy man.

Silverbear and the eagle shared the majestic silence of the Stinking Country. Then the eagle spoke to him. "You are free," the eagle said in Silverbear's own language. "The white man who steals the lives of the animals will be stopped; his actions avenged. The yellowlegs with their false law and heavy weapons of shining metal cannot help you. They are prisoners. The Shoshone people are free."

Silverbear heard the words but said nothing. This was the final answer to their Bear Dance and the culmination of his quest. Now was the listening time.

"Your freedom is guaranteed by your respect for the land," the golden eagle said, staring at him from his stately position upon the rock. "All things work out as the Earth would have them, for the Great Spirit has created a balance in all things. The wrongs of those that have injured you will be righted in their time. Tell this to the Shoshone people."

The eagle spread its wings. It leapt from the rock, dipped slightly in its flight then, stroking the air mightily, soared high. Brown and gold, it gleamed in the sunlight of Silverbear's second day.

It was a happy message to take back to his tribe. Now he knew that Norkuk had been right. The white men had told the Shoshone, "Stay on this land we give you and we will provide for you." Norkuk had known, however, that the land had not been theirs to give and their poor excuse for food was not needed or wanted. His were a proud people, a self-sufficient people. The white man was a lesser creature hardly deserving of the name 'man.'

Washakie, Chief of the Shoshone Nation, had wanted to get along. He wanted peace for his people. Washakie was a good man and he did what he felt was right but Norkuk said Washakie was weak. Silverbear agreed with the young leader. Treaties were simply lies put on paper.

Within the last cycle of the moon the yellowlegs had broken their promises again. Nearly a thousand Arapaho had been marched onto the Shoshone Reservation beneath the stern eyes and many guns of the pony soldiers. The Arapaho and Shoshone were bitter enemies. Even so, Norkuk was disgusted with the way in which those people had been treated. The Arapaho were nearly starved, their clothing tattered and offering little protection from the harsh weather. Among them were less than two hundred braves. The rest were women, children and aged, sickly men. All that they owned, even their horses, had been stolen from them. The yellowlegs pointed to the Shoshone Reservation and told the Arapaho, "Live here."

Chief Washakie should have refused. Instead the chief said his people would endure. Norkuk would not endure. He'd had a belly full of the white man's presence and their lies. Gathering his party, of which Silverbear was the spiritual leader, they left the reservation and returned to the land the Great Spirit meant for them to occupy.

Washakie was now telling the whites that Norkuk and his people had gone to Utah "to get washed." Norkuk and Silverbear believed it was their chief who was in need of washing. Washakie was dirty with the filth of the white man and his lies. Norkuk had known his ancestors were unhappy with the conditions of his people. Now that the eagle had sent its message of freedom for the Shoshone, Silverbear knew Norkuk had been right all along.

Though the holy man had received his message from the eagle, one day yet remained of his journey. The Great Spirit had asked for three days. Silverbear walked on.

*

"In the Stinking Country," Two Ravens said, "Silverbear became an animal. Thereafter he roamed the land protecting it from the white thieves."

"Wait," Glenn said. He couldn't help but wonder if Johnny was messing with his head. "He turned into an animal?"

"Indian legends are replete with stories of shape-shifting and animal spirits intervening for men. Mankind itself is said to have come from the Coyote when it was in human form."

"And you wonder why I think it's all bull?"

"Think what you will. It's no secret that all legends are based in some part upon fact. What if my people were more right than they knew?"

"More right then they knew... about what?"

Two Ravens sat forward in his chair. Glenn was growing annoyed, and he was sorry for that, but he felt his own thoughts growing clearer. He wanted his friend to see what he was beginning to see. "About the spiritual world," the outfitter said. "It's no secret we're screwing up this world. Maybe the Great Spirit has decided to punish us for what we've done."

"You can't be serious?"

"I spoke with my father about this," Two Ravens said. "He is concerned and thinks that you and I should talk with Snow on the Mountains."

"Who is Snow on the Mountains?"

"A powerful shaman. A medicine man. His given name is Bill Pope, but his Indian name is Snow on the Mountains. He is a wise man and a great healer. I think you should meet him."

"What for?"

"Maybe he can help us to understand what is happening in Yellowstone?"

"No, thank you." That would have been an exit line for most, but Glenn settled back and cupped his glass with both hands. He and

158

Two Ravens were friends more than anything. They could say what was on their minds. "There's a real explanation for what is happening, Johnny. I just haven't found it. But I will. When I do this situation will be solved with good police work – not with beads and rattles."

Two Ravens nodded. "Answer one question, will you?" he asked. "I ask because you have not said and I would like to know. At Firehole Falls, where the white rancher was killed, did you also find the feather of a golden eagle?"

Glenn's features tightened. He emptied his glass and closed his eyes. Then slowly, almost painfully, he nodded and whispered, "Yes. Yes, we did."

*

Glenn Merrill knew every sound in Yellowstone. He was familiar with the hollow, high-pitched warning issued by the stalking bobcat; had filed into memory the misty thunder of the Upper Falls; the clockwork whoosh of Old Faithful; even knew the muddy whine of a tourist's RV mired axle-deep in a rain-soaked No Parking area of a campground. Yet as he sat in his leather recliner, bathed in the rhythm of Tumbling Tumbleweeds crooned by Roy Rogers and the Sons of the Pioneers, and sipping the foam head off a mug of freshly poured beer, Glenn heard a sound that was rare indeed in this neck of the Mammoth Hot Springs complex; the chime of his doorbell.

He caught sight of the microwave clock, declaring 8:00 pm in bright red digits, and wondered who it could possibly be. Who did he know that could operate a doorbell? The chief's second surprise of the evening came when he opened the door. J.D. stood in the entryway wearing exhausted eyes and a nervous smile. He couldn't help but ask, "Slumming?"

"I thought I'd see how the other half lived. Is this a bad time?"

"Not at all. I'm just trying to unwind a little. Would you like to come in?"

"Well, okay. Yes." J.D. shuffled her feet. "If you're sure it's all right?"

"Well, what do you know," Glenn said, grinning. "The little lady is bashful after all." He stepped back, opening wide the door, and bowed as he waved her into the room. "Enter, please."

J.D.'s face flushed. She hesitated, took a breath, and stepped in.

"Make yourself comfortable," Glenn said headed back toward his recliner. "I'm having a beer. Would you like something?"

"Sure."

"Everything is in the kitchen." He pointed. "Help yourself." He sat and grabbed his mug. "You'll have to excuse me. I'm a terrible host and a worse bartender."

A lot of women might have felt less than flattered. But Jennifer Davies was not a lot of women. Glenn's casual manner was just the ticket and already helping to ease her tensions. She found the small kitchen, a glass and, by snooping, tasty ingredients. All was suddenly right with the world. Except... "Do you have ice?"

"Ice?" Glenn repeated. "That's made of water, isn't it?"

She poked her head out with a questioning stare. Glenn laughed. "Never mind," he said. "It's an old Indian joke. Try the freezer."

"I tried the freezer."

"Well, try again. Behind... whatever's in front of it."

Victory. J.D. cracked ice from a tray, calling, "I hope you don't mind the intrusion," above the noise. "But it dawned on me tonight that if I watched one more cable movie or ate one more deli sandwich in that musty old apartment of mine, well, I'd lose what little bit of sanity I still possessed." She emerged with drink in hand. "Besides, chief, I hate to admit it but I don't know a soul here. You're the closest thing to a friend I have. Pathetic, huh?"

"Flattery will get you everywhere."

"I didn't mean it the way it sounded."

Glenn laughed and took a long swig from his beer. Following the heavy conversation with Two Ravens, he needed both. And he didn't mind J.D.'s company at all. "Have a seat."

To their mutual surprise, talk came easy. They visited a dozen topics; old jobs, old friends, old adventures, and even new hopes. It had been some time since either had indulged in the luxury of hope. It was nice to forget the park's problems for a while. But, as they knew it would, the subjects of Yellowstone, and Yellowstone bears, eventually found their way into the conversation.

"Bear have been my life. Bear, specifically," J.D. confessed, "for as long as I can remember. This is the first time I've ever been afraid. The fact that people have been killed is horrible, horrendous, choose your adjective, but that rancher, Walton... From what we found, from what his friends said, it's clear that he was hunting. He was experienced, he was armed, and he was hunting for the bear when it killed him."

Glenn shook his head. "I'm missing your point."

J.D. sighed, disgusted he was going to make her say it. "You're hunting the bear too, idiot. I'm worried for you, okay?"

Glenn opened his mouth and then closed it without speaking. He didn't know what to say.

J.D. shook her head. She forced a laugh but it couldn't disguise her fear either. "I just hope you're a better shot than the drunken rancher."

"My gun isn't meant for bear," Glenn snapped. "I carry a weapon to protect myself and others from the kooks of this world. None of them are covered with silver-tipped fur."

J.D. looked up in surprise.

"I'm sorry," Glenn said. "I'm not acquainted with the notion of someone being afraid for me. And, despite the fact that I often am, I don't usually admit to being afraid myself. Your comparison of me to Billy Walton is a little cattywampus. His hunting is not my hunting. Besides, have you any real idea how little use a handgun would be against a grizzly bear in the wild?"

"I study bear. I sometimes sedate them. I don't blow their brains out."

"I said I was sorry."

J.D.'s stare softened. She blushed and nodded.

His apology accepted, Glenn went on. "We're talking about nine hundred pounds of enraged muscle. It's faster than a racehorse. And, coming at you, its head would be bobbing like a toy dog in the rear window of a '57 Chevy. I'm a marksman and I'd have a better chance of hitting a ping pong ball swinging on a string than I would of hitting a charging bear. Drunk or sober, this Walton was supposedly a heck of a shot. He got off one round with a scoped rifle and we're trying to explain what happened to his widow. That says something." Glenn sank back in his chair, bone-tired. "We've both seen too many people hurt over the years out of sheer ignorance. You know, better than I do, the best defense against a charging grizzly is to eliminate whatever it is you're doing that he perceives as a threat. They protect their own like any other living creature. Remove the threat and the bear no longer feels the need to charge." Glenn rubbed his temples. "Somehow," he said. "Somehow we've got to remove whatever it is that's threatening this bear."

"This bear?" J.D. asked. "These bears, plural?"

Glenn shrugged. "Who knows? My old pal, Johnny Two Ravens, thinks it's one. But not a bear made of flesh and blood. Add that to the mix. What good is a piece of lead going to do in the brain of a bear that doesn't exist?"

"I don't know what you're talking about," J.D. said. "But I wish you hadn't said that."

"Yeah. I'm not sure what I'm talking about and I wish I wasn't thinking it. I have to admit, J.D., this is one of those times when I feel like I should pack up and go. We're in over our heads and I don't know what to do next."

"Glenn," she said, "the day we met you told me something that stuck with me. You said, 'If you take the time to let it, Yellowstone will help you cope.' Do you remember?"

"I do," Glenn said with a chuckle. "You're not going to haunt me with my own words, are you?"

"Did you mean them? Do you believe it?"

"Yup."

"Then maybe you should take your own advice."

Glenn nodded. The conversation and the night slipped away. Then Glenn nodded off. J.D. nursed her last drink until the bright red digits on the microwave read 12:30 am. Glenn was sunk, sitting up, in the corner of the couch, breathing softly, sleeping peacefully. The first peaceful sleep, J.D. imagined, he'd had in some time. That was how she left him when she let herself out.

Chapter 16

Well before the sun appeared, Glenn awoke, alone but no longer lonesome. How many people, after all, had friends like Two Ravens and J.D. to tell their troubles to? He showered, shaved, and dressed in a clean uniform; his ritual of 'putting on the game face.' But today would be different. His friends had given him direction. That, and his own words, offered back by J.D. when he was lost; Yellowstone will help you cope.

He needed some time, in and with the park, before anyone else arose that morning. To make sure he took it, his logical brain had even invented an excuse. The lakes and waterways needed checking. With the run-off from the rain they were getting the water levels could become dangerously high and put tourists at risk. In recognition of the favor J.D. had done him the previous night, and wanting very much to return it, he made an early stop to ask her to join him.

Together they traveled south through Norris and then east through the Canyon Village. For the first time, as they passed the developed areas, Glenn saw his surroundings with a more judicious eye. In the midst of paradise, they had erected suburban malls with gas stations, gift shops, cafeterias, Visitor's Centers, ranger substations, campgrounds, and even a post office. He wasn't a hypocrite, he was a modern man. But the ravages of progress could not be denied. They were intruders and, in many ways, offenders. Mankind had a right to live but needed to find a balance. There was a balance to all things. To help the park, he needed to return to the park, to draw strength from all it was and had been.

They continued to a one-way loop road and made the first left at a directional sign that read: Inspiration Point. The road narrowed then twisted down through a heavy green pine forest to finally open into a clearing and a small parking area. Glenn parked and shut off the Suburban.

"Inspiration Point?" J.D. asked.

"I assure you," Glenn said, "my intentions are entirely honorable." He winked and then grabbed a pair of binoculars. "One of my favorite spots in the park. Come on."

The Grand Canyon of the Yellowstone snuck up on you. From thirty yards away, all that could be seen were a few odd-shaped and colorful rock formations surrounded by a vast canvas of open air. On an approach to the edge of the north rim, however, the Canyon reached up and grabbed you – pulling you into its depths.

The Minnetaree Indians called the area "Mi tsi a da zi," the Rock Yellow River. A more fitting name could not have been found. The sheer canyon walls, set afire by the early morning sun, glowed in spectacular golden hues. The contrasting bands and bars of orange, rust, brown, red, green and other molten colors only enhanced their beauty. Falling off for hundreds of feet below, the Yellowstone River snatched the mind and sucked the viewer into its turbulence as it labored, eternally carving the canyon deeper into the earth.

In the extreme distance to the right was the Lower Falls. Its muted roar mixed and danced with the canyon winds singing a song of power and domination. The three hundred foot drop of the Lower Falls dwarfed even the famous Niagara as it spilled its contents in a crashing, swirling riot of motion at its base. The mists rose like spawning salmon, fighting a hundred feet and more back up its face, then fell again to the pool below. The water then coursed its way in sparkling serpentine fashion for twenty-four miles between the towering walls of its own creation. Below their position on the rim, an osprey soared on lifting thermals. The mind took wing with the magnificent bird gliding on the wind in that last bastion of Eden.

They stood in silence and awe as nature unveiled its beauty and power below. Holding the railing to maintain her balance, J.D. finally broke the silence. "It's unbelievable. It's beyond words."

He nodded his agreement, then smiled, took her arm and said, "That isn't all. Let me show you something."

"Where are we going?" J.D. asked as he led her away from the falls and into the timber.

"To see the pride of Yellowstone," he answered with a grin.

They'd gone some distance into the trees, down a rise then up again, when Glenn stopped and, using the field glasses he'd brought, scanned some high, open meadows. "The time," he said, adjusting the focus, "should be about right for his morning appearance."

"Who?" J.D. asked.

"Why, Hercules, of course. And there he is; as reliable as Old Faithful."

Glenn handed the binoculars to J.D., held the branches of the nearest tree back to clear the way, and pointed toward a distant ridge. She searched. She rotated the focus. She gasped. "An elk. He's huge and... Oh, my God," she lowered the glasses and gawked at Glenn. "He's completely white."

Glenn nodded. "He's an albino."

J.D. gasped again and returned to the glasses. Hercules was beautiful; an enormous animal, with a brilliantly white coat, and a towering rack of antlers like a crown. He was a king.

"Do you have any idea," Glenn asked, "what the odds are of an albino bull elk living to adulthood in the wild?"

J.D. was suddenly all biologist and all business. Staring through the binoculars, still captivated by the sight of Yellowstone's prize, she replied, "The odds of any albino mammal being born is something like one in ten thousand. But they rarely survive. An adult bull elk? I doubt if it's even calculable."

"Actually, J.D., I was just being funny," Glenn said. "You see, I ask what the odds are. Then you're supposed to say, 'I don't know, what?' Then, I say, 'I don't know either, but they must be really small.' Then we laugh, because it's a joke. What nerd would really know the odds?"

J.D. lowered the glasses and gave the chief ranger the undivided attention he apparently wanted. Then she rolled her eyes and returned to the binoculars.

Glenn laughed; his first real laugh in a long time. "Here's one stat I do know," he said, returning the spotlight where it belonged. "Other than Old Faithful, Hercules is the single most photographed image in the park."

"I can see why. He's beautiful!"

"It's what I tried to tell you, but told you so badly, without emotion, the day we met. This is a hard place to work. The hours are long, the problems immense, and the people all too often tiring. Forget the incredible things that have been happening. Just the daily grind can make you want to pack up and go. Then I visit a place like the canyon, or stop and take a look at Hercules, and I remember why I have to stay. And just now I remind myself why it is so important we stop whatever is happening here. It is a magical place. If you take the time to let it..."

This time they finished it together, "Yellowstone will help you cope."

Glenn and J.D. returned north by the Dunraven Pass. Both felt renewed, as if the river had taken their cares down that gorgeous canyon and into places unknown. J.D. kicked off her boots, to put her feet on the dash, but found her comfort crimped by the maps, papers, and random items she could only call ranger brick-a-brac. She moved a handful and, on the top, found a copy of that morning's Billings Reporter with the headline: YELLOWSTONE'S 'CHIEF' CONCERN and a kicker asking: 'Should Merrill Resign?' She read several sentences into the first paragraph before Glenn interrupted.

"Is ouster even a word?"

"Not a good one," J.D. said tossing the rag aside. "Who's Howard Lark anyway?"

"You remember, that big mouth that chased us through the hall at Mammoth the other morning."

"Oh, him."

"Yeah, him. My own personal devil, it seems."

"Well, if you ask me," JD said, "he's trying to make a name for himself. Don't let him get to you."

"He's not. What bothers me is, as far as the poaching is concerned, the pretentious cretin seems to know what he's talking about."

*

The Roosevelt Lodge was behind them and Mammoth not far ahead. But neither Glenn nor J.D. were quite ready to jump back into the fray. The road offered one last chance to disappear for a few minutes and together they decided to take it. Glenn pulled off the road at Apparition Lake.

They climbed from the Suburban, easing their doors shut until they clicked. It would have been sacrilegious to announce their presence just then. The soft orange glow of sunrise brought out surreal colors in everything it washed. The human world slept while the natural world never rested. Were it within his power, it would always be sunrise wherever Glenn stood.

The Yellowstone River passed below him running nearly even with the state line at the spot. He stared north over the river at the rising slopes in Montana, bathed in the golden touch of the sun, while he stood in Wyoming where the dark shadow of the ridges to the south and east shaded him from that same warmth. Nature always seemed to keep things in balance. Good and evil, life and death, even warmth and cold. We have so little control over most of it, Glenn thought, and that's the way it should be. It works the way it is.

Glenn breathed deeply of the mountain air and then turned toward the object of his interest. The cool of the morning created wisps of light fog over the surface of Apparition Lake. Glenn understood the scientific principle behind morning fog over water in the high country but that explanation meant little now. The rising mists were a mystical part of the atmosphere and he preferred to think of it as mountain magic. He'd seen what he came for at the Canyon, still Glenn was drawn to Apparition Lake. There really was something different about that place.

As much as his logical policeman's mind told him that Two Ravens' theory was over the edge, there was something about it that troubled Glenn. Hocus-pocus didn't cut it in his world. Everything was supposed to be black and white; gray areas meant trouble.

Without purpose but feeling that same draw, Glenn and J.D. walked the shoreline chilled by the breeze, mesmerized by the rolling mists, and more than amazed at how the lake level had risen in so short a time. The chief couldn't remember when the lake was so deep. Summer grasses grew thick around the edges of the water and, submerged, in the depths as well. The strangeness they'd felt at the close of their first visit came back tenfold. Neither of them would have been surprised if it were to vanish right before their eyes. The phantom lake; Apparition Lake.

Behind them, distantly, the radio squawked. It stabbed the silence like a knife and startled both Glenn and J.D. They shared nervous laughs. "I left my portable in the truck," he said. "Are you okay if I..."

"Of course. Don't be silly."

He started away. "I'll be right back."

J.D. watched him go. She turned back to the misty lake and drew her jacket tightly about her.

*

Glenn pulled the mic through the driver's side window and took the radio call beside his vehicle. "Dispatch, one-oh-one, did you have traffic?"

"Ten-four, one-oh-one. Another elk carcass was found in the Canyon area. Do you have any special instructions?"

Immediately angered but needing to concentrate, Glenn failed to notice a fog curling through the trees. "Get hold of Franklin," the chief said. "He's heading the poaching investigation." The first white wisps thickened to gray rolling clouds that filtered the sunlight and threw the area into gloom. "Find out where he's got the chopper flying right now. Have them rerouted. Tell Franklin I want him to work grids on the Canyon. And keep me apprised." Dispatch acknowledged the order.

As Glenn hung the mic up, he suddenly noticed the dark. More, he felt a sudden chill as if Old Man Winter had arrived early. The hair stood on his arms and neck and he rubbed the goose flesh. With the cold and gloom came something else, something he'd never felt in all his thirty-one years; an unseen presence. The rising darkness and descending fog crowded in on him. He turned to the trees, straining to see through the gray, searching, for something real, something he could put his hands on. Suddenly the presence was upon him.

It came, literally, out of nowhere and was lurching from the fog-bound trees before him, not even appearing to touch the ground; an enormous grizzly. Glenn's mind raced, rejecting what he was seeing as real. It couldn't be. Yet on the monster came, moving at a terrifying speed, its eyes aglow in the sudden dark. It released a roar like a thousand screaming demons from the pits of Hell. Glenn's ticket was punched. He saw the face of death.

But the chief ranger was not afraid. He was startled, absolutely, even stunned, but most of his surprise came from realizing that he was not afraid. A single thought repeated itself in his mind, over and over again, the thought he'd had at sunrise, the same thought underscored at Inspiration Point: There is a balance to all things. It works the way it is.

The bear was almost upon him when, as suddenly, it ceased its charge and stopped. The creature rose up on its hind legs, towering over him, and stared down at Glenn. His prey? Time, like the marauding bruin, stood still. Even the sounds of the forest came to a halt as if there, on the shores of Apparition Lake, a vacuum had formed around him and the animal. The monster's burnt sienna coat glowed hot, while the silver-tipped hairs blended with the shroud of mist swirling around them.

Death took leave. Glenn felt it go.

For reasons he did not know, and couldn't fathom, as certain as he was that the bear was there, Glenn was suddenly just as confident he was not going to die. The threat remained, the animal as deadly but, for now at least, he knew it would do him no harm. Glenn looked up in awe at the massive creature, waiting. Then, unspoken but burning in his brain, he heard a voice, fragile with age yet ringing with authority. "Prepare your Death Song, white warrior," it said. "The time is near."

In that instant, the bear was gone. It did not flee. It did not walk regally away having proved itself the king of the beasts. It hadn't even dropped back down onto all fours. The animal simply stretched out its mighty paws, reared back its head as if praying to the heavens and then, taking the fog and darkness with it, vanished into thin air.

Worried by his long absence, J.D. returned to the Suburban a few minutes later. She found Glenn just standing there, clearly shaken by something that had happened but refusing to elaborate. She saw something at the ranger's feet, gasped in disbelief, and bent to retrieve it.

J.D. lifted the object into the now brilliant sunlight; the feather of a golden eagle.

Chapter 17

Glenn sat, staring out the window at the passing reservation, outwardly silent but with thoughts screaming in his head. It was insane. What he was doing was absolutely insane. Two Ravens was at the wheel, driving toward... what? The chief couldn't believe they were on their way to see a shaman. Worst of all, he'd requested the meeting himself. The bulging packet of tobacco in the inside breast pocket of his jacket was a reminder of just how crazy the whole business had become.

"It is customary to bring a gift," Two Ravens had told him. "Tobacco would be appropriate."

Glenn bit his lip. We're going to see a holy man, he thought. We're going to visit a kook. We're off to see the wizard. His black and white mind screamed, What are you doing? Turn around. Go home. He would have voiced those thoughts to Johnny Two Ravens had he not been completely out of sensible options. But he was and he knew it. He was also out of time. Two Ravens had just brought his pickup to a stop in front of the shaman's house.

Had it been kept up; mended, tended, or even just painted the house of the Shoshone shaman would have looked like a cottage from a child's storybook. It had not and it did not.

The house was small, with a second floor that could only have featured a single bedroom. A door occupied the center-front of the ground level atop three crooked wooden steps with no landing. Two windows, one on each side of the door, looked out over a faded picket fence that separated the brown yard from the brown road; weary eyes and a smile missing teeth on the house's sad face.

A little dog, its species generations lost to mutt-hood, yipped at the end of a rope tied to the sagging gate. A second dog, half husky, half school bus, lay like a sack of potatoes across the top step. The big one had no leash. There seemed no need; you couldn't have lifted its tongue with a corn shovel.

"Hello."

The voice, though friendly and gentle, startled Glenn by the simple fact it seemed to come from nowhere. Two Ravens was rarely startled by anything and after the incident at Heart Lake probably wouldn't be again. Scanning the yard Glenn located the source of the greeting.

Half a dozen cars filled the small enclosure, some on blocks, some buried hubcap deep in overgrown weeds. Several were in varying stages of repair. None looked operable. One of them, a rusted Skylark with a spidered windshield, had two occupants. The shadowy figure behind the steering wheel waved in their direction.

Two Ravens waved back, as if sitting in a junked car were a perfectly normal activity for a resident of Crowheart, but he did not move toward the vehicle. Several uncomfortable minutes passed while the two in the car continued their conversation. Eventually they exited the wreck. The passenger was a young Indian in his late teens. He pocketed both hands, passed Two Ravens and Glenn with a silent nod, and left the yard. The other was the shaman, known to the locals as Bill Pope.

Glenn wasn't sure what he had expected but it wasn't the stooped old man who approached them. He wore faded jeans with the right pant leg tucked into his worn cowboy boot and the left riding over, a western-cut red shirt with a slip rope tie, and a straw cowboy hat with a black eagle feather pointing to the rear. He walked slowly not, it seemed, because of any physical infirmary but because it was his way. The copper skin on his sallow face had been sun baked for over sixty years yet, even from a distance, his blue eyes danced with life and energy.

He shook hands with Two Ravens genuinely pleased to see him. "Hello, Bill," the outfitter said.

"Johnny. I haven't seen you for a while." The old man turned to Glenn. "Who are you?" While blunt, his childlike question was friendly and asked out of what seemed true curiosity.

"Glenn Merrill," the ranger said extending his hand. "National Park Service."

The Indian shook his hand, appearing more pleased with the ranger's name than his affiliation.

"Glenn," Two Ravens said, "this is Snow on the Mountains."

The silent moment that followed seemed awkward to Glenn. If the Indians noticed his discomfort, they didn't show it. Snow on the Mountains, in fact, looked to be deeply contemplating something and, had he not still been standing there, you'd have sworn he'd gone somewhere else. Finally, the shaman said, "I think we can go inside and talk."

He led them to the house and swung wide the frame of the screen door. It struck Glenn as funny because the screen was missing entirely and they could easily have walked right through the door. Snow on the Mountains led the parade over the sleeping dog as if it weren't there. The animal did not stir in their passing.

The living room was an extension of the house's worn exterior, with two old chairs and a sagging couch making up the furniture. A portable TV sat on the floor in a corner unplugged and seemingly unused. With the exception of three bright paintings of Native Americans, hung about the faded walls, the room was colored in shades of worn drab. Through an open door, in the small room beyond, Glenn saw a stuffed bald eagle hanging from a pedestal on the wall. Its petrified wings flew outstretched and its talons seemed poised to strike. Beneath the creature stood a glass case, its shelves were dotted with intricate charms, amulets, trinkets and feathers. Glenn longed for a closer look but thought better of the idea. He took the offered seat on the couch instead while Two Ravens and the shaman deposited themselves in the chairs.

"Oh," Glenn said, remembering. He pulled the packet of tobacco from his duty jacket and handed it to the shaman. "I brought you some tobacco."

A surprising look of delight registered on the old Indian's face. "Let me get my pipe." He jumped up like a six-year-old heading for the playground. He was back a moment later, sending great bursts of gray smoke to the ceiling and nodding between puffs as if tasting a fine wine.

Glenn was unsure how to begin. How, after all, did one start a conversation about murder, evil spirits, Indian curses, and the like? He didn't even know if he had the capacity to believe any of it, no matter what he had seen.

Two Ravens began in a different direction. "The Bureau of Land Management is brush beating the sage south of Lander."

"It is their way," Snow on the Mountains said. "They chain cut the forest lands, knocking down all the pinyon trees, to starve the Indian. Then they revitalize the sage to save the mule deer."

Glenn didn't know but he was about to learn an important lesson regarding Native Americans in general and Indian holy men in particular. They took their time getting wherever they were going. The three had a long visit, their conversation drifting between politics, business, and pleasure but always returning to Indians and Indian affairs. Several times, Snow on the Mountains appeared to fall asleep. His head lolled and then he jerked up as if startled. He ended the movement by nodding to Glenn's right as if communicating with somebody on the empty cushion beside the ranger. Each time, he smiled and rejoined the discussion as if nothing at all had happened.

Snow on the Mountains seemed pleased about his talk with Two Ravens. He repacked his pipe and sat back in his chair as if sated by a Thanksgiving meal. "What is it you want of me?" he asked Glenn while relighting his pipe.

The ranger was taken aback by both the change in topic and, again, the abruptness of the question. The holy man seemed not to notice his hesitation. He simply waited enjoying his smoke.

"As you probably know," Glenn said. "There have been some strange, terrible things happening in the park."

"I read the papers," Snow on the Mountains said noncommittally.

Glenn briefly recounted the bear attacks and explained how the incidents made no sense. Despite feeling ill at ease, he even described his own encounter at Apparition Lake, ending with an emphatic, "I know what I saw. The bear simply disappeared!" He did not mention the voice or the warning. There were some things you just didn't tell people. Outside of his nature, the put-upon ranger finished his story with a plea. "Can you help me understand this? Why the killings? And why wasn't I killed?"

There was further talk between the three but Snow on the Mountains seemed reluctant to say anything of substance. Save for an occasional sigh or grunt of acknowledgment, he said nothing at all. He continued to smoke and listen until the conversation between Glenn and Two Ravens finally died and the silence that seemed to make up most of Snow on the Mountains' world surrounded them.

From that silence, the shaman finally spoke. "Go outside, will you, while I talk with Johnny."

Glenn was surprised by the request but stood immediately to go. He stopped on his way out. "The Park Service," he said, "will, of course, pay you for your services."

"You can sit in one of my cars, if you like. It's a good place to think."

Glenn stepped over the dog and into Snow on the Mountains' yard. The animal was awake this time and looked at him without interest. It had one blue and one brown eye both of which, after the cursory examination, it again closed. The afternoon had only gotten hotter and, despite the wide-open space, the air was close. The dirt road was empty. The quiet was all encompassing. Glenn looked to the cars in the yard, shrugged, and headed for Bill Pope's Skylark.

"Your friend seems to be a man of character and honesty," Snow on the Mountains told Two Ravens.

"I believe he is."

"What is your reason for wanting me to help him?"

"I think the things happening in Yellowstone point to the Indian as much as the white men. Mother Earth is angry. The whites call it coincidence and happenstance. My friend does not believe or understand but is willing to listen that it might be more. If we have offended Mother Earth we should make amends."

Snow on the Mountains puffed slowly on his pipe. "Tell your friend I will take three days to consider it. Then I will let you know if I will help."

Two Ravens nodded. That, he knew, was all Snow on the Mountains would say on the matter. He stood to go but was stopped by a final word from the shaman.

"Tell him he must withdraw his offer of money."

*

Glenn waved to Two Ravens from the passenger's seat of the Skylark. The Indian chuckled and crossed the yard to meet his friend as he stepped from the car.

"What did he have to say?"

"We'll know in three days."

"What do you mean 'three days'?" Glenn asked. "You mean he won't help us for three days?"

"No. I mean in three days he'll have decided whether or not he's going to help us."

"What does that mean? Whether or not he's going to help? This isn't a game. People are dying up there! We need to know what this is now." Glenn took a step toward the house.

The outfitter stopped him with a hand on his chest. "Where are you going?"

"I'm going to tell him we don't have time for this."

"No," Two Ravens said with a deadly serious look in his eyes. "You're not going to do that. I didn't bring you here to treat a Shoshone medicine man like a white drunkard who's broken your fishing regulations."

"If there's anything he can tell us..."

"It's not a question of what he can tell us," Two Ravens said with controlled menace. "It's a question of what he chooses to tell us. He's not your partner and he doesn't work for the white man's government. If he chooses to tell you anything it will be because he trusts you and believes you have the best interest of the land and the people in mind. And he couldn't care less about your schedule."

"What am I supposed to do," Glenn said. "Sit on my hands until he's had his nap and decides to help whitey?"

"Who do you people think you are?" The look on Two Ravens face was no longer one of anger. He was genuinely hurt. "Always the white men say, 'Do it in my time.' There is a time for all things and that is not your time. It is the earth's time."

With no idea what his friend meant, Glenn looked the question.

"Why did you offer Snow on the Mountains the tobacco?" Two Ravens asked. "What were you trying to buy?"

"To buy? What are you saying?" Glenn asked. "Are you saying I tried to bribe him? I gave him the tobacco because you told me to."

"Then the gift was of no value," Two Ravens said simply. "You did not respect Snow on the Mountains or the sacrifice made by the tobacco for you. You did not respect the reason I asked you to give the gift."

"I can't follow all of your Indian mysticism."

"My words have nothing to do with your feelings, for my people or our land."

"Look, Johnny, I don't know what you're angry about. I don't know what you're talking about."

Two Ravens took a deep breath and exhaled at Snow on the Mountains' pace. "The tobacco is a living thing with a spirit. It is given out of respect and should be given with understanding. A holy man has three days to decide if he will heal; a person or a park. Yellowstone needs healing."

Glenn raised his hands in surrender. "I'm sorry," he said. "We'll wait three days."

"One more thing," Two Ravens said. "You must take back your offer of payment. You cannot buy Indian medicine. It is not for sale."

Chapter 18

Glenn sat miserably in front of the television sucking on a beer and channel surfing with the remote. He absentmindedly switched the set off, having gone through the channels twice without seeing what was on any of them. He selected a CD, placed the disc in the player, then changed his mind and turned the power off. He went to the refrigerator for another beer. Nervous energy coursed through him like electricity through a power plant. He had no outlet and felt he was going crazy.

He'd been on the road all day to no avail. He'd sat in his office for hours more, going through the rangers' reports, studying crime scene photos, seemingly for nothing new. A chopper was in the air around the clock. And the reporters would not let up; one reporter in particular. In total, the day had been one more dung heap on top of the mountain he'd already shoveled that week.

When the doorbell rang, all Glenn could muster was an exasperated, "What now?"

"Hi there, ranger," J.D. said as he pulled the door open. Three plastic bags hung heavily from her arms.

"Hi," Glenn said. "What's up?"

"Well, my hands are ready to fall off... otherwise..."

"Sorry. Come on in." He stepped back from the door allowing the biologist room to pass.

"That store was a mess." J.D. made a beeline for the kitchen. "Everyone and his brother must be out. I swear I stood in line for an hour. The traffic is really heavy too." Without slowing, she began unloading the grocery bags. "Is it always like this during fall around here?"

Glenn didn't answer and J.D. didn't seem to notice.

"I hope you're hungry. I'm starving, so I probably bought way too much food."

Glenn stood watching, arms crossed, with a quizzical look on his face.

"Where do you keep your fry pan?" she asked going through the cupboards. "Oh, I didn't stop to think. Do you eat fried food? Oh, well, you will tonight. You look healthy enough." For the first time since entering the apartment J.D. paused to look at Glenn. "What's the matter?"

"Nothing," he said, his arms still crossed. "I'm just a little surprised."

"By what?"

"All this," Glenn said nodding into the kitchen.

"Well, don't get excited. I can cook, I just don't do it often."

"So... why are you doing it?"

J.D. stopped, fry pan in hand, and stared at Glenn. "I'm sorry," she said. "I guess I stepped on a toe, huh?"

"I didn't mean it the way it sounded. I just..."

"No," J.D. said. "You're right. I presumed an awful lot."

"It's okay," Glenn said. "I've just had a hard day. I'm not sure I'm ready for all this right now."

"All what?"

"This," Glenn said, sweeping his arms out to take in the makings of a feast. "I think you're jumping the gun a bit on this relationship."

"Relationship?" J.D. made a face and laid the pan on the counter top. "You must have had a hard day, Mr. Ranger. I think you're having delusions of grandeur."

"What is that supposed to mean?"

"Look, Glenn," J.D. said growing angry. "I enjoyed our hanging out. I enjoyed Inspiration Point and our walk in the woods. I was looking forward to doing it again. But that doesn't mean there's any big relationship budding here. I like your company and tonight I wanted to cook for you." J.D. paused for an instant. That was all the time it took for her to come to a boil. "I thought you were different," she said shaking her head. "But you're just like all the other creeps." She pushed past Glenn.

"J.D., wait."

She turned quickly. "What?" Her hands went to her hips and she glared.

Glenn suddenly pictured her stomping from her truck toward Bear #113 on the first day they met. He grinned at the memory. That was a mistake.

"What is so amusing?" she snapped.

Glenn dropped the smile. "Nothing. I was thinking of something. I'm sorry. Look, I don't want you leaving like this."

"Oh, I see. Don't go away mad, just go away."

"That's not what I meant," Glenn said. "I've never seen this merciless side of you."

"Merciless! You're the cold one in this room."

"I'm not cold. All I said was I wasn't ready for all this."

"All this... is a meal," J.D. said. "What are you afraid of?"

"Who said I'm afraid of anything?"

"You don't have to say it. You radiate fear like a... a radiator. And don't laugh at me."

"Why would I laugh? You're making me mad."

"Yes. That's because the truth hurts," she said. "Face it, Glenn, if it's not in Chief Merrill's big book of standard operating procedures, you can't deal with it."

"What is..."

"Oh shut up!" J.D. screamed. "I'm not through yet. Why does everything with you have to be so structured? Johnny suggests something supernatural is happening in the park and you say, 'No, it can't be.' We have a nice quiet evening together and you're thinking, 'What does she want?' We're not in your rulebook, Glenn." He stared with no clue what to say. She wasn't surprised. "You won't take a chance on anything unknown. You're afraid of not being in control." She grabbed her coat and headed for the door. "Well, guess what, Chief Merrill. You have no control over me whatsoever. And whatever is killing people in your park isn't sweating you either."

*

Yellowstone slept.

The lights had long been extinguished in the tourist shops; the doors locked and barred, their keepers off to recuperate in anticipation of the long day to come. The boardwalks surrounding all the favorite attractions stood empty. The fumaroles continued to steam and Old Faithful kept its clockwork timing but no one was there to admire their splendors.

Long, barren strips of asphalt cut their way across rolling sagebrush and mountain meadow grasses then into deep, black lodgepole and fir forests. Nothing rode them save a yellow stripe that glowed in the light of the full moon. The chill night air carried a deafening silence broken only by the stirring of gentle winds in the pines and the creaking of widow makers; standing dead boles in their midst.

The sun had disappeared and Yellowstone no longer welcomed intrusion. There was no glow from city street lamps or noise from passing trucks on distant highways. The park stood, a primordial world, where only the predators and their prey roamed its inner depths. Fred Black, a human predator, came there only at times like these.

People feared the unknown. Nothing was more unknown than the wilderness of the high mountains at night. Yellowstone at night was a fearful place. Fred feared neither the unknown nor the dark; both gave him power over others. When he suggested a party at Apparition Lake, Fred expected frightened complaints and got them, answering each with a smile and an accusation of "no spine." He was the boss and he used fear like a cattle prod. It kept him in charge; bent his followers' individual wills so that now, regardless of the terrors he cooked up, their worst fear was being without him. That was the way of the human predator and its prey. And why, when Fred led his group to the park that night, they followed.

Several cases of cheap beer later, they sat around the light of a glowing fire set back in the trees near the shoreline of Apparition Lake. No one was afraid of the park now. They had Fearless Fred, they had a warm fire with its comforting light, and they were too drunk to know the difference. It was a party!

Seated in a circle close to the fire, the group sucked on aluminum cans and spewed nonsense. They rattled on to each other, over each other, about who was doing what, and who was doing who, and where they were going to get their next rush of adrenaline, or their next handful of cold cash.

"Man, you sure gave them what for at that Tribal Council," William Jones said with a laugh. "We should have stayed for more."

"Why?" Fred asked. "Those scared rabbits were just going to cry at each other about nothing. With Two Ravens on his high horse it was probably going to turn into a prayer meeting. I swear he goes on more about Great Spirits and healing the world than any idiot I've ever known."

"Yeah," Bull Tarken said jumping into the conversation. "Who needs prayer meetings? No Great Spirit ever did nothin' for me."

"That's because you never make offerings," Fred said with a grin. He stood, grabbed his crotch, and headed for the lake. "I'm going to make one now." The others laughed as they watched their leader disappear into the dark.

Away from the warmth and light of the fire the night air was chill. The weather had been strange lately with the heavy rain and now, as Fred stepped to the edge of the lake, a fog was settling in. He staggered, misjudged the bank in the swirling mist, and nearly fell into the water. Wouldn't that have been slick? He reeled slightly from the effects of the alcohol, spread his feet to get his balance, and unzipped his ratty jeans. Across the dark body, between the shifting lines of gray mist, moon glow reflected off the ripples created by the breeze.

Another, fiercer, chill ran up Fred's back. He needed more antifreeze, he thought. He laughed. "Here's an offering for the Great Spirit," he shouted as he sent a golden arc of urine cascading into the mist-covered lake. He whistled a tune, rotating his hips to write Great Spirit on the water with the stream. He thrust forward, dotting the 'i's and crossed the final 't' with a gruff laugh.

The surface of Apparition Lake exploded.

A huge, brown and gray grizzly erupted up and out of the lake from the midst of Fred's desecration. Its powerful forearms shot forward with claws extended towards the drunk Indian. Yellow-white fangs shone in the moonlight as the bear delivered a roar that shook the timbers of the lodgepole forest around them.

Fred had no time to react and less time to scream. The bruin slammed into his gut, propelling Fred backwards and down to the rock-strewn shore with the force of a jackhammer. The bear leapt atop the Indian, snarling, dripping icy lake water. Fred felt the hot acrid breath of the monster as he struggled for air beneath its crushing weight. He saw the hatred in its hard steel-gray eyes and felt excruciating pain as the animal sank its fangs into his throat. Fred was gone in an instant. With one tremendous snap of its supernatural jaws, the grizzly decapitated the desecrator. It flipped its bloody snout sending the offending head sailing toward the orange glow of the fire. The party was over.

A great roar echoed through the trees, into their small circle, and deep into the conscious minds of the remaining six young Indians. An instant later the bloody head of Fearless Fred bounced into the light and rolled to rest just outside their circle. Stunned disbelief numbed their minds and then, one by one, panic set in and took over.

The Crow brothers, like reflections in a mirror, simultaneously dropped the bottles they'd been holding. They stood, mesmerized and quaking, while the liquor gurgled out onto the ground at their feet. Ed White released the pillowy softness of Angel Adam's left breast and wordlessly withdrew his hand from the warmth inside her shirt. The movement was accompanied by the music of the girl's ear-shattering scream. Bull, the former all-star linebacker for Wyoming's brown and yellow fighting Cowboys, fell off the log they'd been using as a bench and landed face-down in the mud, while William Jones vomited down the front of the silk shirt he'd donned with such pride earlier in the evening.

The grizzly didn't lose a beat. Its roar of death still echoed through the trees when the beast turned on the group in the firelight. It unleashed another growl and bounded in their direction. "No, no," the Crow brothers said in unison, as if mouthing a well-rehearsed duet. "Please, no." William Jones tripped over Bull and fell too smearing the puke on his chin. The odors of vomit and alcohol splashed across his chest, combined with the looped image of Fred's severed head arcing through the air, made him heave again. Stumbling, retching, he made it to his feet and ran into the dark.

"Get down," Larry Crow hoarsely croaked to his brother. "Play dead!"

Larry fell to his knees, grabbing his younger brother's arm as he went. He pulled Lawrence to the cold ground, whispering, "Don't move." Behind them, Larry heard Ed yelling backed by Angel's incessant high-pitched screams.

The swiftness of the action was incredible. The enraged animal closed the distance from Fred's mutilated corpse to the area of their campfire in seconds. The monster pulled up, loomed over the prone bodies of the Crow brothers, and sniffed briefly at the air around them. Unimpressed by their pretense of death the bruin grabbed Larry Crow by the back of his neck. The Indian screamed and was silenced as his spine cracked. Lawrence Crow couldn't remain still. He tried to rise and was instantly smashed to the ground by the bear's right paw. Its left slashed and blood spurted from the gaping wounds opened on Lawrence's throat. The bear flipped Lawrence onto his back, reared up on his haunches, and plunged back down on him.

The younger Crow felt Fred's pain and joined his brother on the far side of eternity.

The grizzly, its muzzle drenched in the brothers' blood, rose and turned on the remaining prey. It roared again, angrier even than a moment before. Ed White pulled a thick limb from the fire and brandished it before him. Flames fluttered at the end of the club as he swung it back and forth. The enraged bear glared at the Indian holding the burning log and the young girl behind him.

Then it turned on the linebacker. Bull hadn't moved a muscle. Wearing a mask of mud, he was frozen in place on the ground near the fire. "I'm sorry," Bull said. He didn't know the meaning of his own words but repeated them anyway. "I'm sorry." The bear roared and nailed Bull with a pounding strike that paled every hit he'd ever taken on a football field. The linebacker tried to scream but had no voice. The grizzly snapped Bull's face and crushed his head like a ripe melon. Then the animal swung around to Ed White.

"Come on!" the Indian yelled. "I am Eagle Feather. My ancestors killed a thousand of you. Come on!" The animal stalked forward hatred beaming from its fiery eyes. Ed slashed out with the stick, striking the bear's coat and throwing up a shower of sparks. Each swing of the burning club received a growl in reply. Firelight threw dancing shadows on the silver-tipped fur of the beast. It peeled back its lips displaying gore-covered teeth in a death's head grin. Ed swung the stick with all of his might, lost his balance, and fell to the ground. As he scrambled to rise, the bear struck his head a fearsome blow. Ed heard a snap. He toppled to the grass like an empty burlap sack unable to feel anything below his shoulders. Ed screamed; a gut-wrenching cry of terror and despair that started in the pit of his soul and raced up, threatening to shatter the very fiber of his sanity. He screamed and screamed and screamed. Yet not a sound made it to the outside world because Ed's broken body could not push the air to make his horror audible.

Angel Adams had stopped screaming when she heard Ed's neck snap like splintering firewood. She stood now, unmoving at the edge of the circle of firelight, her hands up as if pleading for mercy. Tears streamed down her face. "Please," she said. "Please."

Ed heard the growling bear. He heard Angel's final words. Then he heard the indescribable.

A moment later, through moist and blurry eyes, he watched as the bear appeared and towered over him with Angel's crushed body in its jaws. A bloody scrap twisted about her shoulders was all that remained of her shirt. Her torso was slashed and bleeding. Her face, once as angelic as her name, was torn beyond recognition. The monster released her and she toppled, though Ed felt nothing, onto his chest. Several minutes later Ed quit breathing.

The grizzly bear circled the fire, reared up, and roared to the full moon. The unearthly mist from the surface of Apparition Lake enveloped him and the monster disappeared.

Forty yards distant, and thirty feet above the ground, trembling like a newly hatched baby bird, William Jones sat perched on the sagging limb of an old pine tree. The screams, the shouting, the earth-moving roars from below had all faded into silence. The only sounds about the ghostly lake bank were his own as he softly but uncontrollably cried. What seemed like a very long time, but might not have been at all, passed and Jones unclosed his eyes, dreading to look below but knowing he must.

What he saw beneath the tree in a wide circle about their campfire defied description; all of his friends lifeless in a tableau of horror. What he saw floating past his hiding place was just as strange in its out-of-place beauty; a feather. It shown gold, streaked with white, as it drifted on the breeze. It vanished in a cloud of fog that was lifting away as quickly as it had come, reappeared beneath, and dropped gently down to land in silence near the campfire on the blood-soaked ground.

Chapter 19

The Tribal council was in an uproar. Nearly 150 years had passed since the last Indian massacre. To many of the distraught men in the room that is exactly what had happened near Apparition Lake; a massacre. These men felt the same people were responsible, the white man. The tomahawks, spears, and other decorative accouterments around the room had taken on a whole new symbolism. They seemed to speak less about what had been and more about what was to come. War drums beat in the chests of every man present, red man's thunder amid a white man's storm.

William Shakespeare banged his gavel trying to bring the room to order but order was out of the question. Battle lines were quickly being drawn and Indians were on all sides of those lines. Behind Shakespeare stood a nervous stranger whose navy blue suit screamed "government man." He was dark skinned and had jet-black hair, but was not an Indian. The fellow said nothing and was apparently content to stand quietly watching from behind the table and the council chairmen.

Two Fists stood lecturing wildly to a handful of Arapaho business owners. Time and again, he drove one fist into the other to emphasize a point. Across the room, Sam Coyote suffered a similar outburst from one of his Fort Washakie neighbors. Sam looked pained and seemed to be bracing himself for a physical assault as the angry man shouted on. Joe White sat defeated, his head depending from his rounded shoulders. Gone was the handshaking, smiling businessman. The ghost sitting in his place, the father of the slain son, had nothing to say and no one to say it to.

Shakespeare struck the table again demanding silence. The gavel's head flew off, bounced twice across the council table, and skittered to a stop near the entryway across the room. There followed shuffling, then quiet, as the Indians took their seats.

"I know you're upset," Shakespeare said. "We're all upset about what's happened. That's why we've called this meeting." The room stared back at him. "For those of you that don't know him, this is Manolo Pena, our Agency Supervisor." He indicated the government man and drew a low grumble from the crowd.

"What is the government going to do about this mess?" Two Fists demanded.

The supervisor cracked his knuckles; an unfortunate choice for a nervous gesture. He may as well have drawn a gun for the stares he received. Tucking his hands behind his back, he cleared his throat. "We understand your concern," he said his voice cracking. "We know this is a bad situation and we know how you feel."

"You know how I feel?"

The question had come from Joe White in an unusually frail voice. The filling station owner looked up through red, swollen eyes and slowly rose to his feet. "My son, his girlfriend, and four of their friends are all dead. Their bodies were broken, torn to pieces, and left in the woods like the garbage of some thoughtless white camper."

"Joe, we..."

"No, William Shakespeare, I will speak now," Joe said. "These were not the first. Before my son and his friends, four other people died in the same way." He shook a finger at the government man. "You don't know me. You don't know how I feel. My son caused trouble for everyone, and many are probably glad he is gone, but he was my son. He was all I had of his mother and now he is gone and I am alone. You don't know how I feel."

The government man looked at the floor.

"Each time somebody died in Yellowstone," Joe said gathering steam. "You told the public how rare it was. You gave them statistics on bear attacks to back up your claim that it almost never happened. You told everyone to hang their food high up in trees when camping, to play dead when charged, and to have a nice day. But you did nothing." Joe took a step forward. "Tell me, Mr. White, Government Man. Are you here today to tell us how rare it is for a bear to kill six people at once?"

Tears streamed down Joe's cheeks, brine wetting the corners of his mouth. "There is nothing you can do for us, mister. We are Indians. We do not believe your statistics, we have no food to hang in a tree, and we're already dead. You don't know how we feel. So you have a nice day."

Joe collapsed back into his chair his shoulders shaking as he cried. Several shouts of agreement rang out and the room again was abuzz with a hundred voices at once. Shakespeare had no gavel to bang. He simply looked from the angry crowd to the Agency Supervisor and back again.

The door to the community room came open and Two Ravens stepped in. He showed no reaction to the tumult but stepped to the side holding the door open. Behind him and entering at a snail's pace was Snow on the Mountains. The room grew quiet. It took several minutes for the shaman to cross the length of the room. Not a word was spoken as he did.

Snow on the Mountains reached the side of the Council chairman's table. Ignoring the government man entirely, the holy man nodded to William Shakespeare. The chairman returned the nod and then waved silently to the gathered Indians giving him the floor. Snow on the Mountains turned to those in attendance. "There has been much injustice in the land," he said. "By white men and by our own kind. The Earth has open wounds that must be healed." His tone darkened. "It is time. Go back and warn your people; it is time."

"What is that supposed to mean, Bill?" William Shakespeare asked.

Snow on the Mountains stared in the direction of the chairman's table. Saddened by the lack of respect he'd witnessed in Council, the shaman no longer saw the chairman sitting there – merely his Yankee's ball cap. He turned to the room, speaking in the ancient Shoshone tongue. "That is all I have to say about that."

With that, he had finished. It had taken the shaman longer to get to the front of the room than it had to speak. At the same pace, he walked out.

"What the. . ." Two Fists said, standing with his hands on his hips. The cantankerous trout farmer shook his head. "Two Ravens," he said. "You're one of the few around here who understands that crazy old coot. What was that supposed to mean?"

Johnny Two Ravens turned and busted Two Fists in the nose. The trout farmer took several folding chairs with him as he fell crashing to the floor. Others jumped up as gasps raced around the room. Staring through saucer-like eyes, the Agency Supervisor turned white.

"He means," Two Ravens told the room. "The Spirit Bear has had enough."

*

From their place in Glenn's Suburban, J.D. and the chief ranger watched the Fort Washakie Community House. Glenn had spent a great deal of time apologizing in order to get her to accompany him. His ace in the hole had been the reminder that it was her case, too, and she needed to be there to see it through. She agreed, of course, and they put their personal issues aside. Now, as they waited, Glenn divided the time evenly between listening to Hank Williams, Sr. on the radio and fighting to keep the biologist from changing the channel.

To his everlasting delight, the battle ended when Snow on the Mountains stepped from the building. Johnny Two Ravens followed closely behind the shaman. Glenn and J.D. climbed from the vehicle and crossed the street to meet them. Two Ravens was grave, but the shaman smiled pleasantly.

Daniel D. Lamoreux, Doug Lamoreux

"Chief Merrill," Snow on the Mountains said. "How are you?"

"I'm fine," Glenn said. He nervously produced a new packet of tobacco; a special mixture the Indians called 'kinnikkinnik,' and handed it to the shaman. "I want to apologize for offering you money," he said. "And I'm sorry for misunderstanding the first gift of tobacco that I gave you. There is much I need to learn about the Earth and the Indian."

"There is much you can never know," Snow on the Mountains said. It was not a judgment, simply a fact. "But it is good that you want to try."

"Please accept this new gift. I am grateful to you... and to the tobacco." Smiling, Snow on the Mountains immediately drew out his pipe. "Please," Glenn said, "discard the other."

"You do have much to learn," Snow on the Mountains said, packing his pipe. "Because you wasted the tobacco, why should I?"

Two Ravens found his smile again. That it was at his expense was not wasted on Glenn.

"I have considered your request," the shaman said. "And I will help you."

"I'm very grateful," Glenn said. "How do we begin?"

195

Chapter 20

"Get down," Snow on the Mountains called out.

As a group, they dropped into the overgrowth at the edge of the road. J.D. landed in a hidden depression in the ditch and let out a squeal. Glenn avoided the hole but misjudged the distance in the dark. His chin thudded on the soft earth. It rattled his teeth and he wound up with a mouthful of dew-covered weeds. Momentarily stunned, he shook the feeling away and gave J.D. a hand up out of the hole to lay beside him in the deep grass.

In the moonlight, the chief ranger saw both Two Ravens and Snow on the Mountains watching their antics with some amusement. The outfitter had a finger to his lips signaling for them to be quiet. An arc of amber light split the darkness and grew in intensity as a vehicle on the road approached. Its engine growled as it passed, and Glenn could just see the top of a motor home. The vehicle vanished as quickly as it had appeared taking its light with it and leaving the foursome to their darkness.

"Now you know what it's like to be an Indian," Snow on the Mountains said.

Glenn balanced on his elbow and eyed the two to his right. "What do you mean?"

"For uncounted years we've been chased and hunted, kicked out. Always running, hiding, having to sneak around."

Glenn could see what the old man meant but he'd rather have been debating it in a cozy den with a fire burning in the hearth. The ground was cold and wet. Then again, maybe the cold and wet was part of the reason he understood.

"I think it's alright now," Snow on the Mountains said, pushing his old feathered cowboy hat securely onto his head. He stood, with a hand from Two Ravens, and led the way up the depression and onto the road. They walked the remaining quarter mile, left the roadway, and headed down the bank to the edge of Apparition Lake.

The sight shocked them all. The poor grassy excuse for a pond, thick with colored mud and bursting with marsh overgrowth, was gone. The ghostly temporal Apparition Lake was truly a lake stretching for acres to the south and disappearing into the dark. Still the remained something unreal about it. The unearthly fog Glenn had so recently become personally acquainted with swirled eerily atop the water despite the absence of any noticeable breeze. The gray blanket broke and lifted in spots allowing the glassy surface beneath to catch the moonlight and wink a sparkling acknowledgment of their presence.

"Incredible," J.D. whispered. "It's so... changed. I can't even find the words."

Glenn nodded. "I've never seen anything like this."

Despite his own amazement, Two Ravens, the self-appointed noise police, shushed them both with a finger again held to his lips. Glenn glared at J.D., repeated the motion with his finger, and mouthed the words, "Pay attention." He cocked his head at the outfitter, smiled, and winked at the biologist.

Snow on the Mountains, unphased by the lake, or by the antics of the park employees, had stepped to the edge of the water. He extended his arms, tilted his head back, and closed his eyes. He stood unmoving for several long minutes. Then he began to loudly sniff the air.

Glenn crossed his arms, rolled his eyes at J.D., and shook his head. The chief ranger was beginning to feel more than a little foolish.

Finally the old man dropped his arms, turned back to them, and said simply, "Not here."

"What?" Glenn asked.

"Not here," Snow on the Mountains repeated. "We've got to go further down the bank." The old man pointed into the darkness and started walking. Two Ravens followed.

"Wait a minute," Glenn called out. "What are you talking about?"

Without stopping the Indian called back, "You must trust the land, Ranger Merrill."

Glenn had never seen the old guy move that quickly. They covered a hundred yards before the ranger and biologist caught up with their Native American coconspirators. When he and J.D. got there, Two Ravens was standing quietly in the shadows and Snow on the Mountains was again near the lake sniffing the air like a dog. This time the shaman quickly found what he was looking for and turned to the group with a determined look. "This is it." This is what, Glenn wondered, but said nothing.

The shaman removed his hat and laid it on the soft ground at the lake's edge. Then, he began to unbutton his shirt. Two Ravens followed suit, starting to undress.

"Whoa," Glenn said, hands up as if to stop traffic. "What are you doing?"

"This is the beginning of the purification," Snow on the Mountains said, removing his shirt. "The first step."

"This is National Park land," Glenn said. "You can't skinny dip here."

"Keep off Indian," Snow on the Mountains said. "This land belongs to the public."

"That's not what I meant."

"You've come this far, Ranger Merrill," the shaman said. "Do not let your fears stop you now."

Again with my fears, Glenn thought. He looked at J.D. for help.

"You've risked a lot, Glenn," Two Ravens said. "You've come this far."

"I still don't understand why we're here."

"We are here, Ranger Merrill," the shaman said, "because the land is crying out to us. All that you have experienced here in the ancient Stinking Country is happening for some reason."

"So how is getting naked and jumping into a dirty pond of ice water going to help us?"

"You were wrong," Snow on the Mountains told Two Ravens. "His mind is not open."

"I want it to be," Glenn insisted. "I want all of this to stop. I just don't understand how bathing naked in Yellowstone..."

"This is not a bath, Ranger Merrill. This is a serious matter," Snow on the Mountains said. "White men bathe, but do not concern themselves with washing what is inside. Purification means cleansing the body and the mind; reclaiming control over our actions and thoughts."

"You claim that you love this land, this Yellowstone that you guard over," the shaman said. "And I believe that you do. But even though you love it, you cannot hear the spirits of the land crying out. Your mind is full of other things; duties, laws, baseball scores, fears and insecurities. You must purify your body and cleanse your mind, Ranger Merrill, that's the way it is done."

The old Indian pulled his shirt the rest of the way off, folded it neatly, and laid it on the bank. He unbuckled the worn leather belt on his trousers. "You must leave behind your fears, your opinions, and your clothes. The clothes will be here when you get back." Two Ravens followed the shaman's lead, disrobing by the side of the misty lake.

Glenn shook his head and turned back to J.D. The biologist already had her pants off. Glenn stepped to her and whispered, "Do you really think this is such a good idea?"

"I haven't a clue," J.D. whispered back, unbuttoning her jean shirt. "But it's your fault I'm out here getting naked with three men. So why don't you take your clothes off and make me feel the slightest bit more comfortable and stop peeing on the parade."

*

Glenn finished folding his clothes. As he set his hat neatly atop the pile, the sound of rippling water reached him. Snow on the Mountains and Two Ravens, both naked as the moment they were born, were ankle-deep in Apparition Lake and walking slowly away from the bank.

That, Glenn thought, has got to be freezing!

Though the air was still, the chief was already cold. He shivered from bare shoulders to bare feet. Frowning, he turned to J.D. The young biologist too was naked with her arms crossed over her chest. They shared a curious look and turned to the Indians in the lake.

Eight feet out from the bank, the shaman and the outfitter stopped and sat down in water reaching nearly to their shoulders. Two Ravens' back was to the couple but Glenn could just make out Snow on the Mountains features in the moonlight. His eyes were closed and he wore a serene half-smile. The shaman opened his eyes and waved. "Join us."

J.D. took Glenn's hand and stepped to the edge of the bank. Both took a breath and then stepped into the lake. "Oh, my God," Glenn shouted. He was right; the water was freezing.

J.D. released Glenn's hand and ventured farther out. The chief ranger, fighting his flight instincts, ignored the stinging cold and followed after her. They reached the Indians and sat down.

Despite the intense cold, the marshy lake bottom accepted Glenn's hind end like an old familiar chair. His arms lifted of their own accord buoyed up by the water. He forced them down to his sides.

"You do this a lot?" Glenn asked his teeth chattering.

"I have never done it in a lake before," Snow on the Mountains said. "Always in a natural hot spring."

Now I'm mad, Glenn thought. The idea of the soothing warmth of a Wyoming hot spring lit in his mind like a Technicolor movie. He could see the steam rising hot and enticing like a hearty bowl of soup. He pictured his sinuses clearing beneath the sulfurous assault and sweat bursting from his forehead like spring rain. Then his mind screamed the question, what are you doing here?

As if he'd heard, Snow on the Mountains answered, "This is where the trouble is, Ranger Merrill."

Glenn stared, wondering if the old man could actually read his thoughts, but held his tongue. It made more sense to accept it than to question it. What did not make sense was the physical reactions of the Indians to the situation. Neither Snow on the Mountains nor Two Ravens looked the least bit cold or uncomfortable. Both sat, eyes closed, stroking the surface of the water with their outstretched arms. They looked to be in another world.

When Snow on the Mountains, eyes still closed, finally spoke, it was in a strange and resonant tone. "You must be responsible for your thoughts. You must still your minds. Do not question. Do not ramble. Do not dream. Empty your consciousness. Allow it to flow out and away from you. Pick an area of tranquility and nothingness in the distant reaches of eternity and focus your being there."

The thought that the whole affair was a huge waste of time flashed in Glenn's mind. An instant later it was shoved away by a forceful screaming command: "Attend the purification!" He turned to the shaman. Snow on the Mountains looked to be nearly asleep, and the ranger realized he had not spoken. Glenn closed his eyes, feeling a strange and awful fear creeping over his soul. His skin was goose flesh, his body shaking. The notion entered his mind to stand and walk out of the water. An instant later, the thought was forced out of his head by the same command: "Attend the purification!"

Glenn tilted his head back and stared at the startling array of glistening stars in the night sky. He had never seen so many, never dreamed that many celestial bodies existed. He gazed up at a brilliant star above his head; then concentrated on the darkness surrounding it. Glenn's mind began to empty itself. The stinging cold of the lake disappeared. He kicked his feet gently, feeling a soothing sensation in the muscles of his legs. He stroked the surface; the tension vanishing from his tired arms as if someone had pulled a heavy canvas off of him. Unbelievably, Glenn felt the water beginning to warm.

The chief ranger forced himself not to think, concentrating instead on the spaces in the heavens between the stars. "Accept it," he told himself, focusing again on the calm nothingness. He'd lost his sense of time. His sense of motion soon followed. The wild emotional feelings began to leave, draining from his body by his fingers and toes. His anger and fear, hopes and ambitions, dreams and doubts all vanished, washed away by the soothing waters of Apparition Lake.

Glenn continued to stroke the surface of the misty water unable to remember ever having felt so warm and relaxed. He looked to J.D. and saw only contentment on her face. She was feeling it too.

Snow on the Mountains stood and worked his way back to the shoreline, the water glistening in the moonlight as it dripped from his body. Two Ravens followed; then J.D. and Glenn. The chief's skin tingled as the cool night air painted him like a brush. Like the others, he dressed in silence ignoring the water dripping from his body. His senses seemed alive and raced to catch up with his rapid breathing, but the tensions, confusion, and worry he'd brought to Apparition Lake were gone.

He looked to J.D. and she returned his smile. Fully dressed, Snow on the Mountains left the group, heading down the bank into the shadowy darkness. Thirty yards away he came to a stop, no more than a dark outline to the three he'd left behind. They could not see his actions but they clearly heard his voice. Snow on the Mountains began loudly chanting with what seemed a much younger man's voice. His words, in a language with which Glenn was unfamiliar, rolled over the dark and misty lake as the shaman called upon the Great Spirit, Duma Appah. Nature replied with the sound of rolling thunder.

Glenn had no idea how long the shaman was gone. Time no longer mattered. But Snow on the Mountains soon reappeared. As he joined them from the darkness, it was immediately obvious a matter of great weight and sadness filled his thoughts; his brow was furrowed, his jaw set tight, and his eyes weary with some awful knowledge. He looked at the three of them and, for the first time, appeared at a loss for words. Searching, he finally said, "Apparition Lake has spoken to me."

He turned to the chief ranger, as if they were there alone, and said, "Prepare your Death Song, white warrior. The time is near."

Glenn stared at the holy man, stricken. Snow on the Mountains had said it, exactly word for word as the chief ranger had heard it before, in the presence of the attacking silver grizzly bear. But how was it possible? He had not told a soul. "Oh, my God," Glenn said. "Oh, my God."

Chapter 21

It was a forty-five minute drive from Apparition Lake to Norris Geyser Basin, but Glenn made it in less than thirty. J.D. made the trip with him, her knuckles white as chalk from burying her fingers into the dashboard. This was not the same chief ranger who had walked with trepidation into that freezing lake just an hour before. The last words Snow on the Mountains had spoken to Glenn, "Prepare your Death Song, white warrior. The time is near," had an overwhelming effect on him. He'd thanked the shaman and Two Ravens and ushered her to his Suburban as if their lives were at stake. "We've got to get to the museum," was all he would tell her.

On the way, she'd gotten a bit more out of him but not much. "I don't understand," J.D. said. "What's at the museum that's so important, especially at this time of night?"

"I can't tell you exactly," Glenn said. "It's something I should have remembered before but didn't. Something I should remember now but don't... for sure. Do you know what I mean?"

The biologist returned his helpless stare without a clue as to what Glenn was talking about.

"I know I sound confused," he said, pouring gas to the roaring Suburban. "But I'm not. My mind has never been so clear. I've just got to get to the museum."

Glenn felt like a salmon rushing upstream to its destiny.

*

The lights burned in the windows of the Museum of the National Park Ranger, a beacon, as Glenn approached and pulled to a stop in its lot. He had not returned to the Norris Geyser area since the investigation of Bart Houser's death. The chief ranger was grateful for his mission. This was not the time to mourn for Houser or any of the recent victims.

Glenn won the footrace to the museum's front door and then hit a roadblock. There were just too many keys to this park. A moment later, he had the right one and he and J.D. were inside. The race was over. "Now what?" she asked trying to catch her breath.

Glenn moved through the exhibit rooms, searching room to room, back and forth, like a feather carried on the wind. A golden eagle feather perhaps? J.D. followed after, wondering what he was after, watching him as closely as he did the displays.

"Photographs," he finally said aloud. "We're looking for photographs. Something from the late eighteen hundreds."

"Photographs of what? A quarter of the stuff in here must be from that time period."

"They'll be pictures of a lake... or maybe a geyser basin, I don't remember. But look for Union soldiers."

"Soldiers?"

"Yes," Glenn said. "When the park was founded, and through the late eighteen hundreds, Yellowstone fell under the jurisdiction of the War Department. Look for pictures of Union cavalrymen, around either a lake or a geyser basin."

"Why?"

Glenn turned to her in utter desperation. "I don't know, J.D. Just look and trust me."

But it was no easy task. The bear biologist had been right. There were a lot of pictures in that small place, many dating back to before the turn of the century. Nearly half an hour passed before the chief ranger heard her excited voice call out. "Glenn, I think I've found it."

206

He backtracked and located J.D. in a tiny exhibit room off the main entrance. She was on her tiptoes, squinting at a group of photos on the wall in the far upper corner. "Are these..."

"Yes," Glenn shouted like a child celebrating on Christmas morning. "Yes." The chief found a chair, climbed up, and removed three photographs from the wall. He jumped down and laid them atop a display case. Faded and forgotten, the tintype images of Union pony soldiers smiled up at Glenn. They stood with their horses, in varying poses, on a grassy lake bank. Glenn looked ready to dive into the pictures beside them. "I knew it," he said. "I knew it."

"Glenn," J.D. screamed. "I'm going to kill you if you don't tell me what's going on!"

"Apparition Lake," he said. He turned the pictures toward her. "That is Apparition Lake." He tapped the glass. "Their flag," he said as a new light blinked on in his head. He started out of the room hollering back over his shoulder at the biologist. "Their company flag. Can you read it?"

She squinted at the worn photo. "It's a number. Forty-six, I think," she said. Glenn was gone again into the museum. "Forty-six," J.D. yelled. "Or forty-eight, I'm not sure."

"Come here."

J.D. rolled her eyes. "Where are you?"

"In here, come on."

"Do you want the pictures?" she asked, trying to pinpoint his voice.

"No, we don't need them anymore. Just get in here."

She found Glenn two rooms away and staring at a glass display case as if looking through the window of a candy store. Scattered artifacts lay atop its layered glass shelves inside; each marked with a small typed card. "It was forty-eight," he said pointing.

Among the items was a worn brown leather book. Its card read: 'The diary of Lieutenant J. Archer McBride. 48th Cavalry Unit. Fort Laramie.' Glenn pulled out his handkerchief and wrapped it around his hand.

"You're not going to..."

He smashed the front of the display case.

*

For over an hour, Glenn scoured the pages of the Lieutenant's diary with J.D. on his shoulder like a trained falcon. "Unbelievable," he finally said, tapping a worn page of the book. "Absolutely beyond belief. I'm never going to doubt Two Ravens again." He turned to J. D., smiled, and said, "It's all here." Then he began to read aloud, gently turning the fragile pages as he went.

05 June 1879. Just when I feel there is nothing more that can surprise me regarding the treachery of mankind, I am brought round-about to my senses with yet another example of the most despicable of our species. Yet again today, I can but shake my head and be thankful that I was brought into this world by a civilized parenthood with sound Christian beliefs; unlike so many of my brethren who seem deprived of even the slightest nuance of decency, kindness or servitude to their fellow man.

It was with much pride and personal satisfaction that Sergeant Mulhaney delivered to Fort Laramie this day a scoundrel who has avoided capture for nearly eighteen months since that time we were first made aware of his indiscretions and utter contempt for the laws which we are here to maintain. I am compelled to write of this dastardly character for his bearing and mannerisms are of such an unseemly nature as to make him the premiere example of our need for being stationed on this frontier. His name is Jessie Aaron. I am uncertain of his lineage, however, I can only assume from his manner that he was either born in these mountains or was cast out of the civilized world long before it had the opportunity to make any impact upon his process of learning as a child. He is the closest thing to a wild beast that may still hold the illustrious title of "man."

*

Jessie Aaron spit over his filthy, graying beard, rubbed the moisture into his weathered hands and set to work. With a grunt, he rolled the dead bear onto its back. The bear's legs, already stiffening in the cold, jutted toward the heavens like the four corner spires of a Mormon Temple. Straddling the bear, he pinched the fur of its lower abdomen in his left hand and sliced into the pelt below with the gleaming Bowie knife in his right. Moving the blade upward in the direction of the bear's neck, he split the pelt wide, opening it as if it were already a fur coat for one of them dandy eastern ladies.

A heavy stink erupted from the carcass of the animal. It was a smell Aaron was long used to. He breathed through his mouth and kept working, slicing on the down stroke to separate the pelt from the fleshy white under layer. His skill showed in that he didn't scratch the inner cavity nor scar the hide. Save for a slight oozing of capillary blood he'd made no mess at all.

Jessie struggled as he rolled the bear to its side. He was a big man at two hundred-forty pounds; probably over a third of the bear's weight, but the years of mountain life had played tough on old Jessie. He'd ripped a nut trying to role a griz the year before and had just lived with it since. At times it pained him a might but thank God for a good, thick belt.

With the familiar itch-itching sound of the blade, he sliced up the inside length of each limb leaving the valuable pelt in one piece. He peeled the fur off the inner cavity wall from the pit to the wrist. Quickly, almost violently, he severed the paw from the rest of the limb without detaching it from the pelt. Jessie took great satisfaction in the crunch and snap that accompanied the action as bone, cartilage, tendons and ligaments gave way. He pulled both limbs free of the coat on the bear's right side and then rolled the heavy creature again to repeat the process on the left.

Sweat soaked despite the freezing spring mountain air, it dawned on Jessie the bear wasn't the only animal present that was giving off a stink.

That's all right, Jessie thought. This sweaty ol' mountain man would be a well to do ol' mountain man once these furs was traded off. Yesiree, it was gonna be one mighty fine Rendezvous down on the Green River. Jessie was going to get himself the hottest bath ever drawn in Wyoming. He planned to sit in it; all soapy, drinking from his very own bottle of whiskey 'til he either went under and drowned or the water turned so cold he couldn't sit no longer. Then he had plans for one of them fine white dance hall girls.

In an hour's time Jessie had the coat fully separated from the body of the bear, save for where it met the neck. He knelt over the upper portion of the carcass, the dirty knees of his trousers browning the melting snow beneath. The wet felt good; reminding him he'd whipped the big, miserable bruin.

The bear lay dead and staring up through sightless eyes, growling silently and showing a set of vicious teeth that weren't ever going to bite anything again. Skinning an animal wasn't as good as getting paid for the pelt but it ran a real close second.

The bear's body, without its warm winter coat, looked remarkably like that of a human being. A torso of naked muscle with four sprawled limbs; bone white beneath the fading sun and only dotted here and there with pinkish-red splotches of blood. Aaron gave a laugh that turned, all by itself, into a throaty cough. He could think of several folks he wouldn't mind seeing stretched out in just such a condition. Yessiree, lots of 'em.

He dug his hand axe from his satchel and ran his thumb the width of its curved blade. It was time for the money chop. With one blow he'd separate the ferocious looking head from the rest of its dead white body. Then he'd have himself a bear pelt and head, and the Yellowstone wolves would have themselves some dinner. That was the kind of generous fellow Jessie Aaron was.

Jessie raised the axe above his head for the final blow. But before he could deliver it something caught his eye at the edge of the clearing.

*

We had been told of this Aaron, as I indicated, over a year before. His crimes being those of pilfering the wild life in our newly designated national park called Yellowstone. Unfortunately, with the uprisings so evident among the Sioux and the Nez Perce tribes I had been unable to spend any of my sorely inadequate resources in the pursuit of this fellow. Patrols were made aware of his presence in the improbable event that their paths might cross. Such was the case with our fortunate Sergeant, who forthwith brought Aaron to this post for incarceration pending his trial and punishment.

I was quite overtaken by the appearance of this gentleman, and I use the distinction out of kindness rather than respect. His clothing, or what may have passed for such in his estimation, was but rags supplemented with the pelts of a variety of animals... no doubt some of the very creatures for which he now stands accused of killing outside the law. Upon his feet were the tattered remains of what once must surely have been a fine pair of boots, which are today but remnants of their former selves.

He had this irritating habit of picking at the sole of his foot through a cavernous hole in the left. Wholly disagreeable in his lack of manners, he also had the habit of chewing tobacco, which he spat upon the floor beside my spittoon on a number of occasions despite my admonishments against doing so. It has been necessary since his removal from my office to have the floors scrubbed, though the stains will surely remain indefinitely. It was to my utmost amazement that he freely admitted his guilt in the matter of pilfering the animals in the park, his candor being almost to the point of braggadocio. I was compelled to question him regarding the disappearance of a Shoshone medicine man named Silverbear who had been reported by his tribe as having disappeared mysteriously during Aaron's tenure in the mountains.

*

211

It was the evening of the third day now and Silverbear's vision quest was at an end. He'd crossed east from Undine Falls during the night and had spent the day in contemplation and in purification near Blacktail Deer Creek. The Great Spirit had relieved his concerns for his people and given him a great message of hope and freedom for the Shoshone Nation. He set out through the towering lodgepole pines of Blacktail Plateau headed home again.

Traveling through heavy trees, the medicine man stepped out into a clearing. The red sun was fading but the sight before him blemished the absolute beauty of the setting. A dirty white man dressed in filthy buckskin and wearing the long beard of the white hunter, knelt over the partially skinned remains of a grizzly bear. The man held an axe preparing to strike and remove the beast's head.

Here is the taker, Silverbear thought. Here is the white thief with no regard for the animals, the land, the native people or his own white law. The medicine man gripped the talisman staff tightly, lifting both arms skyward.

The Great Spirit had told him that all things would happen in the earth's time. He said the thief would be stopped. Sensing his destiny, and despite his fear of the white thief, Silverbear stepped forward from the shadows of the pines.

On his side of it, Jessie Aaron stood quickly. He was an old man with too big a gut pushed into his worn buckskins but he could still move when he had to. Years of taking game illegally had taught Jessie two things; first, let only your friends watch you work and, second, you have no friends.

At the edge of the clearing he made out the shape that had caught his eye a second before. The falling sun threw shadows among the pines and whatever had come from the woods stood black and undefined. Still it was there. Jessie spit again and squinted into the gloom.

Whatever it was stood upright like a man but without the shape of a man. The figure hesitated briefly just beyond the clearing. Then it rose up full on its haunches and seemed to lift its arms above its head. It started forward in the clearing and with each step gained form.

It was a second grizzly!

Jessie Aaron dropped the hand axe to the ground with a hollow thud. His eyes darted between the stalking bear, now fully in the clearing, and the carcass of the dead bear at his feet. He scanned the surrounding area, wondering where he'd laid his rifle, and was still searching for the weapon when the approaching animal let loose with a terrifying scream.

For the first time that day Jessie Aaron felt the cold. It grabbed his spine, racing up to chill his shoulders and turn his skin to goose flesh. He'd never heard a bear make a sound like that before. It was not a growl or a roar but a high-pitched scream. And the animal was carrying a staff.

Jessie Aaron could not remember ever having been afraid and he didn't recognize the emotion now. Still, his feet refused to move despite his earnest desire to run like the wind.

The creature was still screaming and had closed the gap between itself and Aaron by three quarters. It had fully cleared the shadows and entered the red-orange dusk of the open field. Jessie Aaron finally distinguished what he was seeing. The creature was not a bear at all but a man dressed in the skin of a bear. Beads and feathers appeared and disappeared from beneath the fur costume with each step he took. It was an Indian, an old man at that, charging at him and yelling to bring down the mountains.

Aaron dropped to a knee and grabbed the closest weapon, his hand axe. The Indian had closed to within twenty feet and was still hollering. Jessie Aaron stood, reared back, and gave a yell of his own as he let fly with the axe.

Silverbear had only a second to see what was happening and halt his approach.

Aaron's hand axe struck home with a dull thud, splitting the Indian's sternum and coming to rest buried deep in his chest. The tip of the axe's curved blade had lodge in the base of Silverbear's heart. The medicine man lost his grip on the sacred talisman staff and it dropped like a felled tree towards the ground. The ceramic jar shattered on impact and the blessed cornmeal and carved bear fetish were vomited unceremoniously onto the grass.

Silverbear fell to his knees, his weathered copper face a mixture of sadness and pain. He pawed at the axe handle but did not have the strength to remove it. He lost his balance and teetered to his side on the ground. The holy man stretched out his hand, reaching for the stone fetish.

Silverbear began to pray.

Like the Spirit Bear itself, the talisman had living power. As the grizzly died in hibernation only to be reborn in spring so, too, the medicine man prayed that he be reborn to protect his people and the land. To reap the vengeance described by the Great Spirit's messenger.

Jessie stepped forward and kicked the bear statue out of the Indian's grasp. He picked it up, examined the rude carving and deposited the object into his coat pocket.

Gasping his last, Silverbear closed his eyes.

*

His responses became more guarded upon this subject and, feeling that I might be upon something significant, I lit upon him with ferocity to illicit another confession. That confession did finally come forth. "I was minding my own business," said he. "And this Injun come out of the trees hollering 'til hell won't have it. Well, a white man's got a right to defend his self from them red buggers, don't he?" I was astounded at his lack of compassion or regret. The man went so far as to ask for leniency in his punishment for other crimes claiming that he did us "a favor" in eliminating the Indian. At this point, I questioned Aaron's truthfulness, for it seemed he was but attempting to reduce his sentence by admitting to a crime that he sees as no crime at all.

*

214

It was a chore toting the old man's body from the clearing. Aaron would have left him where he dropped but knew the danger in doing so. The Union soldiers had been hot after him as it was. No, Jessie thought, I have to get rid of the body.

Then he remembered the phantom lake nearby; a lake that came and went with the season. Whether or not it would be there next year didn't matter. It was there now and would hide the Indian's body until late summer. By then ol' Jessie would be enjoying himself immensely and the ravens could have whatever the lake revealed of the old man's remains.

Jessie Aaron reached the lake shore and, huffing like a steam engine, dropped the dead Indian with a muffled thump and the jingle of beads to the rocky ground. Jessie caught his breath.

A blood red reflection on a ribbon of cloud was all that remained of the sun. The pines were no longer trees but grotesque, thin fingers reaching skyward in a vain attempt to escape the ever-increasing gloom. Scattered boulders along the shoreline became disembodied heads peering at Aaron from a swirling gray mist hanging over the water.

For the second time that day, Aaron felt a shiver climb his back. Hurrying, though he didn't know why, the poacher found a heavy rock lying in the brush. It would make a perfect anchor. He made short work of securing the weight to the old man's back. Dragging the body to the edge of the water, Aaron gave it a shove and watched with a wicked smile as the corpse floated slowly into the closing mist.

It had been a great day, Jessie Aaron thought. One good griz pelt and one dead Injun, what more could a fella ask out of a day's work?

As the medicine man drifted further from the shore, the rock shifted and the weight turned him on his side. The rock slid into the water, up-righted Silverbear's body, and started to drag it down. As the water consumed him, the holy man's arms were buoyed up. He looked as he did when he stepped into the clearing, arms reaching for the sky.

He remained in that position for a moment, too long for Jessie Aaron's taste, then sank slowly into the depths. Not a ripple followed the Indian's immersion.

Jessie reached into his pockets hoping to cut the chill of the night air and found the small bear statue dropped by the Indian. He pulled it out and examined it again. Not worth a thing, Jessie thought, and probably more trouble than I need. He tossed the statue into the lake in the exact place where the Indian had disappeared.

From somewhere deep within the black shroud of enveloping pines, the ferocious roar of a grizzly erupted and reverberated across the misty, open water.

*

Nonetheless, it is my responsibility to dispatch a patrol to investigate his claim of having deposited the body of the unfortunate medicine man in a lake in the Yellowstone country. That has been done and I but await their return and report.

Glenn turned the pages, searching the journal. He found another entry and began to read.

12 August 1879. The patrol into the northern section of Yellowstone has returned. The Sergeant has reported that the lake described by the despicable Jessie Aaron, in which he reportedly discarded the remains of the Shoshone named Silverbear, is not a lake at all but merely a marshy depression in the ground. The Sergeant further reports that his unit rode the length and breadth of this depression, their horses slogging down in spots, in a sincere effort at locating the Indian's skeleton. None was found. It can only be my assumption that this dark character is but as well a liar as he is a scofflaw.

"No, no, Lieutenant," Glen said whispering to the pages of the journal. "You were a very intelligent man but you made one mistake. Jessie Aaron wasn't lying."

The chief ranger closed the book with finality and turned to J.D. "Apparition Lake," he said.

216

"How do you know?"

"Because it fits. Silverbear. Silverbear is the name Johnny used." Glenn was staring into the distance. "Silverbear is the medicine man turned spirit animal."

Chapter 22

Glenn would have rather stuck his head in a lion's mouth than walk into Stanton's office and say what he knew had to be said. He and Mike had been friends for a long time; they'd seen a lot together. But the park superintendent was absolutely going to explode when he was told what would have to be done to stop the killings.

Two Ravens, of course, accompanied the chief ranger. He'd led the way to Glenn's understanding of the situation, as little as he'd understood it himself, and had taken him to see the shaman, Snow on the Mountains. It made sense that he would join Glenn now, officially, to try to convince Stanton. They picked J.D. up on the way. She'd been on this ride from the beginning. It was only right she be there for the fireworks that hopefully would bring it all to an end. Besides there was supposedly strength in numbers. How many people could Stanton throw out of his office at one time?

Numbers, it turned out, were not a problem. The small parking lot in front of the administration offices was full to bursting; cars, trucks, mini-vans, all placarded with official logos from every state and federal agency known to man. At least a half-dozen vehicles bore the markings of local and national television stations; their towering blue and yellow transmitters pointed skyward like science-nasty ray guns from the old Buck Rogers serials. Glenn was forced to park a quarter-mile from the building on the side of the road; an act for which he routinely chewed out tourists under normal circumstances. He turned to his companions with a heavy sigh. "Maybe we should just go home."

"Sounds good to me," Two Ravens said.

"Me too." J.D. chimed in.

"You two are a lot of help."

"It's your park." The last was spoken by Two Ravens and J.D., at the same time and couldn't have been better orchestrated had they practiced. Glenn rolled his eyes, shut off the engine, and climbed out of the Suburban.

By the time they reached the lot there was a bank of reporters and news people clustered and waiting for them like a pack of hungry wolves closing in on crippled rabbits. Of course, Howard Lark was in the lead. With the three of them such a photogenic lot, a park ranger and a Fish & Wildlife biologist, both in uniform, with a full-blooded Shoshone outfitter in his worn cowboy hat, the wolves could not have asked for more. Before the trio made it past the first row of cars, the flashes were going off and three microphones were mercilessly stabbed into their faces.

Glenn and J.D. knew the drill. They'd been trained regarding the media and it was part of their job. There was more to it than that for Two Ravens. Appearing on every television set on the reservation, walking hand-in-hand with white government officials and ignoring reporters' questions was not his idea of a great way to start the day. He did not need the pressure of looking like a federal bootlick to the BIAs back home, or the disappointment that would no doubt be felt by his traditional blood brothers. Yet now seemed hardly the time to stop and give a rendition of the plight of the Indian as told by one of the oppressed. The memory of the young people who died at Apparition Lake was of more value than that. He wouldn't use them for a cause. The best answer, it seemed to Two Ravens, was to act invisible. Meanwhile, the ranger and biologist walked before him, smiling, acknowledging the reporters' presence but rebuffing their questions all the way to the front steps.

Then Lark stepped in front of them blocking the door. "Chief Merrill..."

Glenn, reaching past him for the door, was delighted he could finally say it, "No comment."

Lark sidestepped blocking him again. "I haven't asked my question yet."

"The superintendent will speak to the press at the appropriate time. Until then we're not taking any questions. I'm trying to save you time."

"That's awfully sporting of you," Lark said with a sneer. "But how can you not comment about what, for all intents and purposes, was a re-enactment of Wounded Knee at Apparition Lake? How can you not comment about your failure to stop the park's elk poachers? They are taking antlers like they're dime candies. Do you have a clue where they're going to strike next?"

"Are you hard of hearing, Lark?" Glenn asked. "I said, no comment."

"I hear fine," Lark said flashing a smile to replace the one that had vanished from the chief ranger's face. "Fact is, I hear your job is on the line."

"The only thing on the line," Glenn said. "Is your health if you don't get out of our way."

Lark raised his hands in surrender and retreated a step. Glenn pulled the door open. J.D. and Two Ravens entered with neither a word nor a glance up. Glenn followed. Lark caught the door before it closed, and led the reporters in after them, shouting, "Hey, chief. Can we quote you?"

Like invading troops around a medieval castle, Althea's office was soon under siege. The business suits and dark glasses, badges and ranger hats already gathered, were suddenly inundated by note pads, cameras, and microphones, all moving about the cramped space like ants around a stepped upon hill. The din of questions, followed by carefully worded non-answers, echoed off the walls like bad rock music. Glenn found himself immediately grateful for the feds. Their mere presence captured the reporters' attentions and the chief, thankfully, became just another olive-drab hat in the tumult.

Althea, unperturbed as always, rifled files at her desk. Had she been aboard the Titanic, Glenn knew, she'd have rescued as many as she could from the water then cheerily swam laps until help arrived the next morning. She recognized the chief as Glenn's group entered, cast her million-dollar smile his direction, and waved them over. "The super has been looking for you something fierce," she said. "I'll let him know you're here."

Within seconds the office door came open. Stanton stood in the frame looking as if he'd been yanked through the knothole of a wooden fence. Yellowstone's famed "Boy Superintendent" had aged noticeably in the days since Glenn had last seen him. His red eyes hung heavy with baggage. With the plastic smile of a pimply-faced teen working the drive-thru window of a fast food restaurant, Stanton ushered Nelson Princep, a Game and Fish rep, and a lucky AP pool reporter out as if he were shoving bad tuna off the deck of his ship. He waved Glenn over. The Indian and the biologist followed.

Those nearest the pool reporter surrounded her. Those farther away barked like pound puppies at sight of the chuck wagon. They turned their questions and their irritations on Stanton who, despite being ragged and weary, remained ever the politician. "Folks, please." Stanton stepped out, allowing Glenn and his companions passage in then, without missing a beat, returned to the crowd. "As I said earlier, I am meeting with all agencies, department heads, and concerned individuals involved in this situation. Your pool reporter has been given an up-date and I will have another statement for you the minute we have anything to add." He handed the reporters off to the federal talking heads still in the outer office and closed the door on the lot of them.

Stanton dropped into his chair and swept his hand to those opposite, wordlessly inviting Glenn and company to do the same. He gulped from a cup of cold coffee, winced at its chilled bitterness, and then gulped again. He wiped his hands over his eyes, dragging for sand, and then slumped back heavily. He sighed. "What in the hell are we going to do?" He looked past Glenn to J.D., felt a tinge of guilt for the language but didn't have the strength to apologize. "What are we going to do?"

"What is the official story right now?" Glenn asked.

"Official story?" Stanton pursed his lips, blowing a raspberry. "You know it by heart. We've got ten bodies; a park ranger, a local rancher, two tourists, and six reservation Indians. All appear to have been killed by a rogue bear or bears. The Firehole Lake death and that bloody massacre at Apparition Lake were both witnessed. The witnesses described what seems to be the same bear, a huge, silver-tipped grizzly. The same bear you claim to have seen."

"Claim?"

"You asked, Glenn."

Considering Stanton's frustrations, which could not have been more obvious, the chief ranger nodded. He'd shut up and eat a bit of it for friendship's sake.

"Despite the witness reports," Stanton said, continuing on, "and other than the bodies themselves, there is no evidence of a bear at any of the scenes. No bear fitting that description, or unnumbered bears at all for that matter, have been observed in or around the park other than during the attacks."

He paused for a drink but found the cup empty. It was just as well; cold coffee tasted like bad garbage. "In other words," Stanton said, "nobody has a clue what's going on here and the official story is an episode of The Twilight Zone. Three rangers called in this morning with green flu, the Secretary of the Interior wants my head in his briefcase, the media is describing Yellowstone as if it were Iraq, and the entire reservation is on the war path!"

For the first time Stanton actually took notice of Two Ravens. "I apologize," he said, clearing his throat. "I did not mean that the way it sounded."

"Mike, this is Johnny Two Ravens," Glenn said, butting in. "Johnny, Michael Stanton."

"The outfitter," Stanton said, shaking hands. "I've heard about you. I apologize, again."

"There are reasons to be upset," Two Ravens said gracefully. "In the park and on the reservation."

"Which brings us," Stanton said, "right back to, what are we going to do?"

"We believe we have the answer," Glenn said. He looked to his companions. "But you're going to find it hard to accept."

Had he not been totally exhausted, Stanton would have laughed. As it was he simply stared at his chief ranger awaiting the rest.

"There is no evidence of a physical bear, no sightings of a bear outside of the attacks," Glenn said. "Because there isn't any bear. Not a real one at least."

Stanton's eyes roamed over the three people seated before him. "What?"

"The bear only exists when it is attacking."

Stanton jerked up laughing an unfunny disgusted laugh. He tried to drink from his coffee cup again but the thing was still empty. "What are you talking about?"

"Mr. Stanton," Two Ravens said. "He is talking about an Indian spirit that has been unleashed upon people in the Yellowstone area. These murders, and that's what they are, revenge killings, have come about as the direct result of an incident that occurred on these lands over one hundred years ago."

"Oh, now, come on."

"In 1878, a Shoshone holy man called Silverbear..."

"Glenn!" Stanton yelled, no longer even hearing whatever it was the Indian was spouting.

"Listen to him," the ranger said.

"I'm up to my eyeballs in blood and red tape and..."

"Mike," Glenn hollered back. "Listen to him. Just hear him."

The superintendent leaned back again. "All right, Mr. Two Ravens, I'll listen."

Johnny told the park superintendent his ancient Indian ghost story. He related with, Glenn thought, amazing elegance the tale of the great medicine man, Silverbear, and his murder at the hands of the filthy white poacher. He detailed, with heartbreaking sadness, Silverbear's eventual consignment to the depths of the eerie, temporal Apparition Lake. "His spirit does not rest," Two Ravens said solemnly. "Like the grizzly bear, who dies in winter to be reborn in the spring, Silverbear has been reborn to right the wrongs being done to Mother Earth."

"You're telling me a ghost is killing these people?" Stanton asked incredulously.

"A spirit," Two Ravens said. "The spirit of Silverbear, powered by the magic fetish of Duma Appah, and personified as the mighty grizzly."

Stanton turned to Glenn. "Do you believe this?"

"Intellectually, no," Glenn said. "My brain says it cannot be happening this way."

"Then what is this?"

"This is my heart saying something different," Glenn said. "I know what I saw, Mike. I saw the biggest, baddest grizzly bear in my experience that, despite the fact it has been killing everybody else, did me no harm. It wasn't a real bear. It was a spirit. The Spirit Bear saw my heart and knew I posed no threat to Mother Earth. And, instead of killing me, it delivered a warning."

"What about you," Stanton barked at J.D. "You're a scientist. You can't believe this nonsense?"

"Yes," she said boldly. "I can."

"On what basis?"

"On a very scientific basis, Mr. Stanton. We've eliminated the impossible. This is the only explanation left. Therefore, regardless of how improbable it sounds, it must be the answer."

"Wait," Stanton said looking as if he smelled something foul. "That's Sherlock Homes, isn't it?"

"You don't have to believe it, Mike," Glenn said.

225

"I don't," he said. "I think it's lunacy."

"We need your permission to search for Silverbear's body."

"What body?" Stanton rose and paced the length of his office. "There can't be a body. That was a hundred years ago." He pointed at Two Ravens. "You said yourself that the cavalry couldn't find his body when they looked for it; and it had been less than a year. If it wasn't there then, how is it going to be there now?" Two Ravens opened his mouth but Stanton wasn't finished. "He was probably fish food days after his murder."

J.D. looked up innocently. "There aren't any fish in Apparition Lake."

"No wonder you teamed up with Merrill," Stanton screamed. "You're a smart mouth too!"

"Mike," Glenn said sharply. "You said you'd listen."

Stanton reseated himself and took a deep breath. Glenn nodded at Two Ravens.

"Silverbear was cast into Apparition Lake," the Indian said. "He was murdered and denied the sacred burial of our custom. By Shoshone belief, the surface of the water would have prevented him from going to the Creator. Our shaman believes that when the waters of Apparition Lake receded, they took the holy man with them, to hold him and to protect him until the appointed time. The lake has returned and brought Silverbear back. The time is now."

"The time for what?" Stanton asked.

"For balance," Two Ravens said. "Mother Earth has had enough."

Chapter 23

Despite the chaos at the administrative offices the day before, Glenn had hoped beyond hope that their ridiculous program, as Mike Stanton called it, could be carried out without attracting undue attention. But as he eased the Suburban toward the barricades set up west of Apparition Lake that morning, it quickly became obvious that was not going to be the case. There were people everywhere as if the circus had come to town.

Beside him, a flabbergasted J.D. asked, "Wouldn't Stanton love to see this?"

Glenn grunted. "He isn't coming within a million miles of this. He authorized it, and I'm grateful for that, but he doesn't want to see it. He's waiting a report at Mammoth; probably under his desk."

"I don't think I blame him," she said scanning the tumult. "Isn't it funny how people seem to come from nowhere?"

Glenn found it less funny than amazing the way crowds materialized in Yellowstone. And it wasn't a rare occurrence. He remembered an incident near Swan Lake in Gardner's Hole. He'd been out for a drive in his own vehicle and had pulled over, merely to retrieve something from the glove box. In a heartbeat, a camper slowed and stopped near his vehicle, its occupants craning their necks to see why he'd parked. The first vehicle was immediately joined by two more. Someone got out with binoculars. The situation was getting interesting and Glenn decided to sit and watch. Three vehicles became six, and a young couple bailed from their car with cameras. Six became ten. The visitors began to question one another, pointing this direction and then that. When ten rubbernecking tourists became fifteen, Glenn had enough. There was nothing to see; never had been. He was sure that before the adventure was over word would spread that somebody had seen a bear or a moose or maybe an alien spacecraft. Such was human nature.

J.D. broke his reverie. "Who leaked this operation?"

"Huh? Oh, I did, J.D.," Glenn growled. "Everything was going so smoothly, I thought I'd give us all a challenge."

The biologist raised her hands in surrender. "I was just asking."

Glenn flipped on the red strobes and eased into the westbound lane, heading east, past the line of cars, campers and commercial vehicles backed against the roadblock. Gawkers were leaving their vehicles and wandering on the road like herds of bison along the Madison River. Glenn drove slowly, weaving not to hit them, his annoyance turning to anger. He fought the urge to 'moo' out his open window as he passed. The crowd grew denser as Glenn neared the barricades; a wall of arms and legs seemingly attached to a single massive body. Those in the back, on the tips of their toes, struggled to see over the mass in front. Even with lights flashing the crowd seemed ignorant of their presence. He impatiently tapped his horn and a middle-aged woman in front of his grill jumped as if she'd been goosed. She glared back, oblivious to their identities, then ignored them and renewed her attempts to climb the living mountain ahead of her.

"Ordinarily," Glenn said, "I hate the siren."

J.D. took the hint. She squawked the control several times in rapid succession startling the mob. They parted, dashing, jumping, running from the road as if a mad dog had been dropped in their midst. "But you must admit," she said, turning it off again, "it has its uses."

Two rangers on the other side of the barricades were laughing. They stifled it, pulled the roadblocks aside, let the chief ranger pass and then closed them up again. The crowd returned to leaning, including several Glenn recognized as reporters. "Hey, chief," one shouted. "What's going on?"

Glenn threw his vehicle into park and stepped out with a smile, leaning in a like fashion on his door. "Just routine procedures, folks. There's nothing to get excited about. I recommend you all go see the park and enjoy yourselves. For you guys," he added, to the reporters, "I'll have a full, and very dull, Press Release in short order." He turned to the nearest ranger, dropped his voice, and said, "See if you can turn some of these people around and get them out of here. At this rate they'll be lined up to Missoula by noon."

The young ranger warily eyed the crowd. "Yes, sir," he said though his expression suggested he'd just been ordered to join Custer at Little Big Horn.

"Don't be shy," Glenn told him. "It's time to earn your bones, kid." The chief ducked back into his vehicle and, with J.D., drove off toward the lake and the temporary Incident Command Center. The ICC was a converted RV with a communications room, a small conference office, a break room with coffee maker, and a closet-sized bathroom. Glenn pulled up near the vehicle where an agitated Ranger Connolly stood with his mouth hanging open like a landed cutthroat trout.

"Who sent out the invitations to this party?" J.D. asked as she climbed out, the question for some reason heavy on her mind.

"Huh?" Connolly asked his mind occupied. "Oh, uh, your guess is as good as mine, J.D." He turned sheepishly to the chief. "But we've got a problem."

"Only one?" Glenn asked.

"No. I mean a big problem. The press. . ."

"Yes," Glenn said eyeballing the hounds at the barricades. "They were bound to turn up."

"No," Connolly said. "Not them." He chucked a thumb over his shoulder at the RV. "On the other side, talking to the divers, those other two; a reporter from Billings with his photographer."

Glenn looked an angry question while J.D. marched to the end of the RV. She looked to the lake, screwed her face into a frown, looked back to Glenn and nodded. "It's that loud mouth, Lark, and one I don't know with a camera."

Glenn growled. "Where's the Public Information Specialist?"

"Not here yet," Connolly said helplessly. "And not answering her radio."

"What are they doing inside the restricted area?"

"Well, gee, chief. He wouldn't take no for an answer. Started in with that freedom of the press stuff, and the Public Information Act, and... well... I didn't want to get anybody in trouble. I told him he could wait for you here."

"So how did here," Glenn asked, pointing, "become there?" Connolly had no answer which, Glenn decided, was at least better than a rotten excuse. But it was time to get the show on the road and long past time to put a certain news hound in his place. Glenn took Connolly in tow and, with J.D., headed toward the lake and that most obnoxious member of the fourth estate. He used the sixty yards between to build up steam and ready himself for the clash.

The oversized gray van of the underwater recovery team was parked near a group of government vehicles along the roadside and adjacent to the lake. Lark and his photographer were beside it trying, none too successfully it appeared, to bend the ear of one of the divers. Lark turned from the waterdog, saw Glenn, J.D. and Connolly coming, and beamed. "Morning, Chief Merrill."

"Two questions," Glenn said. "One..." He pointed into the distance at the barricade through which he and J.D. had just passed and at the pulsing crowd beyond. "Are you responsible for that crowd?"

Lark took an aborted look and smiled. "The public's right to know, you know."

J.D. glared incredulously.

"Uh huh," Glenn muttered, less impressed than the biologist and fully prepared to ignore him. "And two, what are you doing inside the restricted area?"

"Oh, that would be my right to know. I do know my rights, chief."

"I'm sure of that," Glenn said. "What you don't know is under what circumstances you can legally exercise them. You don't know who has authority here. And, clearly, you don't know who it is that you keep messing with. Now, the park superintendent will have a news conference and statement for the press at the appropriate time. Feel free to go back to Mammoth and wait for it. If that doesn't appeal to you, then you can just get out of my face and go gawk with the rest of the clowns – from outside the barricades."

The photographer snapped his picture.

Blinded by the flash and blinking to clear his vision, Glenn barked, "Do that again and that camera takes a swim. Then you go to jail." He turned to Connolly. "Get them back where they belong!"

Thanks to the Information Specialist being late, and the run-in with Lark, damage control was starting to look impossible. Word was out something big was happening, that was obvious. Glenn hoped that was all. If the public knew they were in search of a corpse missing for over a century, all hell would break loose.

*

Rob Jones stood back and watched with great satisfaction. The rambunctious Cub Scout Troop he'd started out with less than ten days before had actually begun to take on the symmetry and order of a team in the outdoors. They had set up camp near Sulphur Creek in record time, and stood in formation as Jones made an inspection of their work.

"The camp looks great," Jones said. "I'm proud of you boys." The scouts gave themselves a round of applause punctuated with several hardy cheers. "Grab your packs. We'll go for a hike to celebrate. Maybe we can find a moose or something."

As the boys scrambled to get their gear, Greg cornered James beside his tent. "Hey, snot nose," said the bully. James stood to face the larger boy. He felt certain he was about to get his butt kicked but was going to face it like a man. "You did okay today," Greg said showing a rare smile. "What do you say we call a truce for a while?"

A good wind would have knocked James over. "You mean it?" he asked in surprise.

"Sure, I mean it," Greg said. "I guess you ain't such a bad kid." He laid his hand out before the smaller boy. James smiled wide and slapped the palm. They ended the exchange in a handshake.

"You're not so bad yourself," James said. "For a big creep."

For the first time on the trip Greg laughed with James instead of at him. He tapped the smaller boy above the ear. "You don't give up, do you? I guess that's why I like you. Come on, let's go find that moose."

*

With Lark out of his hair, Glenn turned his attention to the dive team leader. "Sorry about that," the chief said. "I hope he didn't press for too much information?"

A military crew cut, sharp green eyes, and a cleft chin above sculpted muscles, the dive leader grinned. "Have no fear. He was still wondering whether or not I even have vocal chords when you started chewing on him." He shook Glenn's hand. "Dave Parker. And if that guy's a problem for you, I'm only going to make it worse. I'm afraid I have no dive team. We were already short personnel because of an incident last night at Bear Lake. Most of my people and equipment are there."

Glenn winced. He knew the place; Bear Lake was just south of the Caribou National Forest in Utah. That's where this team had been summoned from, flown in by helicopter from Salt Lake City to the Mammoth Headquarters that morning. From there, it was over a half-hour drive to Apparition Lake and they'd arrived just ahead of him.

"My partner and I grabbed just the basics and came on alone. I was going to use your people for surface monitors. Now my partner..." He hesitated, trying to think of a polite way to phrase it. "He's laid out in the back of the van, sick as a dog. I don't know if it's sudden on-set flu, or food poisoning, or what. It hit him just as we arrived. He got dizzy as a top, spiked a temp, and he's vomited twice. I'm hoping he doesn't die on me. There's no way he can dive."

As if the gods were listening, a horn began bleating. Glenn, J.D. and Parker turned as one to the west barricades. Having gained no ground dispersing the horde, the rangers were having to hold them back from the gap as they let a pickup with an overloaded bed through.

"How about that? The Indians come over the hill in time to save the Cavalry." Glenn turned to Parker. "That's Johnny Two Ravens, a professional outfitter and, among many other things, a trained and experienced diver."

Parker nodded. "That's terrific. But under the circumstances, chief, he'd have to volunteer."

"When he hears the circumstances," Glenn replied, "try to stop him."

*

Two Ravens did volunteer of course; immediately. He and Parker had a quick conversation and, though they had only met, went about their work with the refined movements of a Swiss watch. Parker unloaded equipment from the van, Two Ravens from his truck. Together they assembled ropes, buoys, and anchors and, in an orderly and precise fashion, placed everything in the staging area on the shore. Having checked with Simpson in communications, and sent word to Stanton the operation was about to begin, Glenn and J.D. rejoined the divers.

"We're looking for a body submerged somewhere in the lake," Glenn explained. "It's been there... for some time... More than likely it will be skeletal remains only." He put a hand on Two Ravens' shoulder. "I don't want you taking any unnecessary chances out there."

Glaring, J.D. butted in. "Glenn, how much diving experience do you have?"

"Me? I can't even swim."

She smiled. "Then why not offer support instead of advice."

The chief smiled back, without meaning it, and turned to the dive leader. "How soon can you be in the water?"

"Ten minutes?" Parker guessed. He looked the question at Two Ravens, got a nod, and told Glenn decisively, "Ten minutes."

They attached regulators to tanks and donned wetsuits. Parker knew his stuff and Two Ravens was no slouch either. Within the promised ten, the pair had entered the water and were inspecting each other's equipment. J.D. and Glenn assumed positions on the shoreline to monitor the search patterns and act as backup in the event of problems.

The divers signaled 'Okay' and Glenn returned a 'thumbs up' to start the search. They swam to the middle of the lake and then split; Parker headed west, Two Ravens east. Still on the surface, they maneuvered to positions that allowed them to cut the lake into thirds. The men set flagged buoys, held in place by small anchors, to mark the starting points for their individual searches. They signaled the shoreline, received the final 'Okay' from Glenn and submerged.

The chief watched silently as the situation slipped from his control. J.D. had been right and he confessed as much to her now. It was out of his control. It was up to the divers now.

*

Sulphur Creek had earned its name. A long stretch of running water framed by washed rock and mixed conifers, with an obvious odor of rotten eggs, it didn't do much to hold the interest of the young scouts. Rob Jones sensed their desire for more exploration and had taken the boys off trail. They climbed up into the lodgepole pines on the south side of Mount Washburn following a game trail through the thick timber. It would be a good learning experience for them.

A half-mile up the sloping terrain, Rob decided it was time to take a break. He was definitely getting too old for this stuff. To the boy directly behind him, Jones said, "Pass the word back down the line. We'll rest here for a while and let everybody catch his breath. Have a snack and tell everyone to be sure and drink some water. I don't need any of you guys getting dehydrated on me."

Rob dropped his pack and took a seat as the boy told the scout behind him and gave instruction to pass the word down the strung out line of hikers. At the back of the line, James couldn't have been happier to hear the news. He was beat. He also had to pee. He dropped his pack into the heavy brush next to the barely discernible game trail and headed into the trees. He'd take care of business in private, away from prying eyes and, in spite of their temporary truce, away from Greg's shenanigans.

*

Young Bass Donnelly and ol' man Gerry Meeks, on horseback and trailing two pack horses, rode to the edge of a timber northeast of Inspiration Point. The conspicuous whomp, whomp, whomp of an approaching helicopter echoed throughout the area, bouncing from one peak to another, making its actual location difficult to pinpoint. Meeks reined in his mount, and signaled Donnelly to do the same, holding up under the cover of thick trees. The Park Service helicopter passed overhead disappearing as quickly as it had come. As the reverberation of its spinning blades gained distance, Meeks climbed from his saddle and signaled for the young'un to do the same.

They moved quietly toward a break in the trees, Donnelly understanding now why the old codger had made him ditch the colorful ball cap. Meeks dropped to one knee, peering through an opening in the canopy of branches, and pointed. The boy sidled up alongside him, removed his new camouflaged crusher headgear, and followed his gaze.

Chapter 24

A small herd of elk grazed through spotty openings in the trees several hundred yards distant. Slowly picking and choosing their morsels, the cows and calves stood for several moments chewing and scanning their surroundings then individually moved on a few yards, dropped their heads to grab a bite, and repeated the routine. Filtering in and out of the trees, their two-tone brown coats and tell-tale white rumps appeared and disappeared from view.

The poachers patiently watched and waited, finally being rewarded with a glimpse of the majestic albino bull, Hercules. As he stepped into view from a thicket of pines, the monarch tilted his head back, pointed his nose in the air and let out a short whistle and several heavy grunts; just letting his girls know to keep close while they grazed. Lowering his nose and pointing antler tines forward, he briefly attacked a small pine releasing a three-second burst of adrenaline and testosterone, then took a mouthful of grass and slipped back into the cover of a dense patch of trees.

*

Two Ravens slid down the rope between buoy and anchor, inhaling slowly from his regulator and acclimating himself to the freezing cold water. Less than ten feet from the surface of Apparition Lake,

237

his vision was reduced to the length of his outstretched arm. The outfitter hated these kinds of dives and imagined that, somewhere in the murkiness over there, his partner Parker felt the same. Lakes fed by snowmelt and the run-off from heavy rain always held suspended sediment so thick a diver couldn't find his butt with both hands. This was going to be a nasty search, Two Ravens thought.

His knees settled into a carpet of thick grass; the kind always found on the bottom of temporary lakes. Silt gently puffed up at his landing and whirled in slow motion in the icy waters around him making visibility all the worse. He removed a line reel from his utility belt and fastened the spring-hook to the buoy line above the anchor. Reeling out line to the first marker, at the five-foot interval, he moved out from the buoy until the line was taught and started working around it in a circle. He worked slowly, stretching his arms forward, kneading the heavy, swaying grasses for anything that might lead to his target. Finding nothing, he stretched his arms to his sides and repeated the action. Still nothing. Two Ravens moved one body length forward following the marker line in a circle around the buoy.

Five long minutes elapsed before he unreeled five more feet of line and began his second lap.

*

On the surface, monitoring the dive from the bank of Apparition Lake, Glenn looked away for a moment to the crowd by the west barricades, including what had become an entourage of television cameras, local news personalities, newspaper reporters, and photographers. "Every reporter in Flyover Country must be here," he said.

"Yes," J.D. agreed. "But there's only one that seems to know it all."

"What's that?"

"Lark," she said.

"Yeah, he's a pip."

"No, Glenn, it's more than that. I'm serious. There's something wrong with that guy. His antics, his attitude, his odd remarks. I get feelings about people; and I've got one about him. Since the day I first saw him, watching him report, watching him hound you; all along it's been about making a name for himself while trying to ruin you. The others ask questions; he fires ammo. Especially about the poaching. He just seems smugly in the know about things he really shouldn't know."

"You're giving him too much credit."

"I'm not giving him credit at all. I think he's dirty. I think he's been parading it in front of us and we've been too busy, and too annoyed, to see it."

"For instance?"

"There are several," J.D. said. "For instance... Has it dawned on you he just all but admitted to leaking this operation? The public's right to know, he called it. But look who's here. The same rubber-neckers that you'd get anywhere you stopped a vehicle in the park; and a ton of reporters. He didn't scoop everyone else with a story. He notified other reporters and gave the story away. He's more interested in giving you a hard time, keeping you busy, than in reporting news."

Glenn eyed the crowd. "There are a lot of reporters here. But I don't see that proves anything about Lark one way or the other. Do you have a fact you aren't using?"

"I have one, yes," J.D. said. "Do you remember the morning after Bart Houser was killed when he stopped us in the hallway at Mammoth? He was razzing you to no end about the elk poachers."

"Yes. I remember."

"Do you remember what he said?"

"The gist of it. I'm not going to ruin brain cells by committing Lark's squeals to memory."

"That's my point. In an effort to ignore him, you haven't heard him. You warned us all about tunnel vision. I think Lark's given you tunnel hearing."

Glenn laughed anxiously. "J.D., what did he say that I missed?"

"He said the elk poachers were making a monkey out of you. That they were running free in Lewis River, Pitchstone, and Firehole."

"Yeah. Well," Glenn said. "Unfortunately, he wasn't wrong. They've hit all those locations."

"Yes, Glenn. But that's just it. He was too right. The poachers have taken game in all those locations... now. But not then. There was the bear at Mary Bay, a handful of elk in the Lewis River area, and another handful in Pitchstone. But, as of that morning, there were no elk poached at Firehole. Firehole wasn't hit until days later." Glenn was listening now. "You tell me," J.D. continued, "on his own, does that loudmouth know anything about poaching, hunting, or wildlife? You don't hold press conferences on poaching incidents alone, so someone has been leaking information to him about elk poaching. Who? And even if it were someone on your staff. How would they have known about Firehole before it happened? How did he know where the poachers were going to strike next?"

Glenn was grim. He signaled to Connolly, who came on the hop. "Head over to the barricade, will you, and invite Howard Lark over here."

"Lark? By himself? The other reporters will squawk."

"Let them." Connolly hurried away. Glenn turned to J.D. with blood in his eyes. "You and I are going to have a chat with Mr. Lark."

*

As white hair fluttered in and out of view through the trees, Meeks calculated the movement and raised his rifle to watch the predicted point of exposure for his shot. Breathing deeply, he exhaled half and held the reticle on the open window of opportunity between trees. As anticipated, first appeared nose, then face, then headgear high. Finally the swollen neck of Hercules eased into view. There the elk pulled up short and stopped. Meeks released the breath and unconsciously whispered out loud, "Just one more step."

Standing with vital organs shielded by the trunk of a large pine, the trophy bull lowered his head and grabbed a mouthful of groceries. Raising it once again, he casually turned to look over his shoulder and skyward. The percussion of chopper blades split the air and Meeks lowered his weapon. Parting the branches carefully, he followed Hercules' gaze and watched the helicopter move into sight, hover momentarily above the albino elk and then bank away.

Looking back to the target, Meeks spit into the dirt and wiped his mouth. The elk had taken that brief moment to step through the small clearing, and disappear back into the trees.

*

Franklin, saddled up on Tuff his faithful horse of many years, rode from the timber near Inspiration Point to a secluded turn-out some distance from the road. There he found what appeared to be an abandoned camper.

Dismounting in the trees just off the road, he approached the cab with exaggerated caution. It was empty. Circling to the rear he un-snapped his weapon, listened for movement inside, then reached for the door on the camper shell. Easing it open, a small bag of garbage fell to the dirt and Franklin's tension subsided. Camping equipment, more garbage, and a piecemeal selection of old clothing clogged the doorway and was oddly stuffed to the interior roof of the camper.

Snapping the thumb-break back into place on his holster, Franklin drew his radio from its case on his belt. "Seventeen to Yellowbird One. I have a pickup with a camper parked and unoccupied about a mile from the Point. Keep an eye peeled. There could be riders on the ground."

"Yellowbird One to seventeen," the pilot replied. "Copy. In the vicinity. All is copacetic thus far."

*

Visibility was declining exponentially as Two Ravens initiated his second lap. Each time he moved his arms in a sweep, sedimentation that had settled on the growth attached to the bottom dislodged, clouding his visibility further. Every action was taking place in darker water and murkier conditions. Johnny considered the last time he had been in those waters. This was no purification. Surely Parker was feeling no more comfortable. A lack of comfort, he thought, in an environment in which we are both familiar. It occurred to Two Ravens he owed Glenn an apology. The chief ranger, his friend, was also submerged in a clouded foreign environment with each new incident adding distraction and compounding his ability to see. He and Glenn were both in a quest for understanding, for clarity... and for a body.

Two Ravens swam on, searching.

*

Rob Jones placed an empty candy bar wrapper back in his pack and shouldered the heavy weight. To the boy behind him, he said, "Saddle up. Let's move on up the ridge a little ways." He took another shot from his canteen as the boy passed the word to the next scout in line. Feeling his age, and regretting his lack of proper exercise, Jones slowly started to climb higher into the dark timber.

Each of the boys got to their feet, passed the word to the next in line, and started up the slope after their leader. The last boy turned to tell James, didn't see him or his pack, figured he'd moved to the front, and continued on with the hike unconcerned.

Of course James wasn't at the front at all. He was still in the timber, forty yards off the trail, and more than a little disoriented. He'd wanted to make sure nobody saw him 'draining his radiator' so he had zigged and zagged through the thick trees to make sure he was out of sight. Now he couldn't remember which way he'd come.

"Mr. Jones," James called out. The dense timber absorbed his words like water in a sponge. "Mr. Jones! Hey, you guys, where are you?"

The only response to his call was the eerie hoot of a great gray owl.

*

242

A less curious ranger would have left the filthy camper be but, after the well-deserved dressing down he'd received over the golden eagle feather, Franklin was not going to leave anything to chance. His uniform could be washed, he told himself. That camper was out of place. And the trash inside was just plain odd. He grabbed the next bag of garbage on top, hauled it out, then started to dig.

Three minutes into the job, Franklin realized the stack of objectionable material was only two foot deep into the camper. He'd been right to take that second look as it was obviously a wall of deception. There was open space behind and he was sure digging further would be worth the effort. He grabbed as much as he could from the lowest tier in the wall, let out a primal grunt, and pulled. A huge pile collapsed out onto the ground at his feet. Franklin peeked through the rift he'd opened and saw the first glint of antler tine reflecting the newly introduced sunlight. Bingo!

Grinning ear to ear, he crawled into the camper shouting, "So I'll shower twice!" He dove over the top of the fallen wall of garbage to retrieve the hidden treasure. He climbed out again a few minutes later with his arms full and set two large antlers on the ground.

He reached for his radio, just as that same device began to squawk at him. "Yellowbird One to seventeen," came the metallic voice. "We've got two pack horses in the trees northeast of Inspiration Point and off the Sevenmile Trail. Suspect riders have got to be close. Those packers didn't get here by themselves."

"Seventeen to Yellowbird," Franklin told his handset. "Copy. The camper contains concealed contraband. Proceed with prejudice, I'm en route! Seventeen to Dispatch, send a unit to secure the camper, I'm en route to back Yellowbird."

Without waiting on the reply, Franklin saddled up and spurred Tuff to a gallop.

*

When the news reports that law enforcement has a suspect surrounded, the general picture that forms in the subconscious is a half-dozen squad cars containing a pair of officers each and a fifteen-man SWAT Team in black uniforms, helmets, and heavy artillery engulfing a crime scene with red lights flashing and bullhorns blaring.

In the case of Howard Lark, the situation was not nearly so flamboyant but nonetheless intense. The reporter was sunk in a chair beside a small table in the ICC meeting room with but two people standing over him, one a mere five-foot-four biologist. Regardless, Glenn and J.D. most definitely had Lark surrounded. "This is outrageous!" he sputtered indignantly, for all the good it did him.

"Yes," Glenn agreed. "So you've said. But you haven't answered the question. Why is it that a pretentious little creep like you seems to have the pulse of the poachers raping my park?"

"I'm a good reporter."

"You're not a reporter at all; you're a muckraker. But even that is beside the point. Who has been feeding you inside information about elk poaching in Yellowstone?"

"I don't know what you're talking about?"

"Assuming that's a lie," J.D. said, cutting in, "how is it that you've been able to report details of incidents not included in Press Releases? Details that have gone no further than shift log reports?"

"Sources. Every reporter has them."

J.D. ignored him. "How is it you have information about poaching incidents before they occur?"

Lark froze, studying the Fish & Game biologist, the toys turning in his head.

"You remember, smart guy," Glenn said. "All the fun you were having at the administration offices? Let me quote you. 'And the elk poachers... they're running free; Lewis River, Pitchstone, Firehole.' How did you know about Pitchstone, Lark? No information had been released. As for Firehole, the poachers hadn't gotten there yet. But you knew they were headed there. How?"

"This is ridiculous. You may as well quit asking," Lark insisted. "I'm not going to reveal my sources."

"Your sources?" J.D. was incredulous.

Glenn chuckled mirthlessly. "We're not asking about your sources. We're talking about your co-conspirators. You've been aiding and abetting criminals in multiple violations of Federal law. We're not talking about a contempt of court charge, Lark. You are in communication with the poachers. You're assisting them. We're talking repeated felonies. Have you ever heard of RICO? You know, racketeering and organized crime. How does a conspiracy charge and decades in federal prison sound? Your only chance is to tell us who these people are and where we can find them. I mean right now."

*

Tick, tick, tick. The clock on Stanton's wall was the only sound he could here. The face on that clock was the only sight he could see. Now that the hordes, who only hours before stood pounding at his door, were on the banks of Apparition Lake, he sat exhausted and despondent.

Divers, he knew, were at that moment searching the depths of that dead phantom lake looking for a one hundred year dead body.

He was beginning to realize how tentative his hold was on the political ladder. He was beginning to see what a very long way down it would be when he fell.

How will I ever explain this operation, he thought, if Glenn, J.D., and Two Ravens fail? If the divers fail? If they don't find that body? And what can I possibly say if they do?

*

"I'm not a co-conspirator," Lark insisted sweating rivers. "I spotted them accidentally near Lewis River. I wanted a story. Then they spotted me. They wanted to put a bullet in my head. I told them, 'You're hunters, not murderers. You don't profit from my death. And

I don't want to be dead.'" He glared at Glenn. "What would you have done?"

He ignored the question. "You agreed to help them? For a story?"

"To save my life, yes! I said if they would tell me where they were going and how and what they did that I would tell their story hypothetically, no names, no suggestion even that they were real. That I would put the heat on the park, on you, and I'd turn them into modern Robin Hoods."

"Who are they?"

"I don't know."

Glenn leaned in, reddening, threatening.

"I'm telling you," Lark shouted, "I don't know. I never asked their names. There's an old man and a young guy, my age I'd guess. I don't think their related. I just think of them as that. Or, sometimes, as the cowboy hat and the crusher. That's what they wear. That's all I ever thought of them as."

"Where are they?" J.D. demanded.

"And keep in mind," Glenn added. "A stay in a federal penitentiary hangs on your answer."

The door was yanked open and an alarmed Simpson stuck her head into the trailer. "Chief, our chopper is reporting riders on the ground; no livestock permits. And Ranger Franklin says he's found the poachers' vehicle. They're both..."

"Inspiration Point," Lark yelled, trying to get it in. Trying to save his bacon. He grabbed J.D. by the arm, pleading, "They're headed for Inspiration Point!"

"Yes," Simpson said amazed. "How did he... ?"

"Never mind," Glenn said looking at Lark in disgust. He turned quickly back to the ranger. "Order the chopper here to pick me up, Gloria. Then hustle back and take Mr. Lark into custody."

Simpson's eyes widened. She said nothing, just nodded and disappeared headed for the radio room. "Come on, J.D.," Glenn said starting for the door.

"What about me?" Lark asked.

"You? Your only prayer is if we stop them before they kill again. Since you aren't going anywhere, I recommend you drop to your knees and help it along as best you can from here."

Chapter 25

The scouts had traveled barely another quarter mile but Rob Jones was exhausted. The game trail had led them into thick blow downs and then had disappeared altogether. Cross-country hiking was not exactly what the Troop leader had in mind when he'd started their little adventure. Finally breaking out of the timber into a meadow opening, Jones decided to regroup and take another rest. He dropped his pack, plopped down on the ground, and waited as the gang funneled from the timber behind him.

The boys had all emerged into the clearing and were removing their packs as they gathered around their leader. Surprisingly, Greg was the first to notice they were short one Webelos. "Hey, Mr. Jones," he said. "Where's snot nose?"

It took a moment for Jones to process the oddly asked question and understand Greg. When he did, and the meaning became clear, a rush of adrenaline shot through Jones' body. He stood up, scanned the group, and quickly took a head count. "Okay, guys," Jones called out, his voice a octave higher with what amounted to near panic. "Where is James?"

*

James was officially lost; lost, and a little scared, and more than a little angry at himself. This would surely be the last straw. First the trouble with Greg, then those stupid post cards, then more trouble with Greg. He wouldn't have a chance now of earning his Webelos Badge. Not after this. Not a chance in the world.

He plunked down on a fallen tree to think out what to do next. He pulled the picture from his pocket, the torn post card of the white elk, Hercules. He wondered what the king of the elk would do. He wondered what Hercules, a leader among men, would do. And he knew they would both stand up, face their enemy, and survive.

James remembered the Webelos' lectures about wilderness survival. Mr. Jones had even had a Search & Rescue Team Leader talk at one of their pack meetings before the trip. What had the man said? To pay attention to the lay of the land. That was it. When disoriented, he was supposed to find and follow a known landmark.

James tucked the post card away and looked around. He scowled, unable to imagine finding any landmarks there. He was surrounded by tall, heavy timber that restricted his vision. The canopy above was garland with heavy strands of lichens, huge masses of green that looked like the beards of old men. The forest floor was thick with fallen timber. What had simply been trees moments before was quickly becoming something far more frightening and the more James looked at it, the more it seemed to close in on him.

*

The sound of the helicopter faded. Gerry Meeks swore under his breath. Them chopper patrols were getting ridiculous, cutting in on his pleasure, cutting in on his money. But it was gone now; for the moment.

Meeks checked his rifle and resumed his surveillance of Hercules.

Eager for some action, hungry with what to him was a natural blood lust, Bass Donnelly moved eagerly to Meeks' side.

Neither of the poachers took any immediate notice of a strange fog settling about them.

*

Sulphur Creek was his landmark. James had worked it all out in his head. If he could just find his way back down the mountain to the creek, he could follow it back. Mr. Jones would probably be pretty hot, but there was nothing he could do about that. Webelos Badge or not, James was headed back to civilization. That was the plan.

James struggled downhill through the heavy timber, climbing over fallen logs and crawling under those too high for him to get over. It was tough going for a little guy and he stopped and sat on another fallen tree to catch his breath.

Going again a short time later, James stumbled through a break in the trees and fell hard to his knees. He looked up to see he was near the edge of a small clearing and to see, right beside him, a man in a camouflage hat, aiming a rifle. James didn't know Bass Donnelly from Adam and he got no introduction. What he got was grabbed by his bright yellow neckerchief, and his young neck all but broken, as the vicious young poacher jerked him to his feet.

"Well," Donnelly said. "Looky here."

*

With the familiar sound of its churning blades, a helicopter appeared above and dropped into a clearing beside Apparition Lake.

Waiting at the edge of the clearing, Glenn told J.D. "You're taking over here."

"Me. How can I take over?"

"You caught Lark. You know the score. And you're surrounded by pros who know what they're doing. Just look wise."

Glenn crouched as he raced beneath the blades and jumped aboard. The copter lifted off, tussling crowd and trees alike, and banked quickly away.

*

Despite a fog that had started to settle into the area, Gerry Meeks had again found Hercules in the trees. Though it made sighting more difficult, Meeks considered the thickening earth-bound cloud a positive development. It would muffle the report of his rifle and add concealment as they prepared and removed their trophy. It was time to bring this hunt to a close. Donnelly, now clutching the Cub Scout with one hand gripped on his blue uniform shirt, waited nearby, his eyes gleaming with all kinds of excitement and anticipation.

The old man was about to shoot when both the poachers, and their young accidental captive, were startled by a high pitched scream.

"Noooooooo!"

Like the Headless Horseman of Sleepy Hollow, a park ranger appeared out of the swirling mist, on horseback, his mount at full gallop. It was Franklin, coming, he thought, to Hercules rescue, his horse throwing dirt from its hooves as it cut back and forth dodging trees in the sparse clearing. He shouted again and, with reins in one hand and rifle in the other, fired a round into the timber near the poachers.

Donnelly dove for cover taking James to the ground with him merely as a matter of course. James gasped, the wind knocked out of him, and tried to sit, struggling for air. Mercilessly, the young poacher shoved him right back down.

Meeks too had taken cover as another round from Franklin's weapon carved its way through the fog and trees in their direction.

The humans weren't the only ones with survival on their minds. At the sound of Franklin's first scream, Hercules had raised his head in alarm and, at the first shot, the elk monarch proved how he had beaten the odds and lived so long. His legs recoiled and sprung, launching him over the first deadfall in his way then, maneuvering like a running back dodging tacklers, he swerved and weaved through the trees to disappear into the timber completely in under three seconds.

*

Like a synchronized swimmer, Two Ravens mirrored his teammate's efforts on the other side of the lake. He'd never seen a lake so devoid of life. There were no fish, no crawdads, none of the usual creatures he was accustomed to seeing on the water or under it. The thought of looking for a dead body in a dead lake made him uneasy.

Returned from the clearing to the lake shore, J.D. felt helpless as she watched the surface bubbles travel in ever-enlarging circles. She and Glenn had been running in circles themselves the last several weeks. Just thinking of it made her dizzy. Now the anticipation of what they might find was beginning to hit home. It was all too bizarre, she thought.

Below the surface of Apparition Lake, trying to act the professional and put his emotions aside, Two Ravens worked like an automaton. Swinging his arms wide, he brushed an object. His reflexes kicked in. He jerked his arm back against his side and felt immediately embarrassed. Was it his first mission, for heaven's sake? He'd looked for bodies before, in the reservation waterways, but there, alone in the belly of the cold dead lake, he admitted now that it had always given him the willies.

He anchored his body, belly-down in the thick grass, determined not to disturb whatever it was he'd touched. Two Ravens drew on his regulator; once for air, twice more for courage, and slowly reached in the direction of the object. Feeling the bump again, he turned his arm to grasp the object. He closed his eyes and tugged it up and toward his face mask.

He opened them again... and rolled his eyes in embarrassment and relief. It was a tree limb.

*

Gerry Meeks had never liked his name. But Geronimo Meeks had taken his namesake's words to heart. He'd decided long ago that he, too, would never surrender. He was far too guilty of far too many things. His age meant once he was returned to prison, he'd never live long enough to see freedom again. Donnelly could do as he pleased. But Meeks wasn't going back to jail. And he wasn't planning on going out alone. He raised up over the log behind which he was hiding, raised the rifle to his shoulder, took aim on the ranger that had ruined his hunt, and fired.

Riding hard, Franklin somehow saw the glint of reflected light on rifle scope just as Meeks pulled the trigger. The bullet hit his horse, and the rider felt the impact through Tuff's reaction as if it had hit him instead. Franklin dove from the saddle as his mount stumbled and started down on its side. The ranger rolled hard as he hit the ground, losing his rifle, and caught himself in a half-crouch. Instinct took over. Franklin scrambled to cover beneath his saddle, behind his horse. He laid a loving hand on the animal and found it was already too late for his faithful partner. The horse was dead. Red with anger, Franklin drew his sidearm, eased over the top of the saddle protecting him, and searched for a target. Any target.

As the ranger's horse went down. As the park cop had run for cover like the coward he was, Meeks jumped up, tossed his rifle aside and ran for his own mount, and his saddle bags. He wasn't running away, no, sir. That's where he kept a loaded pistol.

Donnelly, meanwhile, was a pale mess. He'd never considered the question of surrender versus fight. The possibility of getting caught hadn't entered his mind. Without doubt, the last thing he would have ever dreamed was that he'd be face down in the dirt dodging bullets. He lay flat on his stomach, face pressed hard against the ground, without a clue what to do next.

*

The pilot cleared Dunraven Peak, banked his helicopter hard left, and started dropping altitude. That's when he saw it. His gasp, over his helmet microphone, through the cockpit speakers, sounded like the roar of the grizzly they'd all been chasing. "That's incredible, chief," he yelled. He pointed below. "That fog is where I saw the suspects... But, believe me, there wasn't a fog ten minutes ago!"

Glenn had no trouble believing the man. He knew what it was. And he knew what it meant. "Get me on the ground fast," he shouted. "Franklin's in serious trouble!"

The pilot did as instructed and, as the chopper dropped and cut into the fog rising just off the top of the trees, Glenn saw the first muzzle flashes from gunfire below. An instant later, the plastic bubble forming the helicopter's windshield took a glancing bullet and cracked.

"Jesus, Glenn," the pilot cried. "They're shooting at us."

Glenn couldn't argue. The pilot had called it exactly. Meeks had turned his guns on the helicopter and coaxed the cowering Donnelly to sit up and do the same. Between shots at the whirlybird, they continued to trade fire with the ranger on the ground as well. "We can't let Frankie have all the fun," Glenn told the pilot. "Get me down there."

"What?" the pilot cried back in alarm. "Glenn, I said they're shooting at us!"

"I know. I know." The chief pointed below. "Franklin needs a hand. Just get me close."

The pilot shook his head in irritation, disgust, terror, but he didn't say a word. He pinched his lips to a thin line, grabbed the control with both hands, and started the helicopter down again to a terrifying chorus of ricocheting bullets. It was all he could do, between the barrage, the air currents between the trees, and his trembling hands, to keep his head. When he didn't think he could take another second, he shouted, "This is nuts. They could really put us down, ya know!"

"Try," Glenn pleaded. "You've got to try."

Sucking it up like he never had before, battling the control, the pilot moved again to drop the helicopter down over top of Franklin's position. They were close enough now to see the desperate, terrified poachers turning the battle on, several shots in a row at Franklin, and then several more skyward to pockmark the cockpit bubble and rock the ship. "God!" the pilot screamed.

On his side, Franklin could do little, but he did all he could. With his beloved horse down and gone he had little choice but to stay behind his saddle using the animal, his long-time friend, for cover. He returned the gunfire at the poachers trying to give the chopper what small cover-fire he could muster.

The helicopter hovered ten feet off the ground. It wasn't close enough for Glenn's taste but, clearly, it was as close as they were going to get. Shotgun in hand, the chief ranger jumped. He hit the ground hard and, as he rolled through his landing, the chopper was already climbing fast and banking out of the line of fire. Glenn couldn't blame the pilot one bit. Besides he was too busy. He scrambled back to his feet, snaked his way to Franklin's position, jumped the fallen mount, and dropped into cover beside his junior ranger.

"You okay?" Glenn barked as he chambered a round, raised up, and fired in the direction of the last muzzle flash. "Yeah," Franklin's voice cracked as he also fired into the growing cloud of mist. "Tuff took the one with my name on it."

Glenn nodded understanding and squeezed Franklin's arm. "Hercules?"

Franklin jerked his head in the direction of the woods behind them. "Smart and fast as ever."

*

James, had been curled up, fingers in his ears to block the explosive sound of gunfire. As the chopper had flown in and the poachers turned their attention on it, the young scout grabbed his courage with both hands and started to crawl away from the fight. He'd only gone about forty yards when he realized the fog was getting thick and the air had suddenly grown cold. In minutes the temperature had dropped ten degrees. His fingers were getting numb and a chill ran up his frame and made him shudder. A heavy cloud of mist encircled the boy and rose into the drooping boughs as the trees began to take on odd shapes like phantoms in the night.

James trembled. He watched the mist as it swirled in front of him and gathered into a dark mass drawing in from the edges. Darker and thicker it expanded until a distinct form took shape; the head of a bear with a huge muscled body forming below. Gray hair appeared and the silver bear stared at James with piercing steel-gray eyes. With a tremendous roar the creature emerged from the trees.

"Help me, Jesus," James whispered as his mind raced. A bear! Don't move, he thought. Don't move.

The great silver-tipped grizzly started to charge.

*

Two Ravens had covered an area forty feet out from the buoy and was starting another round. He stroked his feet rhythmically, fining himself slowly along the bottom. Visibility had been rotten from the get-go. Now the slightest motion stirred silt from the bottom and clouded the water darker yet. It seemed he'd been down for hours in the icy water, though he knew it hadn't been that long.

Two Ravens lifted his gauge to check his air supply. Distracted from his course, he strayed out from the circle and felt the tug of his line reel beckoning him back to the center. He dropped the gauge, letting it float slowly to his side, and turned to correct his course. Concentrating to get his bearings straight, he looked into the grassy bottom... and sucked water.

Mother of God, he saw a face. Or was it an animal? It was both. He was seeing a bear's head with the face of an old man, an Indian, jutting from beneath its ferocious jaws as if eaten whole and feet first. He had steel-gray eyes; wide open and staring through Two Ravens to the back of his brain. The diver jerked back violently, off balance in the weightless environment, and choked on inhaled water. He stumbled backward, flailing his arms and legs, trying to recover. The bubbles from his regulator circled his head like a swarm of angry hornets. Panic had taken charge. Two Ravens was the victim of vertigo, losing all sense of up or down. He struck out in all directions to find his way. Slamming his heel into the bottom of the lake, his instincts took over. His legs folded then sprung, propelling him off the bottom of the lake and jetting him toward the surface.

To J.D. and the startled rangers on the shoreline it looked like a warhead had been launched from a submarine. The calm surface of the dead lake erupted with a mighty explosion of water and Two Ravens cleared the surface, breaching like a humpback whale. His regulator shot from his mouth, propelled by a horrendous scream that was suddenly muffled as he hit the surface again and sank briefly out of sight.

Nobody in the crowd behind the barricades knew what had occurred. They only knew that, finally, something had happened. At both ends of the restricted area cheers and applause rang out.

*

The grizzly smashed through the brush like a runaway bulldozer. Limbs fell crashing to the ground, brush was torn away. James was frozen, terrified by the explosive charge. Even at his tender age, he recognized death and knew it was upon him.

The charging bruin seemed almost airborne as he closed the gap. Its steel-gray eyes burned into the depths of James' heart. The boy found his legs, turned to run, and fell over a fallen log. He rolled onto his back as the animal's lunge brought him directly over top of the young scout. James stiffened for the crushing weight of the final pounce and let out an involuntary scream.

The monstrous bear passed over him.

The creature landed beyond his head with a thud that shook the earth. And, without slowing, charged straight toward the poachers. At the scream, Meeks spun around, sending his cowboy hat flying, and saw the gargantuan bear closing fast. Donnelly had seen it, too, and was already vaulting over the log he'd been using for cover. He

258

passed Meeks at a dead run away from the bear and straight at the rangers. Meeks dropped his handgun, grabbed the rifle at his side, leveled it at the animal and fired. Though the fur parted and blood spurted from its chest, the grizzly showed no other sign of being shot. It came on without slowing and swatted the old man as if he was a fly. Meeks cartwheeled in his own shower of blood and landed in an unmoving heap.

Donnelly turned over his shoulder just in time to see Meeks smash into the dirt. Already in a panic, he completely freaked, threw his gun into the air, and threw his hands over his head like a groupie at a Stones concert. Screaming his lungs out, he ran toward the rangers that a moment before had been his targets.

What could Glenn do but provide cover? The chief ranger stood, pumped his shotgun, and unloaded a blast. Like Meeks' rifle shot, the shotgun shell exploded as it passed through the bear's side and sent fur, meat, and blood flying in an arc; all to no apparent effect. Showing no sign of the clearly visible injury, the grizzly turned on Glenn. It rose on its hind legs, opened wide its gaping maw, and snarled.

Screaming and crying, Donnelly leapt to the ground behind Franklin's horse. The enraged ranger saw him, jumped on top of him, and shoved his handgun into the back of the poacher's head. "Don't move," Franklin shouted. "Don't you dare move!"

The massive bear was still there, towering over Glenn, roaring like thunder. He pumped the shotgun again. Ignoring his rolling stomach, forcing the terror from his mind, he raised the weapon and aimed.

*

Water rushed... bubbles foamed. Two Ravens and Parker broke the surface of the water with a churning whoosh. An instant later, a Stokes basket bearing the corpse of Silverbear, surfaced between them. The crowd reacted in awe.

From a rowboat J.D. grabbed the basket, controlling it.

Two Ravens ripped off his mask and, treading water, raised his hands skyward. He called out in the language of his people. "Duma Appah created the Earth with the help of the animal nation. In the name of Appah, we ask forgiveness of Silverbear and of Mother Earth. He-agh. He-aghhhh."

*

Towering over Glenn, the grizzly let out a mighty roar.

The chief ranger looked from the weapon in his hands, up to the bear, and back again. He took a deep breath, clenched his teeth, and threw the gun to the ground. Then he threw back his shoulders and stood before the grizzly unarmed.

The massive silver bear shimmered and, to the echo of its roar, vanished.

Glenn stared in disbelief. He swallowed hard, bunched his hands into fists, and then collapsed to his knees. The feather of a golden eagle suddenly appeared, from nowhere, on the ground before him. The chief ranger began to tremble.

Chapter 26

Below the teeming wonder of the Owl Creek Mountains lay Dry Cottonwood Creek, a silent and lonely place little known and seldom visited. In the early days of the Shoshone it was a sacred site, a keeper of dark secrets, and a door to the afterworld. Its silent, slow-moving waters drained into the Wind River to the east long before there was a dam and a Boysen Reservoir. Though many things had changed over the decades, this was still sacred ground.

The red light of the fading sun set the surrounding cliffs afire in a conflagration of color. In the midst of the reflected glow stood a single, stately cottonwood tree, encircled by a handful of Indians from the reservation. They stood quietly and solemnly, waiting.

The still air soon filled with dust and the noise of approaching vehicles as Johnny Two Ravens pulled his truck up the two-track dirt road toward the gathered people. Parking a discreet distance from the tree, Johnny climbed out of the driver's side and Glenn from the other.

Several government cars arrived immediately after parking behind and further back from the gathering. The latecomers were greeted only with silence and blank stares from the mourners. Glenn spoke momentarily with Two Ravens and then crossed to his companions in the government cars. Michael Stanton shook Glenn's hand somberly. He had aged a great deal in the last few weeks and Glenn would

261

never call him the Boy Superintendent again. At Stanton's side was Nelson Princep. No longer an official observer; for the moment Yellowstone Forever was the furthest thing from his mind. The park still needed changes but Princep's heart told him they would need to start elsewhere. Rangers Franklin and Simpson stood behind, in full dress uniforms, accompanied by two shopkeepers from Gardiner. All were silent.

"You'll have to wait here," Glenn said waving Stanton, Princep, and the others back toward the vehicles they'd arrived in. He held up his hand, silencing any protests before they began. He looked to the watchers encircling the tree, aware of the importance in their not making a scene, then turned back to the white men. "This cannot be completed by us. It is a Shoshone matter. You can show your respect by honoring their request. You'll have to wait here."

Glenn returned to the truck as Johnny Two Ravens opened the tailgate. In the bed, the body of Silverbear lay covered by a gray blanket on a stretcher handmade of lodgepole and tanned leather. They eased it out, Glenn backing out with the head, Johnny taking the feet at the front. It was important that Silverbear approach the tree, and the afterlife, walking towards the Great Spirit.

Johnny paused momentarily, turned back over his shoulder, and quietly told Glenn, "J.D. can come."

Glenn looked to the Feds and called his biologist friend. She stepped reverently to his side. The ranger cast a final look at the group of agents, reaffirming with his glance that they were to remain beyond the sacred ground. Johnny Two Ravens started slowly forward. Glenn followed with his end of the stretcher as they made their way up through the sagebrush and buffalo grasses toward the tree.

What had appeared as dark shadows in the branches were revealed as two young Shoshone braves in the limbs overhead. A bed of wood had been secured between them and they waited to lift Silverbear's body home. Three young braves joined them at the base of the tree and assisted Johnny in lifting the stretcher on high. Glenn stepped back from the immediate circle, taking J.D. to his side, as the men in the tree took hold of the stretcher and lay it to rest on the bed of wood.

Before the ceremony could begin, another vehicle arrived and the mourners turned to the road. William Jones, Fred Black's right hand man, stepped from his truck and silently approached the gathering. Snow on the Mountains left the tree and met Jones at the edge of the sacred ground.

"I'm sorry," Jones said. He turned his reddened eyes to the ground unable to look at the shaman.

"Perhaps now is the time to heal many things," Snow on the Mountains said. The young man nodded silently. "Some days I feel too old to learn new things," the shaman said. "Then the Earth tells me something new, something I did not know about her. She shares her secrets, saying, 'Come learn about yourself.' When that happens I feel young again. Do you feel old or young today?"

Jones looked up crying openly. "I feel old."

"What is the reason you wish to come here?"

Jones thought very deeply. "I want to feel young again."

"Come," Snow on the Mountains said, taking the young man by the shoulder. Together, they returned to the foot of the burial tree where the ladies from the reservation stepped forward, lifting ornamental items to the men above. A carved wooden box of herbs, feathered drums and bells, a horsetail and others; things Silverbear would need in the afterlife. From inside his jacket, Glenn removed and opened a packet. He took from it a handful of golden feathers, those found at each scene throughout the park's ordeal, and handed them to the women. They were tied, with the other items, to branches above the body and left to dangle in the still air. All of this was accomplished without sound.

Silverbear had been a powerful medicine man. He had lived and died, and lived and died, in the image of the Spirit Bear. There would be no burial. A covering of earth would, as a covering of water had, separate him from his Creator. He had earned the reverence of the tree burial. As time and the elements of Mother Earth decayed his body, a body that had been denied its return to the Earth in his former life, the holy man would be free to return to that from which he had come.

As the fading rays of the sun took their wishes to the Great Spirit, each of the elements would take back those parts of Silverbear they owned. The holy man's journey had finally ended; the Stinking Country's healing would begin.

This we know: the earth does not belong to man. Man belongs to the earth.

About the Authors

Daniel D. Lamoreux is an outdoor writer and freelance photographer with over 350 articles and columns, and nearly as many photographs, in more than 40 state, regional, and national publications. His online magazine can be found at OnStand.net. Dan is the founder and CEO of Master Hunter Products, MasterHunters.com, and is on a mission to provide information, education, and entertainment products to fishermen, hunters, outdoor enthusiasts and the industry that provides for their needs. His expertise in the wild has been developed during over 40 years of pursuing the outdoor sports. He lives, plays, and works in the mountains of northwest Wyoming.

*

Doug Lamoreux is a father of three, a grandfather, a writer, and actor. A former professional fire fighter, he is the author of four novels and a contributor to anthologies and non-fiction works including the Rondo Award nominated Horror 101, and its companion, the Rondo Award winning Hidden Horror. He has been nominated for a Rondo, a Lord Ruthven Award, and is the first-ever recipient of The Horror Society's Igor Award for fiction. Lamoreux starred in the 2006 Peter O'Keefe film, Infidel, and appeared in the Mark Anthony Vadik horror films The Thirsting (aka Lilith) and Hag.

Other books by the Authors:

Daniel D. Lamoreux

- The Fireside Collection

Doug Lamoreux

- The Devil's Bed

- Dracula's Demeter

- The Melting Dead

- Corpses Say the Darndest Things: A Nod Blake Mystery